CONTRACT EXECUTION

CONTRACT EXECUTION
THE AGENT OPERATIVE™ BOOK 2

MARTHA CARR
MICHAEL ANDERLE

This book is a work of fiction. All of the characters, organizations, and events portrayed in this novel are either products of the author's imagination or are used fictitiously. Sometimes both.

Copyright © LMBPN Publishing
Cover by Fantasy Book Design
Cover copyright © LMBPN Publishing
A Michael Anderle Production

LMBPN Publishing supports the right to free expression and the value of copyright. The purpose of copyright is to encourage writers and artists to produce the creative works that enrich our culture.

The distribution of this book without permission is a theft of the author's intellectual property. If you would like permission to use material from the book (other than for review purposes), please contact support@lmbpn.com. Thank you for your support of the author's rights.

LMBPN Publishing
PMB 196, 2540 South Maryland Pkwy
Las Vegas, NV 89109

Version 1.01, December 2022
ebook ISBN: 979-8-88541-850-8
Print ISBN: 979-8-88878-042-8

The Oriceran Universe (and what happens within / characters / situations / worlds) are Copyright (c) 2017-22 by Martha Carr and LMBPN Publishing.

THE CONTRACT EXECUTION TEAM

Thanks to our JIT Readers:

Christopher Gilliard
Dave Hicks
Wendy L Bonell
Diane L. Smith
Jan Hunnicutt

If we've missed anyone, please let us know!

Editor
SkyFyre Editing Team

CHAPTER ONE

Norah put her tea down on the crystal lid of the coffin she was using as a coffee table, wrinkling her nose at the face frozen beneath three inches of clear quartz. Even unconscious, the light elf looked like a bastard.

"I wish he'd frozen with worse-looking hair." Norah was jealous of the light elf's silky locks. Maybe being evil made your hair extra glossy.

Officially, Saxon was taking a sabbatical to work on new projects after the unraveling of his pet Henry VIII project. Plenty of people in Hollywood had their doubts. Fortunately, none of them had come sniffing around Los Feliz.

"Do we *have* to keep him here for the party?" Cleo flew over and kicked the crystal above Saxon's face with one winged foot. Norah's mug rattled against the stone, and she held it steady. "That's dwarf-mined quartz reinforced with black-hole onyx you're kicking. If you want it gone, *you* carry it. And you can pay for your own chiropractor," she added.

Hoofbeats echoed on the terracotta tile. Pepe the goat clomped over, wrapped his mouth around the corner of the crystal coffin, and bit down. Pepe had rigorously tested all of Norah's furniture for edibility, and every so often, he re-sampled the coffin to make sure he hadn't made a mistake.

She shook her head at the jaunty black-and-white goat. He huffed off to the corner, where he plopped himself on a dog bed that her client Duncan had gotten from a TikTok collaboration with The Pampered Pom, LA's most luxurious pet supply company. According to the embossed tag, the woven-rope bed was made from non-toxic, organic materials. That was good since Pepe started eating one of the corners as a bedtime snack.

"Don't blame me when you're sleeping on the cold floor," she told the goat. "You can't have your cake and sleep on it, too."

Pepe's slitted pupils flicked to the tile, which he contemplatively licked. *Eating me out of house and home* was literal with a goat.

"You should have taken Minnie up on her offer to store the coffin in her Hollywood Forever crypt," Cleo said.

The pixie wasn't wrong. Saxon made her shiver, like fingernails scraping across a chalkboard but for the soul. Besides, this was Cleo's party.

"What if we throw a tablecloth over it?" Norah asked.

Cleo's runes glowed skeptically. "Do you own a tablecloth?"

"No. But I own some festive bedsheets. I think. Somewhere."

Cleo sighed and fluttered up to the colorful *Goodbye, Cleo!* sign that hung across the door to the kitchen. It was uneven, and she nudged it into position.

Norah went to her bedroom to look for the bedsheets, a journey made much quicker by the massive hole in her bedroom wall. She sighed. Duncan had given her a business card for a contractor a few weeks ago. Apparently, if you lived in a house with seventeen twenty-something influencer bros, you needed a reliable hole guy. Maybe she'd finally take Stan up on his offer to fix it.

Choking on dust bunnies as she rifled through the shapeless back-of-closet pile that served as linen storage, Norah only half-heard the knock at her door. When she emerged with cowboy-themed sheets after intimate encounters with two different spiders, she found Quint already inside.

"Pepe let me in." Her brother eyed the goat with suspicion. Pepe nodded in acknowledgment. Quint leaned in to whisper, "I don't think he's a normal goat."

Norah waited for Pepe to start chewing a hole in her sofa before nodding in agreement. "Where's Hazel?" she asked. The supermodel had come to their rescue in a pinch during the battle with Saxon, and Quint had brought her up in every conversation since.

His expression cooled. He wended his way to the sofa, pushed the goat gently aside, and flung himself face-down on a crocheted pillow. Bad news.

"She's ghosting me." His words were muffled by the pillow.

"What did you bring for the potluck?" Norah asked in an attempt to keep things cheerful.

Quint moaned. "I was too sad to bake."

Norah wrinkled her nose. Quint's complaints about women tended to be of the "Ugh, why do they keep texting me when we've only gone out on six dates" variety. She cared about him, but she also cared about the success of this potluck, and Quint was the only reliable cook in the family.

"Vesta, play Leonard Cohen," Quint said into the pillow. Norah's magical virtual assistant blinked to life and floated into the middle of the room. The opening bars of *Avalanche* cast their gloom over the room.

"Vesta, ignore my brother's depressing music suggestion and play something fun," Norah corrected. The music changed to an upbeat pop song by Rusalka, America's #1 siren pop star.

She shouted to Cleo, "Hey! This is the pop star who gave me your sneakers!" Cleo twirled in a zippy spiral. The song was catchy, and she was distracted from spreading the bedsheet on the coffee table/coffin.

When Norah was done, she sneaked into the kitchen to snoop on Hazel's social media. Her brother and the fire elemental had seemed mutually smitten, but maybe things had cooled.

She found the answer. Hazel had posted a series of photos from her second Alexander McQueen campaign. In the muted, ethereal images, Hazel posed with a water elemental in a series of increasingly intimate portraits. In the last one, she floated in a mountain lake, on fire, entwined with the water elemental model. Steam rose from where their skin touched. Norah blinked away the urge to take a cold shower.

She slipped her phone back into her pocket and returned to the living room, then plopped down on the arm of the sofa and patted Quint's head. "There, there. I'm sure you'll meet another model."

"I don't want another model. I want *Hazel*," he whined.

Norah rolled her eyes. "Buck up, bucko. People are going to be upset when they find out you didn't bake, so try not to drag this party down."

Quint groaned and buried his head in the sofa cushions. There was another knock on the door.

Norah sighed and pointed at her brother. "Pepe, can you get him up?"

The goat's slit-pupiled eyes brightened. He leapt gracefully onto the sofa and poked Quint's prone form with a small hoof. Cries of "That's my kidney!" faded as Norah opened the door to Stan and a person in an opaque black head-to-toe suit.

"Hey, Norah," the muffled female said.

Norah's eyebrows rose. "Hey, Minnie." Having the vampire don a full-body blackout suit was a huge honor. She had, on multiple occasions, referred to the protective suits as "sweltering death traps from the brightest pits of hell" but had made an exception for the cube-shaped pixie.

"Minnie! High five!" Cleo zoomed into the room and slapped one of her Hermes tennis shoes against Minnie's black-gloved palm.

Stan raised a lemon tart and a bottle of wine. "Where should I put these?"

Norah ushered the two new arrivals into the living

room, where horses galloped across the bedsheet draped over Saxon's coffin.

"Is it a theme party? I should have dug up my old chaps and spurs from the 1950s."

The woman in the blackout suit snorted. Stan in chaps would be a striking image. Maybe Norah had missed an opportunity.

"It's not a theme party," Norah replied apologetically.

Within the hour, the rest of the guests arrived. Leaf made a beeline for Pepe, and Jackie barely prevented the seven-year-old from riding him like a pony. The goat was surprisingly tolerant.

"You can have him back any time you want," Norah offered. She regretted it when Pepe whipped around with a disapproving glare.

"Oh, he's exactly where he wants to be," Jackie told her. "And our house doesn't smell like goat anymore!" Norah had gotten used to the faint musk. In hindsight, that might not be a good thing. "Besides," Jackie continued, "I'm glad you'll have company when Cleo's gone. And protection. That goat is worth six German Shepherds."

Pepe puffed out his chest.

"Well, Leaf is welcome to visit any time." Norah's nephew whooped and ran over to the hole in her living room wall to touch the crumbled brick.

"Is this from when you fought off the bad elf?" he asked, awed.

No, this is from where we...over-enthusiastically tapped a dwarven keg while we were celebrating fighting off a bad elf. "Sort of!" Norah told him. She declined to point out the plant Leaf's father had puked on during the subsequent bacchanal. Cleo had been right about covering Saxon's crystal coffin. Leaf didn't need to be any more frightened. None of them did.

When Leaf completed his inspection of the destroyed wall to his satisfaction, he raced over and wrapped his arms around Norah. "My dad got a new tattoo!" he exclaimed. Andrew flexed a bicep, and a dashing pirate grinned at the tattooed mermaid on the other arm. "Ah, young love," he said. Norah rubbed the shining sun tattoo on her wrist, a reminder of her family's shared commitment to taking down the Dark Hound website.

When Leaf ran away to pester his grandmother for cookies, Andrew bent and flipped up the corner of the cowboy sheet to peek at Saxon.

"He hasn't moved?" Andrew asked.

Norah shook her head. "Frondle says the enchantment won't wear off. Ever. I trust him, but Saxon was powerful, and he had powerful friends. The coffin's a precaution."

Andrew lowered his voice. "Speaking of his powerful friends, I've been obsessively checking Dark Hound. Seeing Mom's and Dad's faces on that hellsite makes me sick."

"I know," Norah agreed. Checking the website was like picking a scab. Sometimes she caught Madge looking at the site when she walked back into the office after lunch.

Lincoln came up beside them. "We scoured the grimoire you found in the Old Zoo for a way to talk to Saxon without reversing the Sleeping Beauty enchantment."

Norah sucked in her breath. "You didn't get trapped by the control spell?"

"No. To be fair, we cast pretty sturdy protective wards

before we opened it. Total pain in the ass. I think the spell has been less powerful since that beacon broke."

The mermaid on Andrew's bicep flung herself disconsolately across her clam shell. "Someone is tracking down and killing witches and wizards, and Garton Saxon is our only lead," the tattoo's owner said. "Is there any other way around the enchantment?"

"No," Lincoln replied. "The only way to wake him is to find someone who loves him to give him true love's kiss."

"Seriously?" Norah asked.

The dwarf who had warned Norah that Saxon was coming might have more information. He had seemed attached to his boss, though not in a way Norah would describe as "love." However, no one had been able to find him.

A small figure flew down and kicked the sheet out of Andrew's fingers. "Ow," he said.

Madge ignored him. Today the pixie wore a white-sequined turtleneck jumpsuit. With her round figure, she looked like a small disco ball.

"Don't worry," Madge said. "I've got an idea. If this miserable sad sack had a freckle of love in his life, we will root it out!"

"It's not hopeless. Ted Bundy got married in prison," Norah offered.

Quint sighed, a pathetic sound that stretched across several seconds and multiple registers. "See? Even Ted Bundy had more love in his life than me!"

"Maybe Ted Bundy put in more of an effort, son," Lincoln said cheerfully. Quint sank lower in his seat.

An hour later, Cleo whispered to Norah that it was

time. Pulling out her blue gum eucalyptus wand, which was back at full power after its recent break, Norah conjured an enormous image of a champagne glass and summoned every spoon in the room to clang against it. The utensils glinted.

"Everyone!" Norah called. "I'd like to propose a toast to my dear friend Cleo. She's been a wonderful companion for many years, and I appreciate you all coming to help send her on her flyabout. This pixie is solid, and she's constantly revealing new sides of herself —way more than six. Many exciting adventures await her."

"Norah hopes they include paying rent," the subject of the toast said. Everyone laughed.

Norah raised her glass. "Bon voyage, Cleo!"

"Bon voyage!" everyone in the room shouted. Norah took a sip of her champagne. There was a slurp from the corner, and blood flowed through a clear plastic straw into a port in Minnie's blackout suit.

"Are you sure you want to do this next part?" Norah asked.

Cleo glowed brightly. "You bet! It's tradition for a maiden voyage."

Norah opened the big window on one wall and hesitantly pulled a bottle out of an ice bucket. According to the label, it was a bottle of sparkling grape malt. *From the grape malt region of France.* It had been the cheapest one at the liquor store. Taking a deep breath, Norah smashed the bottle against Cleo's side. A cheer spread through the room, along with a fair amount of glass.

"Woo-hooo!" Cleo cried as bubbly liquid dripped off

her planks onto her winged shoes. "Thanks for everything! Laters, alligators!"

The pixie rose into the air and sped out the window. Norah watched her get smaller and smaller until the speck disappeared in the clouds.

"I'm going to miss that pixie," Norah said. The apartment was going to be quiet.

Andrew, wand out, directed pieces of broken glass into a nearby trash can. Something soft bumped Norah's calf. Pepe had leaned his head against her. Norah patted his side as he leaned in to eat a piece of the broken bottle.

CHAPTER TWO

As Norah stared at the oil painting, Winston's eyes burned into her, searching for a positive reaction. The carved wooden frame was painted a cheerful gold, which somehow made the subject more alarming.

"It's as if Lisa Frank painted Edvard Munch's *The Scream*," Norah murmured. "With glitter."

"Exactly!" the fidgeting gnome exclaimed. "It's deep but also *fun!*"

"And very large," Norah added. At five feet wide and almost eight feet tall, she had barely avoided taking the door off its hinges to get it into the office. Hung, it dominated a whole wall, sparkling threateningly across the carpet.

"So? Is it right for Gnome at Home?" Winston asked, shifting from one buckle-booted foot to the other. The TikTok star was trying to enhance his revenue stream by launching a new product line of magical homewares in partnership with a major retailer. The gnome pulled a thread out of his crisp tweed blazer.

"It draws the eye," Norah stated.

Winston's shoulders sank. He was so short that this brought him close to the floor. Madge winced.

"Aesthetics are one thing. Why don't you show me how it works?" Norah asked.

Winston trudged over and pressed a gilded flower in the upper right corner of the painting's frame. With a hiss, the canvas detached and sank seven feet back, revealing a queen mattress.

Norah walked around and peeked at the back of the painting, which was regular brown paper. The distortion of reality wasn't visible from the side, and the painting was no wider than it had been before.

When Norah flopped onto the mattress, it puffed around her, cloud-like. She rolled from one side to the other, lulled by the astonishing softness. It was dreamy but not suffocating. When Winston asked, "How is it?" she jolted upright, having fallen into a half-sleep.

Norah rubbed her eyes. "That's tremendous. Is it magic?"

"The mattress isn't. It's just very comfortable. Quality control was a huge hassle. Our product testers kept falling asleep instead of filling out their reports."

"Katie!" Norah called.

The door into the waiting room opened, and a cheerful twenty-year-old witch popped in. The UCLA film student was First Arret's only intern. Hollywood's intern tradition demanded that Norah be horrible to the young woman and scream unreasonable demands at her until midnight. So far, however, the only hazing she and Madge had managed was asking the young witch to meet the increasingly arcane coffee demands of the company's burgeoning client list.

"What do you think?" Norah asked, pointing the intern at the painting-turned-Murphy-bed. Not that it was possible to miss the pastel rainbow figure screaming behind that bed.

Katie walked around the painting, then perched on the edge of the mattress.

"It closes from the inside," Winston said helpfully.

Katie pulled her legs up, looked around the frame, and pulled a black velvet curtain closed. Less than a minute later, a muffled snore filtered through the curtain.

"A rave review," Norah said cheerfully.

"Really?" Winston asked. The gnome's TikTok was going strong, but advertisers had been wary of working with him since his disastrous unicorn-grilling stint on *Iron Chef*. His morning show appearances had tilted the scales back into the green zone, but just barely. Winston's hopes and dreams were riding on this collaboration.

"Tell me about the thought process behind the art," Norah said.

"Goblin's balls, you hate it." Winston groaned.

"No, no. Hate isn't the right word. If I was decorating a haunted gay bar, this would hit the spot, but it's going to look insane on the wall of the average studio apartment."

She didn't need to turn on her empathy to understand how badly Winston wanted her approval.

"We hired six of LA's hottest teen street artists to design it," Winston said, cheering up as Katie snored again.

Norah nodded. "Fire two of them and hire some grownups. People who have been roughed up by life enough to develop some restraint. Dial the art back a notch. Okay, a couple of notches. Look, the overall concept is fantastic. If you can nail the design, every barista-slash-whatever in a studio apartment is going to want one."

A muffled snort was followed by the jangle of the velvet curtain being pulled aside.

"I live in a studio apartment," Katie said. "But I can't sleep while a melting rainbow screams at me. Its eyes do that thing where they follow you." She shivered and took a step out of the portrait's eye line.

Winston perked back up and pushed his pointed wool cap to a rakish angle. "Can you help me find the names of some boring grownup designers?"

Norah closed her mouth around a protest. "No problem. Want some help carrying this back out to your car?"

Winston shook his head. "Please, keep it as a thank you."

A protest died on Norah's tongue under the painting's vibrant anguish. "Thank you very much," she said, mustering a heroic sincerity.

When the door closed, Katie and Madge circled the painting. Norah tapped the frame with her wand, and blue magic shot through it. A moment later, it sizzled out.

At least I tried.

Norah sighed. "The magic is baked into the portrait, so there's no painting over it. Would you like to keep it?" she asked Katie.

The young woman hesitated, then shook her head.

"Madge? Interested? You could build a full pixie dreamhouse in there."

Madge hovered near Norah's cheek. "Imagine that

screaming face being the size of your whole body," the pixie said. Norah had had nicer nightmares.

"Fine. I'll take it. For now." Norah smiled brightly and tossed her keys to Katie. "You can load it into my car!"

The young woman stared at the painting, which was over five feet wide. "Isn't your car pretty small?"

"I'm sure you'll figure it out. We have a meeting in a few minutes."

Maneuvering the painting out the door took four tries. It was very entertaining.

"We should have gotten an intern years ago," Norah said. Madge grinned.

"Wait, what meeting do we have?" Madge asked.

"You're going to meet me by the hallway window to watch her wrestle that painting into my Prius."

"I'll make popcorn," Madge offered.

A knock on the office door interrupted their valiant attempt at hazing. A young man in a neon ErrandBoy t-shirt stood in the waiting room.

"Hey." He held a manila envelope out to Norah. It was sealed with wax embossed with an intricate design.

"Who sent this?" Norah asked.

The young man shrugged. "Whoever booked the ErrandBoy hour. Some lawyer, I guess." Norah pulled her hand away from the envelope like it might burn her. Her lawyer terrified her. *Buck up, kid.* Resigning herself to a wide range of terrifying scenarios, she signed the proffered tablet.

Inside her office, she pushed the envelope to the farthest corner of her desk.

"What's that?" Madge asked.

"Legal documents."

"Uh-oh."

"Yeah."

Reluctantly, Madge poked the design on the wax seal with her toothpick-sized wand. The second she made contact, there was a crackle of magic on magic. Thrown off her wing rhythm, Madge dropped onto the wooden table with a thud.

"Are you okay?" Norah asked, readying a protective spell. She looked at the envelope, whose wax seal had melted into a starburst of tiny rivulets.

Norah backed against the bookshelf. "Is it cursed?"

Madge landed next to Norah's head. "No, but there's some powerful magic there. Not dangerous, but there's a lot of it." Her voice wavered, and the pixie edged behind a jade bookend.

The manila envelope burst open, and Norah raised a quick magical shield. The envelope gushed a stack of legal paper that slid onto the floor. The documents unfolded into a large square and then stretched up origami-like into an elegant paper box the size of a large cupboard. Light from inside illuminated delicate scrollwork cutouts.

The sound of ripping paper almost drowned out a faint pop, and an elegant figure burst through the side of the box. A drow woman in a paralyzingly white pantsuit stepped out, prompting Norah to reach for her sunglasses. The drow's briefcase had cost more than Norah's car. Outside of the faintest glint of humor in her eyes, her expression was blank.

"Good afternoon. I'm Cyprine Gunkel. Do you have a few minutes to talk?"

Norah closed her eyes and tugged on the knot of magic inside her that allowed her to read other people's intentions. By sending it out in a small radius, she learned two things. One, the drow intended no physical harm. Two, Madge wanted to punch this showoff in the face.

Through the paper door, Nora saw a phone-booth-sized cubicle, complete with a laptop, a printer, and a ringing phone.

"Wanna get that?" Norah asked.

"It'll go to voicemail."

The pixie narrowed her eyes and spiraled around the room, testing the threshold of the cubicle. "Are you in a cult? We're not buying," Madge said with extra gravel in her voice.

"My religious affiliation has no impact on my current work, and I doubt you could afford me," Cyprine said.

"I see you haven't come to make friends," Norah stated.

"That wasn't an insult, merely an observation. A boutique entertainment company *could* hire me, just as the Fugaku supercomputer in Kobe *could* be used to play solitaire."

Madge grabbed the edge of a scrollwork cutout and tugged, then rode the resulting curl of ripping paper down to the floor.

"Apology accepted." Norah snorted. Grudgingly, she reached for the business card glittering between the drow's French-manicured nails. *Cyprine Gunkel, Esq.*

Uh-oh.

Norah's threat level shot back up to fire-engine red. The drow might not intend physical violence, but she was still dangerous. Dalloway & Gunkel was infamous in

Hollywood. Calling the law firm sharky was an understatement. *If more sharks were Dalloway & Gunkel-y, maybe they wouldn't be going extinct.*

Norah dropped the shield. Magic was great, but it was no match for expensive lawyers.

"I'm here on behalf of Silver Lion studios," Cyprine continued.

Norah mentally added up the property damage she had done on her foray to Garton Saxon's *Henry VIII* film shoot but stopped when she exceeded three times the value of her bank account. "Is suing us really necessary?" she asked. "Can't you talk them into sending bloody-minded Kilomeas to break our kneecaps?"

"Yeah! Please?" Madge let go of the ripped paper. "I barely use my kneecaps. They're jelly cups at this point." She poked one with her wand to demonstrate.

"You are not being sued at this time," Cyprine corrected. "Although that statement is not legally binding upon any future Dalloway & Gunkel actions."

"How reassuring," Norah said. Madge muttered something under her breath that might have been the opening to an actual curse, but Norah cut her off with a glare.

"How can we help you?" Norah asked.

"I'd like you to join me at Silver Lion studios to discuss a business proposition," Cyprine said. "There's a car waiting out front."

Norah and Madge exchanged a look. If the studio wasn't suing her, what did they want?

"Do I need to update my will?" Norah asked, only half-joking.

"There is always a small but real chance of dying in a

car crash on the 101." Cyprine's voice was flat. The drow was unreadable.

"I've rolled those dice before." Norah sighed. "Clear my schedule, Madge!"

"But there's noth...er, of course, Miss Wintry."

With a crisp spin, Cyprine led her out the door.

CHAPTER THREE

With Cyprine beside her, every obstacle between Norah and the Silver Lion warehouse disappeared in a haze of fervent helpfulness. In retrospect, not having to balance on unruly flying shoes also made a huge difference. Norah had passed the twenty-minute drive in an antiseptically-clean Escalade watching Cyprine's motionless silver hair. Norah could probably shave her legs with the edge of that blunt bob. Not a single strand moved the entire time. Norah resisted a wild impulse to reach out and check if it was a plastic helmet.

The envelope Cyprine had arrived in folded out into a mobile workstation, and she spent the ride working on a legal document.

The driver dropped them off at the warehouse from which Norah had escaped from her confrontation with Saxon just weeks ago. This time, she entered through a door like the civilized witch she was.

Cyprine led her to the Hampton Court palace interior that had been meticulously reconstructed inside the warehouse for Saxon's film. Norah remembered explosions and flying splinters, but the rooms were intact. An intense silver-haired woman surveyed her through thick glasses. To underscore the situation, she was perched on a gilded throne.

Where had she seen this woman? Shattered green glass flashed across her mind. That was it! *The Wonderful Wizard* premiere. She had taken Frondle as her date. Norah's spine straightened when she realized the woman was one of the most powerful executives in Hollywood. Marina Macavoy; that was the woman's name. A brief biography scrolled across Norah's brain. The youngest woman ever to head a studio—the studio Norah had smashed only weeks ago, whose *Henry VIII* film she'd gotten canceled.

Fear of being kneecapped had shotgunned an excess of adrenaline into Norah's body. Before she could stop herself, she dropped one foot behind her in an imitation curtsy while tugging out the sides of her yoga pants. "Your Majesty."

Marina stared, then gracefully crossed her legs. "Is that a joke? You're an agent, not a comedian. You're probably funnier than some of the recent dilettantes, but that's not a compliment."

Norah's spine straightened. "You were at the *Wonderful Wizard* premier."

"You were the little witch in Spanx. You know who I am? Good. Then we've done introductions and can get down to business."

Norah swallowed. Had the woman blinked yet? She felt flayed.

"Please don't sue me. Cyprine said you weren't going to, but maybe she was lying?"

"Cyprine never lies. I'm not sure she can." Marina glanced over Norah's shoulder. The drow lawyer was taking a call inside her fold-out cubicle. The clipped words "indemnification for bodily injury" echoed toward the roof.

"Oh, God, it's the kneecaps, isn't it?" Norah wondered if she could make it to the door. She might be able to beat Marina, but Cyprine had the bone structure of a greyhound. She wouldn't make it halfway across the room. The blue gum eucalyptus wand shook as Marina stared contemplatively at Norah's kneecaps.

"I have a lot of skills!" Norah insisted. "Can't we solve this? Do you need any curses removed?"

Marina narrowed her eyes. "Does menopause count?"

"According to my mother, yes." Norah wondered if she should curtsy again. She was about to try it when Marina cut her off.

"There *is* something you can do for me."

"Dry cleaning?" Norah hated dry cleaning.

"What? No. I need you to put together a package."

"Like, a muffin basket? A really apologetic one?"

Marina clicked a fingernail on the armrest of the throne, and an obedient silence dropped over the room. It wasn't magic, just force of personality.

"I'm not in the repentant baked goods business. I'm in the movie business. When I say package, I mean a *movie* package. Are you getting this?"

Norah gulped. She was in deep, but she didn't have to keep digging. "I'd love to hear more about it."

Marina waved her around the corner to a breathtaking

bedroom set. Norah ran her hand over the carved wooden posts and touched the embroidered velvet curtains with one finger.

Sweeping her hand across the room, Marina said, "Before you stands a mostly accurate replica of Hampton Court palace. As you can see, Saxon's horrible *Henry VIII* project sailed fearlessly past its production budget."

"It's very nice," Norah remarked.

"It's very stupid," Marina corrected. "Period-accurate sixteenth-century carpentry? Ridiculous. Someone with real talent would have used spray-painted particleboard and made it work, but here we are. The set lives, unlike the movie."

"And you want a movie," Norah finished meekly.

"Bingo. But I want more. I want a showcase for Hollywood's magical talent. Garton was a shitheel, and his disappearance is a blessing to the city. However, his project had more magical talent in it than Long Wands."

Norah blinked. Long Wands was an all-male, all-wizard strip club in West Hollywood. Norah had been there for three bachelorette parties. Two had ended in tears and one in blood.

"Don't get distracted, Wintry," Marina barked. "The point is, if I don't launch a new magical project to replace *Henry VIII*, Gen Z is going to hammer me. Not in a fun way."

The look Marina had given Frondle at the film premier wafted through Norah's mind. She frowned. "Is that all? You need a magical smokescreen?"

Marina shrugged. "That's half of it. The other half is that

I'm interested in what you're doing. You have a good eye for talent. I have a location, and just to put a number in the air, one-point-five million bucks. I don't want you thinking big, Wintry. Think small. Adapt some play where rich people walk around opening doors and looking out windows."

"Sounds architectural."

"I'm not going to hamper you artistically by giving you good ideas. Do whatever you want as long as it's great and cheap. Or make it shitty and cheap."

That might be possible, Norah thought.

"As long as it blows the top off the box office," Marina finished.

Norah puffed out her cheeks. "Let's set up a meeting."

Two silver eyebrows drew together. "You don't have time for a *meeting,* Wintry. You'll be too busy working. Two weeks for pre-production. That's what you get. You'll have eighteen days on set before we raze this palace to the ground."

"What?" Norah tripped on the edge of a hand-knotted carpet. Twenty-three days would be tight. Eighteen was cruel and unusual.

"Think small, Wintry. A small, perfect, box-office darling."

"Is that all?" Norah asked. She was tempted to say no. She had seen films unravel under much better conditions than the ones Marina was proposing. She'd be stupid to decline, but she'd be even stupider to accept.

"Can I sleep on it?" she asked.

Incredulity covered Marina's face. "No, you can't *sleep*. What in this conversation has led you to believe you're going to be *sleeping* for any healthy interval of time in the next..." She paused to do the mental arithmetic.

"Thirty-two days?" Norah supplied.

Marina nodded sharply and jabbed her finger at a gilded doorframe.

"Sit on the throne for eight minutes and see how it feels."

Norah imagined someone coming through the doorframe and looking out the nearby window.

"Go! Your eight minutes have started!" Marina shouted. Norah jumped and scuttled out. The throne was uncomfortable, but she could tolerate it for a month. Doubt nagged at the back of her mind.

After what Norah assumed was eight minutes to the second, Marina emerged and pinned Norah to the velvet cushion with a hard stare.

"Why didn't things work out with Frondle?" Norah sputtered. "He was sad, you know."

Marina's eyes narrowed. "Not for long, I bet. It's hard to keep a goldendoodle down. Although I knew a depressed goldendoodle shifter once. Anyway, Frondle is charming and a staggering tower of beef, but he is clearly in love with someone else."

"Who?" Norah asked, mystified. Frondle's personal life was a mystery.

Marina shook her head and gave Norah a look that was generally reserved for young children or old pets. "Have you made up your mind?"

Norah grinned. "I have one condition." Marina raised an eyebrow. She had an expressive face, which was rare for a woman in Hollywood over sixty. One of the ravages of

Botox was visible emotion.

Norah continued carefully. "I will put together a package, but I need to know that you understand this will be an absolute shitshow."

Liquid ocher eyes drilled into her. "One hundred percent," the silver-haired executive agreed. "We've got a deal? Good. Cyprine's gonna take you through a forest's worth of paperwork now." By the time she finished talking, the drow attorney was halfway across the warehouse.

Marina walked away, delivering a few choice closers over her shoulder. "Have fun! Make sure it's a small, great, sellable shitshow! You can polish a turd into a perfect orb. They tested it on *Mythbusters*!"

Cyprine handed her a clipboard. Norah was still watching Marina's back. *I feel like I've been hit over the head with a beautiful marble sculpture.*

"Miss Macavoy has that effect on people," the drow commented, then she drowned Norah in paperwork.

"*WHAT?*" Madge yelled. The pixie was a blurry halo.

"We don't have time for questions," Norah replied. "We need to call every writer on our list and ask if they have a single-location project. Focus on horror. Women fighting off a chainsaw, that sort of thing."

Madge flapped to a full stop and poked Norah in the nose with her wand. "You said sixteenth century."

"Yes."

"They didn't have chainsaws in the sixteenth century."

"So make it a regular saw."

"A regular sixteenth-century saw?"

"And Renaissance Faire-ify the dialogue," Norah continued.

"In two weeks?"

"No." Her guilt twinged when Madge looked relieved. "It's gonna have to be way quicker than two weeks."

"How are we going to do this?"

"*STOP ASKING QUESTIONS!* You should be making a call and writing emails while the phone rings!"

"Um, Norah?" a small voice called. Katie peered in from the waiting room. "Do you want coffee?"

Norah declined to stop typing.

"For the next thirty-one and a half days, don't ask. Just bring the coffee."

"Got it. Okay. Do you need anything else?"

Five hundred critical tasks scrolled past at race-car speeds.

"I'm promoting you to second assistant. Take some of the names on Madge's list."

"Ask about contained scripts?"

"Yeah. When you're done with that, hire a new intern. Maybe two. *And bring me some coffee!*"

CHAPTER FOUR

"Are you going to join the party?" Norah's mother asked gently.

Norah jumped out of her skin when Petra's hand touched her arm. During her four hours of sleep the previous night, she'd dreamed about losing her phone inside a pitch-black circus tent. It dinged with alert after alert, but she never found it.

"I'm here! I'm at the party!" Norah peevishly snapped the elastic on her party hat. A bad script about sexy nuns tugged her attention back to her phone. "I'd give my left kidney for a *good* script about sexy nuns," she muttered.

Petra tried to take her phone, but Norah's grip was too strong.

"Hah! You'd have to train for weeks to defeat my superior hand strength," she said.

"It's just that Leaf asked me if you're mad at him," Petra said quietly.

Abashed, Norah tucked her phone into her pocket. "Okay, I'm present." *While I'm being present, I can think about which nun script is the least bad.* A vast expanse of emerald lawn stretched out around her. What had it cost Jackie to rent a full-on estate? A temporary corral had been set up at the edge of the lawn under some large trees. Sun dappled the shiny coats of three miniature horses, their manes and tails braided with colorful ribbon. Their horns were painted gold.

Wait, horns?

Norah walked closer, but a bounding figure cut her off.

"Auntie Norah!" Leaf said and flung himself around her leg.

"Happy birthday, Leaf! Great party."

"Fly me! Fly me!" He tugged on the leg of her pants.

Norah gave Petra a questioning look, and Leaf abandoned her.

"Fly me, Grandma!" he shouted.

Petra smiled indulgently, pulled her wand out of one billowing purple sleeve, and pointed at a corner of the lawn. She shot a stream of hay-colored magic out of her wand into Leaf's tennis shoes. The little wizard flew up into the air and soared toward a patch of grass, then caught himself with a jolt of magic from his wand and landed lightly.

"Nice trick," Norah said.

Leaf beamed. "We've been practicing! Do you want to ride a unicorn with me?"

Taking her hand, he pulled her over to the edge of the corral. The nearest unicorn glared at her and stamped so hard its hoof sank an inch into the ground.

The young light elf running the concession, who was

no older than thirty, tipped his hat. "If your conscience is clear, you've nothing to fear."

"Um. Why don't you go without me, Leaf? I thought unicorns were bigger," Norah said.

"They're miniature unicorns," Jackie said, sidling up. When they hugged, a small baby bump brushed Norah's stomach. "Hop onboard if you want. They're rated for up to five hundred pounds. Magical strength, you know."

A huff at Norah's feet provoked a boyish squeal.

"Pepe!" Leaf shouted. The goat, who was wearing a jaunty purple bowtie and a party hat, nuzzled the boy's arm.

"Can Pepe ride the unicorn with me, Mom?" Leaf asked, pushing on Jackie's leg. The nearest unicorn looked through its forelock with slitted eyes, ears plastered against its head.

"I don't know. Have fun finding out," Petra said. Leaf grinned and tugged the goat toward the corral.

"Are you sure that's safe?" Norah asked.

"Pepe's not dumb," Jackie said. "For what I paid, those unicorns better be prepared to carry more than one measly goat. Apparently, being half the size makes them twice as expensive."

There were at least a hundred people in the rented garden. In addition to the unicorns, there was a chocolate fountain and a circulating troupe of clowns.

Norah waved. When the clown in the bright orange mask waved back, he lost his balance, tripping into an expert tumble.

"How are the kids responding to classical Italian *commedia dell'arte*?" Norah asked, trying not to laugh.

"The one in red is wearing a lot of padding, and they seem to enjoy kicking him." Jackie's expression was neutral.

Norah nodded sagely. "They're good clowns. Is the caterer I recommended working out? I told him firmly to treat you right, and he's still angling for the craft services contract for the film."

A young woman in a starched white shirt offered a tray of translucent green orbs studded with purple flowers. "Mint orb with edible bouquet? It's the chef's conception of Earth before the arrival of man."

"Um, sure," Norah said. She and Jackie each took an orb, and the server swept away.

It was like swallowing a field of wildflowers at midsummer. Very sophisticated and tasty.

"Is there food for the kids?" Norah swallowed the last of the flowers.

"Oh, yeah. There's a chicken finger trough. Literally a trough. Leaf is in heaven. However, half the tiny weirdos are eating the canapes. One of Leaf's classmates grilled the chef about the tasting menu. Anyway, there's a proper sugar-on-sugar pink cake, and if they don't eat it, I will."

A man in a top hat approached them. "Are you Jackie?" he asked. "I'm the Amazing Ambrose. Quite a party you've got here."

Jackie shook a white-gloved hand as she swallowed the second half of her orb. "Yes. Nice to meet you. Um, there's a little stage behind the chocolate fountain. The clowns are going home in about twenty minutes, and I thought you could circulate with some card tricks until then."

"Your wish is my command, madam." He swept the top

hat off his head in a deep bow. Norah choked down a giggle as the black cape billowed toward the chocolate fountains.

"You hired a magician for a wizard's birthday party?" Norah asked.

Jackie tugged at the waistband of her pants. "Okay. I might have overdone it, but we just told Leaf he's getting a new sister, and I wanted him to feel special."

"It's a girl?" Norah squealed. Jackie beamed.

"I'm going to buy her so many dolls," Norah stated.

Jackie cringed. "Not the creepy ceramic ones. Please."

"Oh, yeah. Uncountable glass eyes will follow you around your house. I'll enchant them so that they *can* blink, but they never will." Norah finished with her creepiest laugh.

Jackie's pleas fell on deaf ears. A tall figure appeared across the lawn. Jackie saw him first and sighed in disappointment. "I was hoping he would wear the elven armor again. I was going to take a picture of him on one of the unicorns."

Alas, Frondle was not attired for battle. He had donned sky-blue pants, Birkenstocks, a metallic shirt, and a pointy brimless navy hat embroidered with stars and moons.

"Conical hats are traditional for an American birthday, yes?" Frondle asked. Norah stared up—and up and up—at the Himalayan quantity of blue velvet on his head. The hat was at least four feet tall.

"Sure," Norah said. Even in a stupid hat, he was dashing.

"Where is the birthday boy?" Frondle asked. "I wish to present him with a boon from the elves."

"Ooh, how formal!" Jackie said.

The miniature unicorns were riderless, so Norah led Frondle through the party. The light elf's hair gleamed gold in the sunshine. He seemed impressed with the chocolate fountain and prodded it with a wooden skewer while impatient children waited for their turns.

"Do you want a strawberry?" he asked. Twirling one on a stick until it was more chocolate than fruit, he held it to her lips. Norah bit down, and a shiver ran up her spine at the look on the light elf's face.

"Has your home recovered from the battle?" he asked.

Norah's mouth was so full of chocolate that her response came out as a gurgle. She chewed, then replied, "Mostly. The hangover from the dwarven beer finally went away, at least!"

"So soon? It must have been a weak batch," Frondle said apologetically. Norah shuddered. She didn't want to taste whatever the dwarven equivalent of a triple IPA was.

"Thank you for your help that night." Norah met Frondle's ice-blue eyes. "You saved my life. Twice, as far as I know."

"It was an honor." Frondle swept a deep bow, a lock of his golden hair dangled into melted chocolate.

"Hey! No mouth-drinking from the fountain!" an angry voice said. As Frondle bolted upright, the chocolate-covered lock whipped across his face. A stocky man with a loud spray tan ran over to cut him off from the fountain.

"There's no dipping your face in. You wanna do that, buy your own. Stick whatever you want in it, but not in my house. Be an example to the kids."

The man was a full head shorter, but he leaned in fearlessly until Frondle stepped back.

"Please accept my apologies," Frondle said. The chocolate smeared on his face undercut his sincerity.

"It was an honest mistake," Norah protested.

The man turned, and his face widened with a smile. It was Angelo, the caterer. "Norah! My favorite current target for bribery. This your boyfriend? I didn't realize. By all means, stick your full face in there."

Heat crept up Norah's body. "Oh. Um. Frondle is my client."

Angelo was the son of an LA craft services magnate named Domenico Consoli. On his third trip down the aisle, Consoli had married Angelo's mother, a drow named Jessa. Now, Angelo ran the business's day-to-day operations. Over the past year, he had started incorporating Oriceran foods into his menus.

"The food is fantastic," Norah said. "Great balls. Very green."

"If I had a quarter for every time a woman said that, I'd be screwed on laundry day. You made any big decisions about the flick?"

"Not yet." Norah smiled. She'd let him grease the wheels until the party was over.

"Okay, okay, I see how it is. You gotta let the competitors wine you and dine you, like on *The Bachelorette*. I want that rose. A little birdie told me the production is mostly magical. No one does Oriceran food better than me."

Norah laughed. "I'll keep that in mind."

"You're the boss, boss. I dearly hope. Want me to set up a chocolate fountain for you two in," he lowered his voice to a barely audible whisper, "one of the *private* rooms upstairs?"

Norah's face joined her ears in turning a nice bright red. She managed to splutter, "What? No, that's not... I have a lot of work." She noticed Frondle's crestfallen face. The tip of his hat flopped to one side. *Oops.*

"Maybe another time," she said, trying to sound casual. Angelo grinned, and Frondle licked chocolate off the tip of his nose. "Let's find Leaf. Actually, let's find you a sink, and then let's find Leaf."

Ten minutes later, a pretty garden path stretched before them on the return from the main house. Frondle had gotten all the chocolate off his face and most of it out of his shirt.

"I wondered, Norah," the light elf started. Her breath caught in her throat. "Could I take you out sometime? Have you ever gone diving?"

"Like, SCUBA diving?"

"I was thinking of the magical kind. I have some Oriceran bubblegrass we could eat to help us breathe while we look for dolphins in the kelp forests."

"What about sharks?" Norah asked.

"I'll cover us in light bubbles so they'll think we're large jellyfish. That frightens them."

It wasn't as comforting as "Don't worry, there are no sharks out there." Diving sounded cold. And murky. And kelp-y. Frondle's face was hopeful. Norah couldn't ignore the flutter in her stomach.

"Sounds great," she said. When he offered his hand, she took it. As they neared the main party, their companionable silence was interrupted by a commotion near the magician's stage. Picking up her pace, Norah ran toward the blue-striped structure. A crowd of interested children had gathered around the Amazing Ambrose, and Leaf was yanking on the white-tipped wand in the magician's gloved hand.

"You're using it wrong!" Leaf shouted. "It's not *doing* anything!"

Miraculously, the magician was still in character. *That* was amazing. Struggling to retrieve his property and his dignity, the Amazing Ambrose yelled, "Young man, if you allow me to continue, you will be amazed by what you see! Arcane secrets! Ancient magic!"

Leaf pulled hard, and the wand cracked. Norah was presented with the broken pieces. Leaf's chin bobbled as he held it out. "He says he's doing magic, but I can't see any traces. Doesn't that mean he's dangerous? Is he here to kill Grandma?"

That provoked a choke from the Amazing Ambrose, then he stopped in his tracks and dropped his bravado.

"Kid, they're not paying me enough to kill someone."

Frondle frowned at the magician and blocked his path.

Norah hugged Leaf. He knew more about her family's recent misadventures than she'd realized.

"Oh, honey, no," she said. "He's not a wizard, Leaf. You know how when you and I do magic, it's sort of easy? Like this!" Norah plucked the pointy hat off Frondle's head. Tipping it over, she pulled out her wand and filled it with blue magic. A moment later, a fluffy rabbit poked its head out of the velvet. It was a simple glamour, but it did the trick. Two kids behind Leaf squealed. Norah turned back to her nephew. "The Amazing Ambrose can't do real magic, but he studied and practiced for a long time to make it *look* like he can. Learning to pull a rabbit out of a hat probably took years. Do you understand what I'm saying?"

Leaf nodded and wiped his face. "He's just pretending?"

"That's right," Norah agreed.

Leaf smiled and leapt up, the kind of emotional pivot only a kid could manage. "I'm going to try to catch him tricking me!"

The scowl on the Amazing Ambrose's face when Norah stood could have cooled a walk-in freezer. "Only hacks pull rabbits out of hats." He spat a little on the consonants. "I use an ermine."

Norah reviewed the speech she'd just given Leaf and cringed. *Solve it. Solve it right now.* "Um, you're not looking for new representation, are you?" She fished a chocolate-stained card out of her pocket.

The scowl vanished faster than a magician's assistant in an Aztec tomb.

"I am! Let's do lunch," the Amazing Ambrose said. Norah breathed a sigh of relief.

"Why don't we come back in a few minutes?" Norah pulled Leaf away. Frondle introduced himself, and Leaf insisted they see the chicken finger trough.

It was true to its name.

"Very authentic," Norah said.

Leaf grinned, and Frondle crouched beside him.

"Young wizard, I have a gift for you from my days in the Solar Vanguard." Dropping to one knee, he presented Leaf with what was either a long dagger or a short sword. The blade shone, and the malachite hilt was carved in the shape of a sleek otter. Leaf's eyes popped out.

Norah scratched her neck. "Is that blade sharp?"

The light elf looked crushed, and he sniffed. "The blade is sharp as the finest Oriceran diamond knife. I would never sully my honor by giving a *blunt* blade as a boon."

"That was a safety query." She scrambled to her feet and ran after Leaf before she finished the sentence. Her nephew was running in a figure eight, brandishing his sword before him.

Clearly accustomed to blades of the plastic or butter knife variety, he swung at a topiary poodle. Although the blade was nearly silent, the topiary head shifted and fell onto the lawn.

"*Vive la revolution,*" Norah whispered. "How's it going, Robespierre?"

"Uh, wow!" Leaf screamed, balanced precariously between enthusiasm and anxiety. He put the sword on the ground, pulled his wand out of his pocket, and attempted to replace the section of bush he'd chopped off. "Sorry," he muttered to the decapitated bush.

"Need some help with that, kiddo?" Norah asked. Leaf nodded and looked down, cheeks turning red.

"Okay. While I fix Fifi, why don't you have Frondle walk you through some basic sword safety lessons?"

"It would be my pleasure," Frondle said when he caught up to them.

"Can I name it?" Leaf pleaded. "People in books always name their swords."

"Maybe you should see what your mom thinks before you get too attached," Norah said.

Frondle shrugged. "It is the custom to name an elven blade."

"I'm gonna call him Steven!" Leaf shouted. Maybe it was

a trick of the light, but the carved stone otter on the hilt smiled.

"Are you sure you don't want a name that's more sword-y?" she said. "Like, Stabby? Or McPuncture?"

"I want to call him Steven!" Leaf's face was stubborn, and for a terrifying moment, Norah thought he was going to cuddle the razor-sharp blade. Instead, Frondle led him onto the grass and hit him with a stern lecture. She walked back to the decapitated poodle when she heard, "And *don't* swing it at anybody until you know the spell for reattaching an arm unless you're in serious danger."

Norah floated the severed topiary head up to its neck and carefully connected the major branches with threads of blue magic. It wound up looking more like a rescue dog than a purebred poodle, but it was good enough for casual inspection. As she was about to leave, a furry creature poked its head out from behind the poodle's leafy tail.

So that was what an ermine looked like.

CHAPTER FIVE

Norah ran her hand through her bristly brown beard while holding up the camera on her phone to check all the angles. If she'd done everything correctly, this glamour would last three hours. She'd need a break by then.

"Hey there, handsome," a high-pitched voice called. The change in Madge's voice was more disorienting than her gossamer butterfly wings.

"This isn't ethical," Norah said. It was a complaint rather than an argument.

Madge spun and checked her temporary backside. "Ethical, schmethical. We're saving lives!"

"I don't know. Have you seen *Audition*? They sort of did this, and terrible things happened."

"It's not gonna go that far."

Put on your game face, Norah. Your bristly beard-covered game face. "You're right. This is good. We will find a way to talk to Saxon. Nice wings, by the way."

Satisfied with how they looked, they pushed through a

door in the rented Burbank studio plastered with a sign that read Untitled Garton Saxon Biography Reality TV Show Casting.

Marina would be furious with Norah for taking four hours away from film production to track down the person behind the Dark Hound website, but what Marina didn't know wouldn't hurt her. Besides, who needed sleep?

Three days ago, she had put an ad on every reputable audition site in Los Angeles, asking people to share happy memories of Garton Saxon. She'd posted on some disreputable sites too. Anyone who actually loved Saxon was unlikely to be walking on the right side of truth and light.

Norah drained the dregs of her lukewarm coffee. "This is good."

Madge, drinking out of a dollhouse teacup, took a lap around Norah's head. "Katie started putting espresso shots in our coffee," the pixie informed her.

"That girl is gonna go to the top in this town."

Inside the featureless near-empty room, Norah looked at her watch and double-checked the camcorder on its small tripod. Fifteen minutes until go-time. Setting her laptop on the wobbly folding table, she tapped the corner with her wand. A glowing three-foot by two-foot screen stretched across the air. The list of names it displayed was long.

"This is going to take a while," Norah said.

Madge nodded. "Every person I called raved about the guy. Was he drugging them? I also heard a lot of loud sighs of relief when I told them he wouldn't be here in person."

"He can't have been horrible to everyone, can he? Filmmaking is a collaborative art form."

Madge raised an eyebrow. "Oh, yeah? Has it brought out the best in you over the past four days?"

Norah considered the number of times she'd screamed at her phone. "I'm passionate. Ugh. I wish I could talk to that creepy little dwarf. Firmly. With thumbscrews."

"Maybe he'll show back up," Madge offered, but not optimistically.

Stan had tracked down the dwarf's last known location, but it hadn't been easy. He'd strongly hinted that he had called in a favor from the Queen of the Elves. The trail had dead-ended in Oriceran's Dark Forest. The dwarf had cashed in some valuable Earth artifacts to buy a Rip Van Winkle box. The devices operated on the same principles as Winston's Murphy beds. The box created a small pocket of unreality, but instead of opening and closing, it disappeared for the number of years specified by the user, and it knocked you unconscious for the duration.

"How many years do you think he set the box for?" Norah asked.

Madge shrugged. "I don't know. Good riddance."

Norah took a deep breath. "Let's go find true love."

"Bring in the cattle!" Madge shouted and flew over to open the doors.

Garton Saxon's former assistant spoke so softly that Norah and Madge had to lean across the table. Hopefully, the camera's mic was picking her up.

"Garton was one of the most brilliant people I've ever worked with," she whispered, twisting a ring on her finger.

Time to turn on the ol' radio. Taking a deep breath, Norah reached inside for the knot of magic she'd acquired from the 1930s radio her mother had given her. Steeling herself to feel the would-be auditionees' emotions, she tugged the loop of magic that turned the enchantment on.

Terror hit her like a Hollywood Hills landslide. The young woman was sweating fear from her pores, and her eyes flicked to the red Record light on the camcorder every few seconds.

"Is Saxon going to listen to this later?"

"This is just a preliminary audition," Madge replied.

The young woman nodded uncertainly. "Because, um, he was really great. The best boss ever. Seriously. Best five weeks of my life."

She proceeded down an extensive list of positive qualities. By the end, her fear had diminished.

Once the door slammed, Norah turned to Madge. "How long do you think it took her to memorize all that?"

"Hopefully, less than five weeks. She seemed pretty motivated."

Madge scowled. "The guy produced former assistants at robot-assembly-line speeds."

"We're going to hear a lot of variations on a theme," Norah said.

In the auditionees' defense, they didn't *all* say the same thing. A light elf assistant's "once-in-a-generation producer" became a witch's "unprecedented Hollywood talent." The fear radiating from them was so thick that Norah thought she could see it.

"Why are they even *here?*" Norah asked. If these people

were so afraid of Saxon, why had they shown up to star in a reality TV show about his life?

"Did he seem like the kind of guy who would run complicated schemes to find out which toadies would unquestioningly obey him?" Madge asked.

"Well, yes."

"There you go!" the pixie exclaimed.

"Would it kill one of them to have Stockholm syndrome?" Norah cried. It was a horrible thought, but she was desperate.

"Would that count as true love?" Madge countered.

"It would be better than this," Norah said, waving her hand at the nebulous mist of terror coming off the cattle-call line. When Norah's watch beeped, she collapsed in relief.

"Glamour time," she whispered to Madge. "You know, I'm thinking about keeping the beard. It suits me."

Human and magical faces lined the hallway, throwing off a persistent undercurrent of anxiety. Norah was about to turn her radio senses down when a strong emotion pinged from the line. Someone was desperate to see Saxon's face again. If they were afraid, the bright, pure desire for one more look had burned it away.

Her eyes swept across the crowd, but she couldn't pin down the source. Too many streams of information were flowing in. She swam through the tangled emotions, trying to find the source of that bright passion.

Above her shoulder, one of Madge's monarch butterfly wings morphed into a pixie wing. *Uh-oh. The glamour!* Norah snatched the pixie out of the air and stuffed her in a pocket, ignoring the muffled screams that deteriorated into curses.

A shifter who had taken cat form to curl up in a sunbeam opened one eyelid and stared at Norah's chin. The left side of her beard was gone. Norah spun, ignoring the pixie's wand repeatedly jabbing her side.

She picked up her pace, but the cat was faster. Claws scrambled across the waxed floor with a loud hiss. Norah's bushy beard shifted to sideburns, which were quickly replaced, to Norah's chagrin, with a manicured soul patch. She slapped a hand over her chin. *I would never.*

"What's going on?" a middle-aged man asked. He grabbed Norah's arm, and her pocket went still.

Pulling free, she sidestepped right. Fur stood on end, and bones cracked and lengthened behind her. As she tried to push through the crowd, a claw hooked her shirt. "What's going on?" the cat shifter asked, pupils still slits.

Norah covered her face with her hands. The last wisps of her beard tried to establish a peach-fuzz mustache. It was like reverse puberty.

"I can explain," Norah said, voice croaking into a higher octave.

A solid barrier of disgruntled ex-employees corralled her against the wall.

A muffled "This should be good" rose from Norah's pocket.

The last trace of her glamour flickered away, the jeans and hoodie she'd selected unraveling into a pair of leggings and a loose pajama top. One of Saxon's bottomless supply of ex-assistants stared at the mustard stain on the gray fabric.

Currents of emotion flowed toward Norah. Turning up their volume, she searched for the person who had wanted to see Saxon.

There! The burning desire flickered, a dimming flame at the periphery of her awareness. Norah extended her senses, but the current ebbed into a trickle. Her chance to wake Saxon up was getting away.

Screw it.

Norah shoved the cat shifter and ran, but hands closed on her. She wanted to scream at the fleeing person to stop, but they were moving fast, and she was distracted by the shouting. She struggled until the last thread of emotion snapped, her target past her range.

"Hell," Norah muttered. The crowd pushed her back, and she retracted the range of her empathy. The mob had a mind of its own, and emotion in her immediate vicinity had blended into two currents. They wanted answers, and they wanted to know exactly how Garton Saxon was involved.

"Here's the truth," Norah said before she realized she'd have to provide a follow-up. *Start with the truth.* "I am not casting for a Garton Saxon biography."

The mob grumbled, and a female voice from the crowd muttered, "I drove from *West Covina*!"

"I'm actually casting for a dating show where legendary Hollywood executives find, uh, love?"

Her pocket rustled, and Madge, once more a pixie, took to the air. "It's called *Greenlight My Heart.*"

The mob stilled. It was time to throw some chum into the water.

"In the show, Saxon will team up with ten contestants to develop romantic comedy short films that, uh..."

"Showcase the true meaning of love!" Madge finished. Time to pull in the line.

"The winner gets a development deal at Silver Lion and a four-carat diamond ring."

"And a new car!" Madge added.

Norah shot her a look. *Don't oversell it.*

"What kind of car?" the cat shifter asked.

"A Tesla?" Norah asked. The mob murmured appreciatively.

"Why the fuck am I here?" The middle-aged man's bald spot gleamed in the overhead lights. Norah had a vision of him in a bikini in a hot tub.

"Loves knows no age or gender!" Madge said and waved her wand. A flashing green heart rose in the air.

"Waste of my fucking time," the man muttered as he stalked away.

"If you sign up for our mailing list, we're having a drawing for free parking for a year," Norah shouted after him. There was an appreciative murmur. They were more likely to get everyone's names.

"Is that a thing?" the cat shifter asked.

"We partnered with the city," Madge told him.

The pixie was a bullshit prodigy. It was lucky for everyone that she had a conscience.

Names were written on the clipboard, and a surprisingly large chunk of the mob stayed to audition. Under different circumstances, their resolute efforts to feign romantic interest in the terrifying light elf would have been funny.

After Norah thanked the last person and cut the camera feed, Madge laid on the desk.

"I'm tired," she said, face pressed into the wood. "Wanna get margaritas?"

"Only if you promise not to spill one on my laptop while we work," Norah replied.

"Fine, but you're buying the first round."

CHAPTER SIX

Norah looked good. The tube top, flowing gray pants, and matching calf-length vest were more fashion-forward than what she usually wore, but it was cool.

Maybe too cool? Screenwriters, as a species, gravitated toward elastic waistbands and coffee-stained everythings. She didn't want to overdress. Norah sighed. She was used to writers having to impress her, not the other way around.

Days of eyeball-burning reading had finally teased a halfway decent script out of the woodwork: *The Players* by Sid Wheatley. Sid was meeting her at Castaway, and she had called in a favor to get a table near one of the crackling fires on the patio. She hoped the view would bring her most difficult client around.

According to Sid's Instagram photos, he had just turned twenty-nine. According to his tax paperwork, he was thirty-six. Norah had reluctantly given him her business card at her first party after starting First Arret, her talent agency. He'd proceeded to send her polite, cheerful emails every two weeks on the dot for six months until she broke down and asked for his script.

She'd been looking forward to sending Sid the business end of a rejection email, but to Norah's dismay, the script was good and written to sell. It was a low-budget black comedy crime movie called *Hoard* about idiot hackers stealing Bitcoins from a dragon. Norah had initially assumed that Sid was a wizard, but he turned out to have no magical powers. He'd said his roommates were magicals, and he'd picked up the lingo from them.

When Norah had set a meeting, Sid had RSVPed to the calendar invite, confirmed by email, and emailed to confirm she'd gotten his confirmation. He'd also sent her brisk updates, links to relevant industry news, and dragon memes on a daily basis until she was almost, but not quite, fed up enough to cancel. It was a superpower. He'd annoyed every person in Hollywood, but not *quite* enough for them to do anything about it. Now everyone knew his name.

A few months ago, she had seeded some not-subtle hints about dropping him as a client, but Saxon's shenanigans had put a dent in her client list, so she hadn't. Instead of going cold, he'd clutched her tighter. The pace of the emails picked up. Now she needed a favor.

Norah threw on a necklace of carved wooden beads from Stan and was debating whether it was cool hippie or uncool hippie when her phone rang.

"Don't freak out," Madge said.

"Don't open with that, and I won't." Norah's nerves were clawing their way up her throat.

"I got you a meeting with Bitta."

The phone slipped and Norah grabbed at it, barely catching it before it struck the hard tile. She was breathing hard.

"*The* Bitta?"

"Okay, well, *Stellan* got you a meeting with Bitta, but don't tell him that. He's been too big for his britches since beard blowouts took Hollywood by storm."

Bitta, a dwarf, was Hollywood's breakout magical director. She had knocked the box office to its knees with three lucrative summer blockbusters in a row and then gone into hiding after an on set breakdown. Oscar buzz had been replaced by strange rumors.

Norah had last heard about the director from a tabloid at her dentist's office. According to the glossy pages, she'd gotten into New Age religion and had sold her Malibu home to fund a thousand-dollar-an-hour astrology habit.

"What am I going to wear?" Norah asked.

"Whatever you're already wearing," Madge replied. "She's joining your meeting with Sid. Are you not in the car?"

Norah froze. She was running five minutes behind, which was fine if it was just Sid, but if she hit traffic...

"Of course I'm in the car." Norah sprinted out the door. Her keys refused to slide into the lock.

"Jesus, Norah, I just heard you lock your door," Madge said. Ignoring her, Norah took the stairs two at a time. She didn't see the hose across the sidewalk until she was face-first on the grass. Stan, blithely watering the lemon tree, waved.

"Stan!" Norah called. "Can I take your Thunderbird?"

The hula dancer on Stan's dashboard was enchanted

with some of the most powerful magic Norah had ever felt. He never took more than sixty seconds to find parking.

Stan looked from her desperate face to the grass stain on her vest and threw her the keys.

"You okay?"

"I'm meeting with Bitta."

Stan's eyebrows shot up. "I love that dwarf's films. I cried at *Pegasus Lasso* for the first time in sixty years. But she's…"

Norah edged toward the parking lot. "What?"

"Mmmm, I guess you'll see," Stan replied.

Madge's tinny shout through the phone, "Why can't I hear an engine?" pushed Norah back into action before she could press Stan for more information.

The Thunderbird cut through LA like an elven sword through an arm. By the time she got there, Norah had developed an affection for the dashboard hula girl that bordered on arousal. Just as she arrived, a car pulled out of the spot directly in front of the restaurant.

She was a full three minutes early, but she hadn't beaten Sid. He was perpetually early to their meetings. She'd once shown up to a coffee spot a full hour early and found him staring at a wall. He'd just been doing some writing, he'd explained, although he didn't have a laptop or even a notebook. Arriving more than minutes early was a social crime.

"Don't freak out," she said as she saw him slip into one of the seats. The fire was warm on her back, and the view over the low green-brown hills was amazing.

"Are you dropping me? Just tell me now, and we don't have to do the horrible lunch dance," Sid said.

"I'm not dropping you," Norah replied, slinging her purse over the chair. "It's worse. Bitta's coming to lunch."

"Bitta who?" Sid asked. Norah had been wrong to assume his face couldn't get paler.

A rising murmur in the restaurant told him who as a stocky dwarf woman in a skintight houndstooth jumpsuit parted the crowds. The mass of crystals strung around her neck on silk cords would make the average natural history museum weep.

Norah was about to extend a hand when Bitta crossed her arms and turned her back.

"Uh," Sid said. Norah shook her head, and the noise died on his lips.

My shitshow, my move. Should she say something? Was Bitta waiting to be announced? Hollywood directors should come with protocol officers. She considered proposing it at the next LA city council meeting.

Everyone in the restaurant had noticed the dwarf. The outfit would draw attention even if she wasn't famous. Amid the open staring, a middle-aged man rose to his feet, having apparently appointed himself the representative celebrity botherer. Halfway across the floor, a nimble server physically pulled him back and spun him toward his table with a fierce warning look. Norah's mouth opened as she stared at Bitta's complicated braids.

At exactly twelve thirty-five, Bitta turned, dropped into her seat, and held out her hand. For the first time in his thirty-six years on Earth, Sid was speechless.

"My astrologer told me this was the perfect time for a new venture," Bitta began. Her voice was as low as most men's but melodious, like rich dark velvet.

From a bejeweled pink purse, Bitta produced a deck of yellowed tarot cards, the once-colorful ink barely visible through stains and tears. In a few places, holes in the cards had been patched using magic.

"This is Madame Blavatsky's original deck," the dwarf continued. The faded ink showed an old woman and a boy on crutches struggling through the snow beneath five pentacles. Bitta held it in front of her face, glared at Sid, and returned it to her purse.

The table rattled as Bitta leaned across it, breath hot on Sid's face.

"Your aura is blue, and I need it to be gold."

Sid's retreat rocked his chair onto its back legs. Norah grabbed it just before he tipped over. The dwarf's breath was like subterranean steam, and Sid looked at Norah for help.

Maybe this was going to be fun.

"You heard her, Sid. Gold it up."

"Uh..."

Bitta let out a disgruntled huff. "I'll send him to my aura guy. *If* this works out." Sid's gulp was audible. Bitta tapped an acrylic-tipped black nail on the table. "Here's the skinny, kid. I've heard of you."

Sid brightened and pulled his chair an inch closer to the table. "Oh! Thank you."

Bitta twirled an amethyst around her fingers. "It's interesting you think that was a compliment. That's good. Buckle on a little more of that oblivious self-esteem, and let's talk about *The Players*."

Sid sat up straight. "You've read it."

"Twice. Look, kid, it's not a movie."

The chair shifted as Sid's soul left his body. Sensing that now would be the worst time to approach, a bored server appeared at their table.

"Do you know what you want?" she asked, voice clipped. Sid looked like he was about to ask if the menu had anything with hemlock in it before Norah cut him off. "Can you get us some coffees and come back in fifteen minutes?"

She had more invested in this than Sid, she realized queasily. She was running out of time to put this deal together. If she had to read another sexy nun script, she might join a convent.

She liked *The Players* enough for this project. The script was about a mysterious force tormenting a troupe of traveling performers trapped inside a castle during a black plague quarantine. The shaggy six-legged beast that stalked the lightless hallways was scary, but the actors were the *real* monsters.

"Yet!" Bitta announced.

Sid tracked her movements like she was a predatory animal.

"What?"

"It's not a movie. *Yet.*" The server brought coffees, and Norah drank hers in gulps to stop herself from making everyone play nice. The broadcast from her guts was unmistakable. They had to fight this one out.

"What happened? You get dumped by an actress?" Bitta continued.

Bingo. Sid's face twisted. He stammered an unconvincing denial, but Bitta plowed ahead. "Your flick's lousy with villains. If *you* hate 'em, your audience will, too."

Norah held her breath. Sid bought some time with a sip of coffee. Bitta rearranged the crystals on the table without breaking eye contact.

"You're right," Sid finally admitted. Norah let out a breath she hadn't realized she was holding.

Bitta nodded. "You drive here, kid?"

"Yeah."

She pulled a peacock feather quill from her bag and scribbled down an address.

"Meet me here in thirty minutes. Bring enough clothes for three days."

"Uh..."

Norah turned on the dwarf. "Does this mean you're in?" she asked, snapping a picture of the address with her phone. Sid slipped the original into his pocket.

Bitta's eyes narrowed, and she smoothed the frizz off her forehead. A Panda Express fortune cookie appeared on the table. Bitta cracked it open, lost in concentration as she surveyed the fortune.

"What does it say?" Norah asked, fidgeting. Her tension had started to ease. *Panda Express has never let me down.*

"Keep your expectations reasonable," Bitta read. Good advice under the circumstances, though Norah had been hoping for something more upbeat.

"Does that mean you're a yes?" Norah asked.

Bitta shook her head. "We'll know in three days."

She snapped her callused fingers, and their server materialized.

"Give me one of everything on the menu. To go."

The server pulled on her collar. Norah had done her

compulsory time in LA food service, and the kitchen was going to be pissed.

The crystals swept off the table, and a glittering jewel the size of a robin's egg plunked down to replace them.

"That's an Oriceran sapphire," Bitta explained. "For the staff."

The server's eyes widened. Norah guessed she'd never had to have a tip appraised.

"Right away, your directorship."

Bitta grinned. "I like that. I'm gonna make that happen. Her Most High Directorship. Leave the food on the doormat in an hour, Norah, but don't bother us." She tapped the scribbled address insistently, looked at her watch, remained still for two minutes, and then swept out.

Sid excused himself to find a restroom, the green terror on his face suggesting an oncoming bout of vomiting. The uproar from the kitchen provided Norah entertainment for the next ten minutes. After twenty, with no sign of Sid, worry set in.

Norah pushed open the door to the bathroom. "Sid?"

Panicked breathing emerged from the second-to-last stall. Hopefully, he was done vomiting.

"How's it going, buddy?" she asked.

"What if I can't do it?" Sid demanded.

When all else fails, tell the truth. "Then I won't get the package together in time to get the picture, and your life won't change." She hoped he would take it as a threat. Sighing, Norah tuned her radio magic to the lowest level and sent it toward the panicking screenwriter. A bottomless hunger for approval grabbed her by the throat. He was terrified she would learn he was a fraud.

"You know what I like about you, Sid?" Norah asked. A hopeful face tipped up. "Almost nothing," she continued. "You're not going to have a career because of your charisma or because people want to do you favors. *You're* going to have a career because you're good."

He blinked rapidly, gripping the toilet paper holder with a white-knuckled hand. "Is that a compliment?"

"It is if your priorities are straight," Norah agreed. That coaxed him out of the stall.

She realized that they weren't alone in the restroom. A man at the sink in a black leather vest looked up. "You know what you need, man? You need some pink fairy."

Offering his hand, he revealed two translucent pink pellets. Some kind of bean? Strangers with magic beans rarely produced positive results. Norah was about to usher Sid back into the restaurant when he snatched the beans from the stranger's hand and swallowed them dry.

"You don't have time to do unfamiliar drugs, Sid. You're supposed to meet Bitta in *ten* minutes," Norah cried. There was no indication that Sid had registered this information. Instead, his expression grew distant, and his eyes turned bubblegum-pink. When he slapped a hand over his mouth, Norah jumped out of the way, expecting another bout of vomiting. Instead, with a muffled choke, his hand flew off his mouth as if pushed by force. A sparkling pink fairy crawled out, shaking saliva off her cotton candy-colored wings. Norah probed the fairy with her empathic senses but felt no emotion. It wasn't a person but an enchantment.

"You're the greatest screenwriter since William Goldman," the fairy apparition whispered.

The man in the black leather vest grinned.

"Whatever she tells you, you *have* to believe. That's how pink fairy works. I'm Chunk."

He handed them a black business card, empty except for a phone number embossed in bubblegum-pink.

"How long does it last?" Sid asked, the end of his question interrupted by a second fairy. The apparition perched on Sid's right ear and lovingly stroked his temple. "You have what it takes," she cooed.

"That card is made of edible paper. Eat it, and you'll never forget my number," Chunk said. Sid waited for a third fairy to climb out of his mouth before swallowing the card whole.

"I *am* the greatest screenwriter since William Goldman. I *do* have what it takes!" Sid sprinted out of the bathroom.

Chunk offered her a second card. "Care to take a spin?"

"Sorry." Norah glared at him. "I'm on a no-paper-from-strangers diet."

"It'll do wonders," Chunk sing-songed. She hesitated for a moment before shaking her head. *I don't have time to do unfamiliar drugs.*

As she left the restroom, her server blocked her path.

"*Bitta's* order is ready." She whispered the director's name at the lowest possible volume.

"Where is it?" Norah asked.

The server pointed at a line of six busboys struggling under the weight of a hundred and fifty heavy paper bags. Fitting them into the Thunderbird was going to require culinary Tetris.

"They'll have to make two trips," the server said with an aggrieved sigh. "We have *got* to shorten our menu."

CHAPTER SEVEN

Over the next forty-eight hours, the radio silence from Bitta and Sid drove Norah so far up the wall that she started going for two runs a day. When her pocket finally dinged at midnight, she scrambled for her phone, only to see what appeared to be a video butt-dial. The screen was entirely pink, and a familiar fairy-like voice in the background whispered, "You are a strong and confident woman" before the call cut off. Was that a compliment for Sid? She called back, but no one answered, which blackened her mood. If she couldn't get a package to Marina two days from now, the wheels would come off the cart.

At least she'd made progress on the Saxon project. The *Greenlight My Heart* ruse had produced four promising candidates. Additionally, a cross-reference between auditionees, fake raffle signups, and RSVPs had produced two names that Norah thought could be the source of the fiery emotion she'd sensed in the hallway.

Asking people to kiss a comatose elf wouldn't be her

finest hour, but desperate times called for lip gloss. Madge had talked Norah out of revealing the truth about their project. Instead, they would disguise Garton Saxon as a gold statue of Garton Saxon.

"It's a stupid plan," Madge said. "Almost as stupid as most people willing to audition for a celebrity dating show."

Norah had rented a studio in Burbank for the audition. She and Madge had come in early to get Saxon situated. It had taken a little brainstorming. The light elf's body was as stiff as a rock, but he couldn't stand upright on his own. Madge had tried a few spells, with limited success. They eventually settled for the expediency of putting Saxon's feet in concrete and using magic to make it set faster. That was both effective and fun. Plus, it would slow him down if he did wake up.

That was another problem. An extremely dangerous light elf wasn't going to wake up from a coma like a ray of sunshine. She and Madge had spent the morning applying protective wards, and Frondle had fashioned one of his Sleeping Beauty arrows into a dagger for her. When he'd dropped it off, he'd told her he was looking forward to their date. Despite the chaos, she was too. Under the waves, the ocean would be green and peaceful.

She just had to watch a bunch of strangers kiss a statue first. Swapping the can of gold spray paint to her left hand, she wiped the sweat off her palms and checked that the tarp they'd brought was stretched beneath him.

"Is this going to hurt his eyes?" Norah asked, holding the nozzle to Saxon's face.

"We need him to talk, not see," Madge said. She was

right, but Norah shivered and pressed her finger onto the nozzle. Within an hour, she had produced a life-sized golden light elf. Upright in an empty studio, the effect was unsettling. Any lingering guilt she had was washed away by the cold expression on that perfect, evil face.

Norah shot a jolt of magic over the light elf to make the paint dry faster and wiped off her hand. "Let's get this toad kissed."

One by one, the candidates filtered in. The first was an industry-standard blonde named Penelope. Norah thanked her for coming to the callback. That was how she'd referred to it over the phone. It was like a magic word for getting actors to go places.

"So, today we're shooting videos that could be used in the show's promotional material if you're accepted. What we're doing here is combining Tinseltown glamor with true love."

"We need you to kiss the statue," Madge cut in.

The actress didn't even blink.

"Just a peck on the cheek is fine," Norah said.

Cynicism flickered across Penelope's face, but she papered it over with a glowing smile and shone such a joyful look on Saxon that Norah sucked in her breath. *It sure looks like love.* Flinging her arms around the hopefully-dry paint, she leaned in. When her lips were a hair away from Saxon's cheek, she froze. "What's my motivation?"

"Your motivation is that you love the statue, and you want him to know it," Norah said. *Feel free to go method.*

Penelope leaned in again. Norah held her breath.

Penelope's back straightened. "Is it more romantic or more sexy?" she asked, searching their faces.

"Let's see romantic first," Norah said.

Norah gripped her wand as Penelope's lips landed firmly on Garton Saxon's cheek.

"Touchdown," Madge whispered. Under the gold spray paint, Saxon was still, then...

Nothing. Squat. Corpses were livelier.

Disappointment mingled with relief. She was prepared to talk to the light elf, but she wasn't looking forward to it.

"That was great! Thanks for coming in!" Norah chirped.

Panic flickered in Penelope's eyes.

"I can do it again! You want sexy? I can do sexy!"

She dropped her voice into a throaty Happy-Birthday-Mister-President register. "Hello, lover!" She hooked a leg around the statue. Even on his pedestal, he was an inch shorter. Stroking the gold chest with her hand, she dove tongue-first for Saxon's mouth.

Norah opened her mouth to object when a small wand poked her in the neck.

"I want to see how this plays out," Madge whispered.

It played out with a lot of slobber. As Penelope walked out, mouth rimmed with an inch of gold, Norah shot twin purification and healing spells into her back.

"See! She'll be fine," Madge stated. "Next!"

Four of the people in the waiting room barely looked at her. The fifth, a light elf whose sign-in identified him as Illio, peered past her shoulder into the room. Was this her mystery Garton fan? Norah closed her eyes for a moment and turned on her radio magic, probing the room's emotions. Four of them oozed a Hollywood hunger for success. When Norah felt the current coming off of Illio, she gasped.

There it was, that bright, burning desire to look upon Saxon's face.

She would do him last, she decided. If Garton Saxon woke up, there would be less chance of collateral damage.

The next four candidates zipped by in a cool twenty minutes. Despite pecks, smooches, and a memorable attempt to give the golden statue a hickey, Saxon remained lifeless.

"Thanks," Norah said to the last of the four, an elegant dark elf in a tweed suit, then approached Illio.

"Ready?" she asked.

The light elf brushed a swoop of chestnut hair behind one ear and nodded. A flowing gray coat of some soft material covered his muscular shoulders, an elven style paired with Earth textiles. Maybe organic cotton. Illio's movements were precise, and his eyes lit up as he entered the room, tugged in by some magnetic pull from the statue.

Madge rattled off the spiel about the audition, and Norah's adrenaline shot up. Illio was the one. According to her empathic senses, all the right signals were there. He was desperate to be closer to Saxon, to hear his heartbeat.

"Let's try a take!" Norah said, reinforcing the wards on the floor with a surreptitious twitch of her wand under the table. The wards were designed to repel light elf magic. Illio stumbled but said nothing.

"Ready?" she asked Madge.

The pixie winged upward, wand in hand. "Whenever you're ready," she told Illio.

Her heart beat faster as Illio approached the body. Currents of emotion flooded her. *Passion. Hunger.*

Revenge.

The line between love and hate was thin, but Illio had clearly left it in the dust some time ago.

"Hey!" Norah leapt to her feet as the elf's coat dropped to the floor, revealing a gleaming elven broadsword.

"For Yverne!" Illio shouted, and the blade flashed from its scabbard. The protective wards would stop offensive magic but not stab wounds.

Norah shot a stunning spell at the elf, but he sensed it and spun, deflecting the line of crackling blue with his blade.

She flung a shield of protective magic between Illio and Saxon. The twirling light elf brought the broadsword down on it, and a sunburst of hairline cracks radiated through it.

Then Illio spun toward Norah. "I don't understand your twisted scheme, but I have sworn an elven oath to avenge my sister. Saxon must die!" Crystalline sweat beaded on his face.

"You knew he wasn't a statue?" Norah asked.

"Three years ago, I set a tracking spell on that vile monster, but he was always protected until several weeks ago, when he disappeared."

When we put him in the crystal coffin.

"This morning, he reappeared. I came at once. It's a stroke of luck to find him defenseless."

Illio had clearly been at this for some time. There were plenty of people in Hollywood who wanted revenge on Saxon, but most of them were too smart to try it. Apparently, the tall light elf was not so hampered.

"You have thrown your lot in with a dangerous enemy, witch!" Illio brought his sword down on the shield again with an impressive flying leap. One more strike, and he would be through the shield. Out of the corner of her eye, Norah saw Madge drop and wing a wide path behind Illio.

"We're not trying to help him. We just need to talk to him so we can find out who's trying to kill my parents."

Illio stabbed the shield, and it crumbled. *Shit.*

As he stepped forward, Madge sprang into the space above Saxon's golden head. Wings a blur and wand out, she fired a stream of magic at the crown of Illio's head. *What is she doing?*

Suddenly, Norah understood. As Illio raised his sword to block Madge's spell, the length of his unprotected body opened to Norah.

Her stunning spell hit the small of his back as he pointed his sword at Saxon's throat. Stiff body unbalanced, Illio fell sword-first toward Saxon.

"No, you don't!" Madge shouted, diving for a lock of chestnut hair. Her wings strained as she held the full weight of his body aloft. If her strength didn't break, the hair would.

Norah sprinted and grabbed Illio by the collar before his sword pierced Saxon's golden guts. She lowered the light elf to the floor and dragged him under the light by the windows, then tapped his mouth with her wand.

"Why do you want revenge?" she asked.

The light elf sputtered. "Saxon married my sister. Halfway through the honeymoon, he revealed his true personality. It took her years to muster the courage to leave him. Nothing happened for a year, then small things started to go wrong in her life. Little things, little curses, but they kept piling up. He layered them on like coats of paint on an old house. It ground her down. She's never been the same."

"Where is she now?" Norah asked. *Surely she doesn't love him.*

Illio pressed his mouth shut.

"I can't let you kill him," Norah said. "Not until we talk to him. Yverne. Is that her name? She might be able to help."

Illio shook his head. "She can't help anyone. Not even herself."

Norah motioned Madge over to the corner.

"What are we supposed to do with him?" she asked.

"I'll tell you what we should do," Madge muttered. "Lock him up until he tells us where his sister is, use her to crack Saxon, and then set him loose to sweep up the mess."

It had a dark symmetry. Norah's mind raced. Stan could help find the sister if they were desperate, but she wasn't keen to take prisoners.

An impossibly loud scream ricocheted off the hardwood floor. Illio climbed to his feet, molasses-slow, shards of magic popping off him like bits of shell off a hardboiled egg.

"Mother of Merlin," Madge muttered.

It was possible to break a stunning spell with force of will, in theory. Norah had never been able to do it. The trick required a burning purpose.

At least she now stood between Illio and Saxon, but they wouldn't be able to flank him a second time. Madge went for it anyway, rounding the room toward the light elf. He raised a wall of gleaming magical darts and herded her toward Norah.

"Two to one, Illio," Norah cautioned.

He nodded curtly. Despite the odds, she thought he would attack again. Instead, he ran at full speed toward the nearest window and launched into the air as the elven blade sliced through the glass.

Norah rushed over, relieved to see that he had broken his fall with a gleaming web of light. He rolled off it and hurtled into the shrubbery at an impossible speed.

Norah turned her magical radio senses up to maximum range, wincing at the chaotic flow from the office building around her. The hole in the window, lined with cruel shards, beckoned.

Geronimo!

She cast a magical cushion as she jumped, hoping Illio hadn't stuck around to pull it out from under her. The landing was soft, and she was quickly on her feet.

There! Burning emotion pulsed behind a row of manicured yews. Norah sprinted toward them, grateful for her recent uptick in training. As she shoved through the bushes, horns honked. Illio ran across a four-lane road, the blade in his hand flashing in the sunlight.

Norah tried to follow, but the traffic had picked back up. By the time she managed to cross, Illio was an ember at the far edge of her range. Light elves were much faster than humans, but she followed him as long as she could until the blip on her empathic radar flickered and died. Panting, she bent over, legs burning and acid rising in her chest. She stuck her face under a nearby sprinkler, then walked back to the building.

Madge was waiting in the car, Saxon already loaded into the back.

"How'd you get him down?" Norah asked.

"I pushed him out the window. An experience I recommend, although getting him into the car took a hefty anti-grav spell."

Norah sighed. "I want to drive around the neighborhood for a bit. See if we can pinpoint Illio's location. If we get close enough, I'll feel him."

"What about *The Players?* Get any closer to that deadline, and you'll have to start picking out baby names," Madge suggested.

"We can work while we drive," Norah replied.

Ten minutes after she got in the car, Norah realized her phone was gone. "I must have dropped it while I was running."

For an agent in Los Angeles, losing a phone was worse than a magnitude ten earthquake. "I'll install a backup on my old phone when we get home," she said. "I don't want to lose time."

They drove around until Norah's gas light turned on. She was hollow with exhaustion, her emotions scooped out by using her radio magic at max range for hours.

When she saw a billboard for a new otter exhibit at the Aquarium of the Pacific, she remembered she was supposed to meet Frondle in Malibu two hours ago. Slamming on the brakes, Norah snatched Madge's phone, ignoring the pixie's protests.

A rapid-fire search through the contacts list proved futile.

"You don't have Frondle's number?" she asked.

"Oh, um..." Madge turned away, fiddling with the window lock.

"What?"

"He's saved as NICE BUTT," Madge explained.

Frondle picked up immediately. "Madge? Is Norah all right?"

"Hey, Frondle, it's me," Norah said. "I'm sorry about our date. Someone at the kiss-a-thon tried to kill Saxon." When she explained what had happened, Frondle's patient understanding restored a little of her energy. She would find a way to make it up to him.

"Would you like to come over?" Frondle asked. "Not to, um… I mean, my roommates are having a party."

She was pretty sure she could hear someone singing along to an acoustic guitar melody. There was only so much of the Great American Songbook her exhausted body could take.

"Next time," she said sincerely. "What about tomorrow? I'll be sending Marina the script tomorrow night, which will give me about five minutes of breathing room." As Frondle agreed, she hit a speed bump, and Saxon's head banged into the roof. Checking on him in the rearview mirror, Norah was jealous. *No one ever puts me in a nice, comfortable coma.*

A couple of hours of sleep would have to do.

CHAPTER EIGHT

It was two hours until Marina's deadline, and Norah's brisk up-and-back jog to the Hollywood sign hadn't distracted her from the fact that she didn't have a script. Her muscles still ached from yesterday's chase, and when she got home, she decided to take action.

The house where she'd dropped off the takeout earlier in the week was a Topanga Canyon aerie whose fragile-looking floor-to-ceiling windows revealed Malibu and the Pacific Ocean. Her new phone rang as she pulled into the long driveway, and Marina's name on the screen made her heart skip a beat. She turned on the speaker and held the phone away from her face as she parked next to a bright blue Japanese motorcycle.

"Two questions, Wintry," the executive said before Norah got a "Hello" out. "One, are you shitting the bed on this opportunity? And two, why am I suddenly producing a reality TV show called *Greenlight My Heart?*"

Norah looked longingly at her car. If she started now,

she could throw her phone over the balcony rail and be in Mexico by midnight.

Don't be stupid. At least wait until rush hour is over.

"I, um… Look, there's some magical business going on, and…"

"Stammering wastes my time. You shouldn't have enough hours in the day to produce reality TV on top of all your other business, but maybe the witches invented some antisleep potion. The idea's not bad. Maybe we could do a collab with Sundance or something. Obviously, it can't be Saxon—you lose your sense of taste or something?—but there's a nugget there. Cyprine will be in touch about the rights."

"I…what?"

"The rights to *Greenlight My Heart.* I have decided to punish you for your weird scheme by giving you the job."

Golden light bounced off the clouds behind the house. *We're going to need more interns.* "Thanks?"

"You deserve it, and I mean that in a bad way. And you haven't answered my first question. Are you fucking up?"

"I'll have more information in a minute," Norah said.

"I don't need *information.* I need ninety pages of twelve-point Courier."

The hillside house was a blocky modern number, one of those places where everything looked expensive, and nothing worked like it was supposed to. Vast expanses of window dwarfed spindly supports. One of these windows looked into the living room, and Norah jumped when a pink flare accompanied by a *bang* flashed from within.

"I've got to go," she said.

No one answered the doorbell, so Norah popped the

lock with a basic opening spell and warily stepped inside. A sugary-sweet cotton candy smell pervaded the room, growing stronger as she approached the recessed living room.

"Hello!" she called warily. Another *bang* made her jump again, and pink light flickered on the walls.

The furniture in the living room had been pushed back. The pillows and cushions had been commandeered for a circular nest in the center. At the perimeter, a laptop was placed on a small wooden pedestal, surrounded by crystals and smoky candles. Inside the hollow of the nest, Sid and Bitta lay on their backs, facing in opposite directions. Between them, a half-empty candy bowl of pink beans emitted a bubblegum-colored haze.

Norah was too far away to read the words, but the laptop showed a page of a screenplay. *At least they've been working.*

She coughed to announce herself. "Hey, guys."

Sid bolted upright, cutting a path through the pink fog.

"Nowah!" he said, garbling her name as a pink fairy crawled out of his mouth. The apparition looked almost as dazed as Sid.

Bitta's eyes were still shut, but the pink haze swirled around her mouth and nostrils. She was still breathing.

Footsteps echoed from the kitchen, and out came the magic bean seller Norah had met in the bathroom three days ago. He had changed his leather vest for a Sex Pistols shirt and held a long-necked glass teapot full of something that looked like Pepto-Bismol.

He nodded nonchalantly at Norah. "Wanna do a pink

fairy neti pot?" he asked. "I just blended it. You could have the world's most confident sinuses."

"Sure!" Norah took the pot from him, walked over to Sid, crouched an inch from his face, and flung the neti pot against the door to the balcony. There was a tremendous crash, and the pink liquid rose in a mist. Sid whined softly. Norah hoped she wouldn't have to physically prevent him from licking the syrupy liquid off the floor.

The pink fairy that had just crawled out of Sid's mouth sprawled like a starfish on his head, running a tiny hand back and forth through his eyebrow.

"When you parallel park, everyone stops to watch and think about what a good father you'd be," the fairy apparition stated.

"The compliments get increasingly specific," Sid explained, voice unsteady. Norah reached for the laptop.

"Don't!" Bitta shouted, eyes still closed. "The words need time to settle into their new surroundings."

Norah edged closer until the page number in the top left corner was visible. Ninety-six. That was good. Almost perfect.

A pink fairy emerged from Bitta's mouth with a soft pop, made three loops through the haze, and burrowed into a coil of the dwarf's shiny braids.

"The folds of your brain are exquisitely functional and aesthetically pleasing," the fairy whispered.

Norah had seen enough. "As much as I'd love to let the words settle in, they need to be exported to a PDF, so we don't piss off one of the most powerful people in Hollywood."

"Wait for it," Bitta insisted.

"How much pink fairy have they done?" Norah asked Chunk. A row of emerald studs glittered in his ear.

"They did exactly as much as they needed to." He winked. "Now that you're here to keep the lid on, I'm gonna peace out."

Norah heard a fairy behind her say, "You can fly through the air any time you want to."

"I *can* fly through the air anytime I want to," Sid repeated, his voice a dazed monotone.

"Have fun with that." Chunk slunk toward the door. When she looked back, Sid was halfway toward the balcony, flapping his arms in long, slow loops. Norah ran after him.

"You can't fly, Sid," she said.

"I *can*, Norah. I can do anything the fairies tell me."

"I hope they told you to proofread your screenplay," she stated.

A motorcycle engine started up and then faded into the distance. Sid's eyes moved slowly back and forth. He made no effort to evade her.

"I think they *did* tell me to proofread," he finally said. "They said I was more detail-oriented than a nuclear safety engineer. No typo can withstand my mighty red pen!"

Norah let out a small breath. She walked Sid back to the nest and sat him down.

"It's almost ready," Bitta said. "Five more seconds."

Norah waved sweet pink mist away from her face. A few seconds later, a faint sound rang out. A small Tibetan singing bowl by the laptop vibrated, throwing off an eerie peal. It crescendoed until it was a clear, bright noise, rippling through the haze of pink fairy dust.

Bitta's eyes popped open, and her torso slowly rose until she was sitting upright in a perfect L-shape.

Leaning toward the laptop, she typed, "FADE OUT."

Norah wanted to hug her.

"It is done." Bitta's voice was an incantation. Norah retrieved the laptop, exported the file, and emailed it to herself and Marina.

With a soft *pop,* two more fairies emerged simultaneously from Bitta's and Sid's mouths. They corkscrewed around each other, linked hands, and whispered, "You can pull off a fedora."

Norah snorted in disgust. Now that she had the script, it was time to pop their confidence bubble. "Nope. Absolutely not. I draw the line at fedoras." She plucked the candy bowl from the nest, marched into the bathroom, and poured the contents into the toilet.

She hesitated for a second before flushing. She had read about pharmaceuticals in the water supply making their way to the ocean. Finally, she shrugged and pushed the handle. *The world can survive a few over-confident fish.*

Two beans remained in the bottom of the jar. Norah started to shake them loose but reconsidered and stuffed them in her pocket.

Just in case.

Back in the living room, she hauled Sid to his feet. "Get in the car," she said, pointing his body toward the front door. A similar attempt to pull on Bitta's arm was futile. The dwarf was as movable as a small hill. Norah pulled out her wand and drew three intricate runes in the air. When the antigrav spell hit, Norah grabbed Bitta by her pointy-toed green boot and pulled her to the car.

She needed to find a safe place to stash these two in the next twenty minutes, or she'd be late to meet Frondle. A vision of blond hair billowing above elven armor flashed in her mind.

"Move it, Sid!" she barked. The screenwriter stomped his foot huffily. Norah had a sudden burst of inspiration.

Norah would not leave actual children with a goat, but Pepe could handle a drug comedown just fine.

"Don't let them onto the balcony," she told the attentive goat. "If Sid wants to try flying again, he can do it on a nice flat surface. Do *not* let a guy named Chunk into the complex. And don't let them do any weird magic." Pepe nodded sharply, stomped his hoof, and trotted around Sid and Bitta like a schoolmaster inspecting unruly students. "Whatever you do, *don't* let them buy any fedoras," she finished, ignoring their crestfallen looks.

Popping into the bathroom, Norah traced the runes on her mirror and sternly instructed the makeup application spell to stick to a little eyeliner and lip gloss. When the makeup had folded itself back up and stacked into neat rows inside its glass box, she headed to her bedroom, where she jumped in surprise at the screaming neon oil portrait that covered an entire wall. She still hadn't gotten used to it. The day she could ignore it, she'd be worried.

Norah threw on a sleek black jumpsuit by a young LA designer. Its only adornment was a complicated set of twining straps across her bare back. Chunky mules completed the look. For half a second, she considered eating one of the pink fairy beans she'd pocketed earlier.

I can be my own pink fairy. "Your work/life balance is the envy of Hollywood," she whispered to her feet, resisting the urge to laugh at this ludicrous statement.

Back in the living room, the bubblegum smell was encouragingly faint. "How do I look?" she demanded. When Sid opened his mouth, she cut him off with "Not you!"

Pepe looked her up and down and stamped an approving hoof. She headed out the door.

Frondle lived with roommates in Koreatown. Fifteen minutes of circling for parking made her wish she had a magic hula girl of her own. Finally, in desperation, she pulled into a small commercial lot and cast a glamour on her Prius to make it look like a cop car. She didn't *think* anyone in Los Angeles would be stupid enough to tow a police car.

Stepping carefully around piles of trash, Norah made her way to a grimy apartment building and called Frondle to let her in. He appeared instantly since he had been waiting just inside the door and ushered her up to the three-bedroom apartment he shared with four roommates. A dark elf couple on the sofa greeted her with disinterest. Frondle pulled her down the hallway to see the rest of the place.

"That's Castor's room," he said, pointing at a shut door. "He made Variety's *Ten Young Puppeteers to Watch* list."

"Impressive?" Norah said.

"He's still at the theater. He's *always* at the theater. Next, we have Ethan's room," Frondle said, tapping on a second door with a mouse hole cut into the bottom. A fat orange hamster emerged.

"Aw!" Norah exclaimed.

It shifted into a ginger-haired twenty-something man.

"Ooh!" she added.

"Check it out," Ethan said and opened the door. Inside was a complex network of tubes, several hamster wheels, and a series of high-end dollhouses. The living room of one dollhouse was furnished around a tablet computer as the centerpiece of a sleek home-theater system.

"I shift into hamster form to use the room," Ethan said. "I have more space than half the working actors in Los Angeles. I don't know how regular people do it. When anyone asks me if they should move here, I tell them, 'Only if you can turn into a small animal.' Seriously."

"That's one way to solve the housing crisis," Norah agreed.

Frondle pulled her down the hall into the last room. It was instantly apparent that this one was his. As Norah walked in, the smell of night-blooming flowers hit her nose. An enchantment made the ceiling look like the night sky far overhead. A clothing rack at the foot of the bed held worn t-shirts, a single dress shirt, a tuxedo, and Frondle's precious elven armor. *Quite the wardrobe.* Small plants potted in glass orbs nestled in the squares of an IKEA bookshelf behind the bed. Their leaves phosphoresced, casting a shifting glow.

The lighting would make a person look great naked. Several potential scenarios crossed her mind.

Frondle reached behind her for the door. Up close, the

light elf smelled like sunshine on hay, and her heart beat a little faster.

It took a full minute to close the door, requiring a process more complicated than most of the serious curses Norah knew. Finally, a simultaneous raise-and-shove procedure made the latch click but rattled the room so badly that several large coins slid off a pile on Frondle's desk. These turned out to be heavy. When she pressed one with a fingernail, it made a small indent.

"Is this *solid gold*?" She replaced the coin on the pile, which was stacked so high as to be in constant danger of an avalanche. Here and there, a brightly colored gemstone peeked out of the pile. "You're as rich as a king! Why are you living with roommates?"

"I wanted the full human experience, like on American TV. Gold is hard to spend here. The first time I asked for change from that taco truck on Western, they laughed at me."

"You bought a burrito with *solid gold*? I hope it was a good burrito," Norah said.

Frondle nodded vigorously, his hair sparkling in the faux starlight. "It *was* a good burrito. Very good. Worth the coin. They haven't let me pay since."

A solid gold coin for an infinite number of burritos was a good trade. "I'm going to make you an appointment with a business manager," Norah said. "Next week. When I'm an agent again. For now..."

Her voice trailed off, and Frondle smiled. Warmth radiated from deep inside her. Sweeping a hand around her waist, Frondle pulled her in and kissed her. His lips were soft, and he tasted like anise and black pepper. Strong arms lifted Norah effortlessly. She wrapped her legs around him and laid her head on his shoulder as he kissed her neck. He was warm, and his muscular body enveloped her comfortably.

Less than a minute later, the sound of her snoring woke her up. Norah jolted awake. Frondle stood still, continuing to hold her. She was horrified to see a bead of spit on the light elf's shoulder where her head had rested.

"Oh, my God! Frondle..."

Amusement crossed his face. "You looked cute. Like a hibernating bear cub."

"I've been working so hard, and I felt so comfortable," she explained guiltily. Afraid to lose the moment, she went in for another kiss, vowing to remain awake this time. The next thirty seconds were extremely pleasant.

Just as Norah was about to propose activities that would utilize the bioluminescent lighting, there was a knock on the door. Before she could shout at the person to go away, it flew open.

Irritated, she climbed down from Frondle's embrace, smoothing her clothing.

A wizard in his late twenties or early thirties stood in the doorway. He had dark hair and bushy black eyebrows that met in the center. Norah suspected he always looked angry.

"This is my roommate Castor," Frondle said. "Castor, this is Norah."

Castor snorted. "So, that's how you get an agent in this town?"

His voice was light, and Norah couldn't parse if his greeting had been an insult or a joke. Frondle had worked hard for what he'd achieved in Hollywood, and the dig nagged at her.

She was tempted to turn on her empathic magic and subject this guy to an emotional X-ray, but she didn't want to violate Frondle's privacy on their first date.

"I hope that's not why you signed Sid," Castor continued.

What an appalling thought.

"You know Sid?" Norah asked. Of course he did. Everyone in Hollywood with an email address knew Sid.

"Norah just sold his screenplay," Frondle announced. "She's a very good agent."

Norah felt a blush creep up her chest.

Castor's expression darkened at the mention of Sid's recent success. Norah shook her head. "The deal could still fall through."

"Sid and I used to be writing partners." Castor's eyebrows pushed even closer together, and he oozed disgruntlement. Seeing your ex flourish after a breakup was never easy.

"How was the rehearsal?" Frondle asked.

"I broke three strings and got a splinter under my fingernail. I swear to God, that Gypsy Rose Lee marionette has it out for me."

"Congrats on making the Variety list," Norah said.

Castor rolled his eyes. "That was, like, two years ago. Do you want comp tickets for opening night? I can get two," he amended, staring blankly at Norah.

"Imagine a sexy nightclub variety show, but with puppets," Frondle clarified.

"It's called 'Evening Wood,'" Castor said. "I named it."

Norah imagined Pinocchio in a thong and decided to leave the imagining to the creatives. Curiosity got the better of her. "How sexy are we talking? On a scale of bell pepper to habanero?"

"Habanero. Definitely habanero," Castor said so confidently that Norah decided she must see this extravaganza.

"I'd love a ticket," she said, warming when Frondle beamed.

"We're making sunfruit margaritas and watching *Frasier* if you wanna join," Castor said. Frondle raised an eyebrow at Norah.

"What time is it?" She checked her phone and saw two voicemails and three texts from Marina. *Shit.*

"I should go," Norah said, assuming that Castor would excuse himself. The wizard didn't move even after she coughed pointedly in his direction.

"Would you walk me to my car?" she finally asked Frondle. He bowed.

Several minutes later, Norah was relieved to discover that no one had towed it. "I'm sorry I fell asleep. I know people say this when they don't mean it, but it's not you. I'm just exhausted."

"You must rest! I was very happy to see you tonight," Frondle said.

"Me too. I'm weirdly looking forward to the risqué puppets."

"I've seen Castor practicing. It's physiologically accurate."

Norah chuckled and put the date in her calendar. "I think I'd enjoy anything with you," she said shyly.

Frondle glowed at the compliment and swept Norah

into his arms for another kiss. Her eyes fluttered shut again. When she opened them a few minutes later, a frowning face greeted her.

"I'm not letting you drive," he said.

"I'm fine!" Norah protested.

"I can't allow you to nod off and crash through the window of my favorite bulgogi place. Give me your keys."

Norah sighed and dialed Marina's number as she climbed into the passenger seat. It only rang once.

"Wintry!" Marina said. "Why aren't you answering your phone?"

"It's nine o'clock at night," Norah replied.

"Nine o'clock is the go-getter's three-thirty. Answer your phone, Wintry. Anyway, I looked at the script, and it's good. Maybe better than good. Rewrites should be a breeze."

Norah, whose neck had started to relax, sat up. *Rewrites?!* Bitt and Sid had barely gotten the script done the first time.

"Get to the studio at seven, and we'll hash out the notes," Marina finished.

"Seven in the morning?" Norah asked.

"Yes, Wintry. Seven in the morning. I swear. How's *Greenlight My Heart* coming along?"

"Great!" Norah lied. She took a deep breath and rolled one of the pink beans in her pocket between her thumb and forefinger. *Not yet, Wintry. You're your own pink fairy.*

"I'm the world's best agent," she whispered.

"That's the spirit," Marina said. "Who cares about the truth? This is show business!"

"We'll be there at seven," Norah said. "Looking forward

to it." Her ever-growing to-do list rose in her imagination. She closed her eyes, thinking about the most pressing tasks. If she could get three of her clients cast in this thing, First Arret would be in the black for another year.

Her imagined to-do list floated away from her, the paper it was written on folding into an origami crane. The bird came at her with an outthrust beak, pecking at her eyes and throat. When the beak dug into her arm, she jolted awake.

Frondle was tapping her elbow. "We're here."

Norah hugged him goodbye. "How are you getting home?"

"I'm going to run!" he said brightly.

She did the arithmetic. "It's four miles."

Frondle shrugged. "It's not going to take more than one episode of *Frasier*. Goodbye, Norah!" With one last peck on the cheek, the light elf leapt from the car and bounded south, his long legs a blur. Norah watched him for as long as she could see him.

Pepe met her at the front door like a babysitter who was fed up with unruly kids.

"How'd it go?" she asked. Pepe's shoulders moved in what she was sure was a shrug, and he let out a noise that might have been *"Shhh."*

Norah pulled off her chunky boots and crept into the living room. Bitta was face-down on the couch, snoring like a power drill. Sid was curled up on Pepe's organic cotton dog bed. The goat trotted over and pulled a blanket up to Sid's neck. Admiring his work, he took a bite of the blanket and chewed it thoughtfully.

Norah set three alarms and slept like the dead.

CHAPTER NINE

Amid the chaos of the film set, Norah felt calm. Her only job from here on out was to babysit Sid and collect her clients' checks. Now that she had gotten everyone to the starting line, she could shout encouragement from the stands.

Her ticket to the opening night of Castor's puppet show was in her pocket, a tangible reminder that soon she would have a well-deserved night off. *Even if there are a few strings attached. To the sexy puppets.*

The hustle and bustle filled Norah with pride. She loved movies, and this one had come together because of her. Her client had written the script and several more of her clients had been cast, including Duncan, who had a small but pivotal role as the first theater troupe member to be murdered. Norah had surreptitiously snapped a photo of the schedule that morning and followed it as the AD called out shots and scenes. She'd released Katie from her internship duties to work as a production assistant.

It was going to be a good flick. It was already lucrative.

First Arret's coffers, which had been depleted by the Saxon kerfuffle to the point where Norah hadn't paid herself last month, were filling up nicely.

At lunch, Norah sidled by the craft services table. The young man working there was about to shoo Norah away when Angelo came out of a nearby trailer, gave her a big hug, and began loading her plate with sliders.

"Norah, you must be a good example for the actresses by eating my beautiful food. Cooking for these people is so depressing. They only want unsalted lettuce and fat-free chicken breasts. Every day, I swear to my father that I'm moving to the American Midwest and catering weddings. They would not abuse me like this in St. Louis. Look at my poor lasagna. Look how she languishes. In Chicago, they'd be begging me for seconds."

He underscored his point by cutting a slice of the aforementioned lasagna and piling it over the sliders. Norah took a bite and was transported by tender noodles into a paradise of perfectly balanced cheese and Bolognese.

When she opened her eyes several seconds later, Angelo was glowing.

"Those are Earth tomatoes, but they were grown in Oriceran. Tell me if you feel weird."

"Angelo!" Norah said. "We're on an eighteen-day schedule. You can't get everyone high at lunch on Oriceran rain-fed produce."

"I'm an artist. These things happen, Norah."

She glanced at the lasagna again. So far, its only effect

was to make her want to eat eight more squares of it. She sighed.

"Is there any salad?"

Angelo clutched his heart. "You wound me, Norah." He pointed her toward a much busier table. As Norah walked away, she heard Angelo bend down and whisper to the lasagna, "It's not you, beautiful. No, don't cry."

Time flew. At the end of the day, Norah found Bitta in a huddle with the cinematographer, a light elf named Sinter, and the first AD, a terrifying fairy named Oleander whose blue morpho wings glittered in the light when she screamed, which was pretty much constantly.

Norah couldn't resist. Drawing runes in the air with her wand, she summoned a glowing magical ear and sent it through the crowd at ground level to the center of the huddle. She had perfected her eavesdropping spell in high school but had sworn off casting it after learning what her friends really thought of her perm. *They were right, though. I did look like I'd been struck by lightning.*

Three voices filtered to her through the spell.

"This is good news," Sinter was saying. "We made our day fifteen minutes early."

"We should keep rolling. Give ourselves a cushion for the rest of the shoot," Oleander said. Her voice was like a diamond drill. Norah probably could have heard it without the eavesdropping spell.

"I've never had a first day run this smooth," Bitta said.

"That's *good*, Bits." Sinter sounded exasperated.

"It's good? Like having your wish come true when you touch the monkey's paw is good?" Bitta said, voice strained and words rushed. "Something bad is coming straight at us. I can feel it in my dense dwarf bones."

"You're being ridiculous," Sinter said. Norah gave it about five seconds before he started yelling.

"We're wasting time, air, and light," Oleander barked. "Stop being a Nostradumbo, and let's shoot the stuff in the tower. It's already lit."

"It is? How?"

"Electrical is running ahead of schedule, too," Oleander said. "Stop suggesting our set is cursed just because I'm fucking fantastic at my job. Put on your baseball cap and woman the fuck up."

There was a long pause. The warehouse was getting restless, and Norah heard a few of the people in the camera department talking about happy hour. The production was shedding momentum. If they were going to forge ahead, they would have to start soon.

"We're moving to the tower. Scene twenty-eight, shot three B!" Oleander shrieked, slicing through any discussion of happy hour. The crew seemed relieved that they were moving on. Almost all of them were seasoned veterans, and they were more worried about the tight schedule than she was.

When Norah's phone rang, she cut the eavesdropping spell with a quick circle and slash of her wand. Madge's gravelly voice boomed out, distorted. "How's *The Players?*"

"Good," Norah said. "Maybe too good. I dunno. How's *Greenlight My Heart?*"

"I found a perpetual Christmas village in Toronto we can rent. They usually shoot back-to-back Hallmark movies, but we could get it for a week. I think we should rent the warehouse in Poland, though. The space is dirt cheap, and the production costs will be a fraction of what they would be here. When are you coming in?"

"We made our day. I was thinking about taking the night off."

"Oh, no, you don't, Wintry. I need you here."

"Ugh. Fine," Norah said. "You know, I don't think this is going to be as much of a shitshow as I expected."

She regretted saying these words almost immediately, and went out of her way to find an authentic sixteenth-century wardrobe to knock on. The words haunted her as she drove home. *I'm being as unreasonable as Bitta.*

She felt vindicated when she got a panicked call the next morning at five-thirty.

"Katie?" Norah asked, rubbing her eyes. "Is everything okay?"

"Bitta won't come out of the railcar, and Security caught some guy trying to sneak onto the set. He said he was friends with Bitta, and then he said he wanted to talk to *you.* He mentioned you by name. Then he ran away and escaped on a motorcycle. Oleander's been trying to get in to see Bitta for half an hour, but I guess she reinforced it with some dwarven metals."

Norah sighed. "I'm on my way."

The first cold light was on the horizon by the time Norah got to the studio. The parking lot was a quarter full even at this hour, and black-clad shapes moved in and out of the building like ghosts. An ominous mist wafted through the air, and the shadows on the concrete spooked her. Paired with the early morning call, her nerves jangled in her limbs.

Then she opened the door and screamed.

An enormous beast got to its feet, balanced on six hairy black legs. It was the size of an ox, and shaggy black fur weighed down its bulk.

When Norah screamed, it raised its head.

The head was flat and wide, with torn ears. Its mouth opened to reveal rows and rows of wet, mucous-covered teeth. The beast's eyes were bleached white with dead red pupils, covered by the same goo.

Then the monster's head sagged, and Stellan stepped out from behind the shaggy body.

Norah, who had pulled out her wand to fire off a powerful curse, sagged against the doorframe in relief. This was the beast stalking the movie's characters. It had an articulated skeleton and was operated by a team of special-effects wizards.

"Pretty good, huh?" Stellan asked. "It just got delivered from the shop. Worked my crew all night, and I think it paid off. We call him Fuzzball."

"You just about gave me a stroke," Norah replied.

"I take that as a personal compliment." Stellan grinned and ran a hand through his breathtaking beard. The thick, luxurious hair had been brushed out until it shone and was sculpted into soft waves. A black-and-white beaded barrette, striking against the auburn hair, caught back a section at the side.

Katie came rushing up, barely glancing at the huge monster.

Without speaking, she took Norah's arm and hauled her toward the railcar at the back of the studio.

Garton Saxon would have thrown a fit to see someone

else using his precious green nineteenth-century rail car, so Norah was happy that Bitta had taken it over. Hopefully, the dwarf would rough it up during her tenancy.

At first, it looked dark. No light shone from the frosted windows. That was because the windows had been boarded over from the inside.

"She fused some kind of metal over them, and the door locks have been reinforced with dwarven mechanisms," Katie explained.

Norah swore under her breath. Stellan might be able to break through, but dwarven workmanship was impenetrable.

Norah's knuckles made a muffled metallic noise on the door.

"Chunk?" a hopeful voice asked.

"I think that was the guy Security tried to catch," Katie whispered.

At least he didn't get through. One less thing to worry about. Norah didn't need Bitta on pink fairy or anything else.

Norah tugged on the loop of the empathic radio enchantment. A steady current of emotion flowed toward her from Katie, and she used it to calibrate her senses. Apparently, the intern-slash-production-assistant wanted to excel in a series of increasingly responsible roles until she was—was that a precise seventeen-year plan?—the top creative executive in Hollywood. The clarity of intention was admirable but chilling. Norah hoped the young woman would elevate First Arret rather than crush it beneath her on her mighty ascent of the Hollywood machine.

She turned the radio enchantment on Bitta.

Black emotions roiled through the door. Two flavors of fear twined around each other. One was the normal fear of an artist doing something she cared about. Bitta was afraid *The Players* would be bad, or worse, that it would be good, and everyone would think it was bad. The other current was a fear of physical harm. The energy was dark, shot through by an occasional bright jolt like lightning.

"Can I come in?" Norah called. "I won't make you come out if you're not ready."

There was a long pause. Then, the door opened a sliver, and a callused hand pulled her in. The door slammed and automatically locked behind her.

Despite the railcar's outward appearance, the interior was warm and well-lit. White dwarven lamps swung from the ceiling, and a magical fire crackled in a protective glass orb at one end of the room. Script pages, schedules, and storyboards were stacked in neat rows on a low, sturdy desk. All of Saxon's spindly, delicate furniture had been tossed out and replaced with functional pieces.

Before Norah could speak, Bitta shoved a deck of tarot cards into her hands. Unlike the cards she'd seen at Castaway, these were new and printed with bright, cheerful animals.

"Offer me the deck," Bitta ordered. Norah shuffled it half-heartedly and spread the cards. Bitta drew one without looking at it and showed it to Norah. Death.

"I thought Death could be good?" Norah asked. "Like, it's about renewal or something? I mean, if everyone who drew Death died, there'd be no one left in LA to teach yoga."

Bitta frowned and tossed the deck in a nearby trashcan that was, Norah now noticed, full of cards. A mix of cheerful and dark, they overlapped in a chaotic jumble of wands and cups. Bitta turned to a corner where a pile of brand-new tarot decks was stacked. The dwarf tossed another one to Norah, this one embossed in black and gold.

"Do it again," Bitta demanded. Norah slipped off the plastic wrapping, took out the cards, shuffled, and fanned them out. Bitta winced as she picked a card. Death again.

"Do it again," she insisted. This deck had woodblock prints. Norah felt queasy when Bitta pulled Death again. *Did she learn close-up magic?* If she had, why would she use it for this?

"I've gone through thirty-seven decks," Bitta said. "You know how many Deaths I've gotten?"

Bitta grabbed her collar and pulled her face close, her breath like a forge. "Thirty-seven, Norah. Thirty-seven Death cards. Something bad is coming."

Bitta's fear wasn't rational, but Norah had to admit the tarot thing was spooky. *I can't talk her out of being afraid.*

"Maybe something bad *is* coming," she said. Bitta looked vindicated. "If that's true, we need you more than ever. You're the captain of the ship, Bitta, but you're not alone. Half the people out there are magicals. They've been working in this business since pictures started moving. Stellan's a special-effects god, and Sinter can bend light to his will. If some evil force comes along, Oleander will probably just yell at it until it slinks away. I'm a pretty good healer," Norah said, brandishing her blue gum eucalyptus wand in what she hoped was a heroic gesture.

"If Death comes for us thirty-seven times, we'll give it thirty-seven one-way tickets to hell. Okay?"

The fear wafting off Bitta receded, revealing a trickle of courage. The dwarf took a deep breath and turned toward the door. As she gripped the handle, an earsplitting crash rattled the train car and shouts filtered in.

Bitta looked at Norah triumphantly. "Hah! I told you!"

Bitta grabbed a heavy-looking silver axe from a hook on the wall—*I didn't see that before*—and retreated into a corner of the car. Whatever faint bravery had started to emerge had been flooded by a river of fear. The dwarf would be useless.

Norah grabbed her wand and ran out into the warehouse.

The source of the noise was easy to identify since people were running away from it with unadulterated terror. Dodging scampering PAs and trundling members of the electrical department, Norah wove around a tower, under a stone arch, and through a small, walled garden. Gravel crunched under her feet as fake plant fronds whipped out of her way.

Near the tower, she passed the last runner and stopped to find the source of the commotion. The chaos had receded into silence. A fountain at the center of the garden burbled peacefully, a flirtatious cherub winking from the center.

Norah was about to write the whole thing off as some kind of mistake, but an enormous furred leg descended from above and neatly decapitated the statue. Water sprayed from its neck like arterial blood.

The great beast named Fuzzball picked up the

cherub's head and chucked it lazily through a nearby window. Norah winced when the glass shattered. The art department's budget lacked a line for "murderous rampage."

The beast skittered to the stone arch and punched through it, then stepped around Norah.

It's bent on destruction, not murder. Or whoever was controlling it was. If this was one of Stellan's pranks...

Between its spindly furred legs, Norah saw a huge stained glass window. This was the most expensive set piece Saxon had built. Its leaded jewel-tone glass formed a portrait of Mary. *The Players* made extensive use of the chapel, and the climactic showdown between the beast and the last player was set there.

That was the plan. Now the monster was trundling toward it, limbs gyrating at unbelievable angles.

Norah was about to shoot a freezing spell from her wand but realized if the beast wasn't alive, a freezing spell wouldn't do much.

Changing course, she sprinted forward and threw an antimagic well in the monster's path.

Its front legs fell in, and Norah felt a burst of satisfaction when the furry black stalks went limp. The monster briefly unbalanced as its four unaffected legs skittered away from the well, dragging its unmagicked limbs behind it.

Norah threw out another antimagic well and backed the beast beneath an eave of the chapel. It scrabbled at the ceiling, and chalky dust turned its glossy black fur dull and gray. After failing to punch through the ceiling above, the monster tried to go around the well, but failed again. It slumped forward, limbs splayed, the light gone from its eyes.

The stained glass window was still intact. There was hope for the film.

Stellan ran up behind Norah, and she could not be polite.

"What the hell was that, Stellan? If this is your idea of a prank, I swear to *God* I'm going to lose it."

Stellan was just as distraught as she was. "It wasn't anyone on my team, I swear. We were having our safety meeting. No one was operating it."

Norah raised an eyebrow. "Safety meeting?"

"Yeah. Ironic." Stellan waved a callused hand.

"The monster couldn't have come to life, could it?" Norah asked.

Stellan shook his head. "It's a prop. A great prop, mind you, but it's an articulated skeleton covered in fur."

"Like a supermodel," Norah muttered.

Now that the immediate danger had passed, Norah ran back to the walled garden to assess the damage. Now it was the unwalled garden. Gigantic chunks of crumbled quick-dry concrete lay everywhere. Accessing her magical sight, Norah saw a thin trace of magic leading to the ceiling.

"Stellan!" she called. "Call Security. Tell them to check the roof."

She knew from experience that the roof wasn't secure.

A few of the bravest crew members crept back into the garden, including Oleander. She had assembled a small, nervous-looking band of black-clad people armed with c-stands and booms. Oleander clutched a salad fork. Norah hoped anyone thinking about tangling with the fairy would think twice.

Seeing Norah, their shoulders dropped.

"It's fine," she said. "I think it was just someone playing a prank."

"If that was a prank, this is a hairbrush." Oleander threateningly twirled her fork.

Norah realized Sid was in the group, butter knife brandished in a loose grip. He took in the destruction with wide eyes.

"You're going to have to set the garden scene somewhere else," Norah told him.

A blood vessel in one pink corner of Sid's eye twitched. "B-but the garden is one of the script's key metaphors for life."

"Not anymore, it's not. Give me that." She snatched the butter knife from his hand. "You know what they say about the pen?"

"It's mightier than the sword?" Sid asked.

"Yeah, and it's *definitely* mightier than blunt cutlery. Go! Get to work."

He ran off, and Norah sighed. So much for her night out.

CHAPTER TEN

Norah woke up to a toothpick poking her repeatedly in the forehead. She swatted it away and opened her eyes.

Oh. Not a toothpick. Not yet, anyway.

"If you don't knock that off, I'm going to take your wand and use it to clean popcorn out of my teeth." Norah glared at Madge.

The pixie buzzed over and sat on Norah's bedside table, tiny gold sneakers swinging over the edge. "Pepe let me in." Appearing on cue, the goat trotted in and dropped a slobbery newspaper on Norah's bed. The front page read Gargoyles Gone Wild: Trouble on the set of *The Players*.

"Shit." Norah felt a headache coming on. "How bad is it?"

"Oleander did an interview with Variety that just went up. It's..." Madge's voice trailed off disapprovingly.

"What?" Norah asked.

"It's weird. Lots of stuff about spirits. There's already a

bunch of TikToks calling it the 'Hauntedest Movie of the Year,' and there's a pretty active subreddit forming."

"Hmmm. That could be good. No one got hurt, right? Sounds like we're getting a lot of publicity."

"That *might* be true, except..."

"What?"

"We still can't find Bitta."

"What?"

"Yeah."

"This is day *two* of eighteen."

"Yeah."

"She can't be fucking gone." Norah clutched her hair.

"That's why I'm here."

Norah finally had the wherewithal to look at her watch. It was 4 a.m.

"Why are you up?" she asked suspiciously. Madge looked sweaty, and there was pixie dust on her hem.

"I was having drinks with some of the costuming fairies," she said, an effort at dignity failing.

"Maybe she's holed up in the railcar?" Norah asked. "I got her out yesterday."

Madge shook her head. "Uh-uh. I got in through the vents and checked. She's gone. You owe me a new blazer, by the way. Disgusting."

"Fine," Norah said. "But nothing from that Victorian dollhouse store. The people there are dicks to me."

"Deal," Madge agreed.

Norah sighed. "Let's go see if we can find anyone who knows where Bitta is."

They got to the set in half an hour. Surprisingly, they found Marina touring it with a gaggle of reporters.

"Apparently, this is the most haunted set in Hollywood!" Marina exclaimed brightly. Norah waved and pushed past. The executive, of all people, didn't need to know that her director had vanished.

This early in the morning, the set was full of low-on-the-totem-pole crew setting up for the day. Norah asked them when they'd last seen Bitta and got her first break almost immediately. Someone in the electrical department who'd been loading trucks the previous evening had seen her flee the warehouse around the time of the attack and drive away. Swerving only slightly, the electrician had added.

Norah abandoned her canvass, realizing that a random costume assistant wasn't likely to know where Hollywood's hottest director was. She went looking for Sid.

The writer had constructed a small blanket fort in one corner of the warehouse and was attached to his laptop by the eyeballs, working on his script. He hadn't heard from Bitta either. Norah was about to give up when a burly figure in a white shirt approached.

"Hey, Angelo," Norah said. The caterer smiled, handed her a cheese croissant, and glared at her until she ate half of it. The buttery flakes were perfect, and the cheese was still hot inside the oven-warm pastry.

"This is perfect, but I have a lot going on," she said.

"If you're looking for Bitta, she's probably with her astrologer," Angelo murmured.

Norah perked up. "Do you know where?"

"I may have catered a solstice or two," Angelo said neutrally, looking around to see if anyone was listening.

Picking up on his anxiety, Norah twirled her wand and cast a cone of silence above them.

"By telling you this, I am breaking client-caterer confidentiality," Angelo half-whispered.

Norah tried to match his gravity. "Of course. I didn't get this information from you." Exasperated, she threw him a wink.

"Hmmm," Angelo continued. "Fine. Okay." He took her phone and typed in an address. "I'll warn you that the woman is impossible. She wouldn't let me cook any pasta. Do you know how much *salad* it takes to feed three hundred people? The sheer volume!"

As Angelo shuddered in dark reverie at this memory, Norah thanked him, then made for the door at a run. It was only when she turned on her Maps app in the car that she realized the address was in the middle of a canal.

It was not, as it turned out, a mistake. The Venice Canals had been built in 1905 as part of a developer's attempt to graft European elegance onto the city of Los Angeles. Norah walked down a greenery-lined waterway, following her phone. Small canoes were tied to docks at intervals, and palm trees swayed in the distance.

Norah's phone chirped that she had arrived, and she looked across the water. Floating in the middle of the canal was a polished wooden houseboat with *The Hierophant* painted in white letters on its side. Mystical symbols fluttered on pennants hung from the sides of the boat, and runes had been chalked around the windows and doors.

If Norah cast an antigrav spell on herself as she leapt, she could probably make the jump. However, a gondolier in a striped shirt dropped a set of tourists along the edge of the canal, and Norah opted to hand him a crisp $20 to pole her over.

The second her shoes thudded on the deck, a tall, silver-haired woman emerged from the cabin, wielding a knife that, while ceremonial, looked sharp.

"Bitta?" Norah asked cautiously. There was a round window in the wall of the boat, and through it, Norah got a glimpse of twisted braids.

"It's the curse!" the dwarf said, her muffled voice filtering through the wood.

"We have taken to running water to shield ourselves from dark forces," the silver-haired woman added.

Norah looked at the brackish water of the Venice canal. She would have described it as napping rather than running.

Norah's phone rang. Marina.

She picked up.

"Wintry! I just got off the phone with Semihill," Marina said, referring to one of the top studios in Hollywood. "They loved your little publicity stunt, and they're coming in with two million bucks."

Relief washed over Norah. Marina didn't need to know that it hadn't been a stunt.

After Marina outlined the new deal, Norah said goodbye and put the phone back in her pocket. *Well, this gives me a little more carrot to work with.*

"I can offer you a pay raise," Norah called. "Half a million bucks."

The silver-haired woman's eyebrow arched hungrily.

"Bitta doesn't want to talk to you," she said. "I will speak for her. I'm Celestia."

Of course you are.

"I'll talk to whoever's name is going on the check," Norah said.

There was a long pause, then the door to the houseboat opened. Bitta's face was lined, and she had dark half-moons under her eyes.

"I was right," she crowed. "We *are* cursed."

"So, are you more afraid of a curse, or more afraid of not having five hundred thousand dollars?" Even at a thousand bucks an hour, that was a lot of astrology.

Sensing she was losing ground to the gravitational pull of boatloads of money, Celestia edged forward.

"I could sage the set to rid it of negative energies," she offered.

Norah rolled her eyes. Great. Distract the murderous dark spirits with a salad.

"Fine. I'll do it," Bitta said. "After Celestia sages the set."

"Great. Now, as much as I would love to swim in Venice's beautiful canals, let's steer this thing to shore."

CHAPTER ELEVEN

Madge alighted on a lily pad, sinking up to her ankles as it dipped into the water. The bright pink lilies bobbed serenely in response.

"It's pretty, but is it *romantic?*" Norah asked. She and Madge were scouting locations for the first *Greenlight My Heart* challenge. A large turtle poked its head out of the water and opened its mouth in a lazy threat. Madge fluttered out of its reach, glaring at the leathery head.

"I'd go on a date here," said the pixie. "Grab an airplane bottle of vodka, hop on a turtle, and tool around the lilies."

It did sound appealing. Norah was tempted to stay here for the rest of the afternoon, but duty called.

"Okay, so it's *genuinely* romantic, but this is reality TV. No one wants authenticity. People want heart-shaped beds and chocolate doves."

A bird preening in the water gave them a skeptical look.

"Pink flowers are close enough," the pixie said, flitting down to dip her feet in the water. She ignored her beeping phone. When Madge's phone stopped beeping and Norah's phone started, the agent sighed and picked up.

"Is this Norah Wintry?" the person on the other end asked.

"Yeah. Who's this?"

"I'm Stewart."

"Stewart who?"

"Hi, sorry. I'm a bartender downtown at Clifton's. We have a situation."

In the middle of the day, Clifton's Republic was open but quiet. The bar, an LA institution that had opened in 1935, had recently closed its cafeteria. Norah's stomach grumbled; she longed for their winsome pudding cups.

The Clifton's interior resembled a redwood forest, with towering fake trees and rocky streams meandering between the tables. Stewart, who had met them at the door, led them across a bridge over a stream to a corner of the restaurant that had been blocked off with Wet Floor signs.

"Is it true there's a pixies-only speakeasy at the top of one of the fake redwoods?" Norah whispered to Madge. The pixie made a noncommittal noise and flew ahead. She landed on a table near a vinyl bench occupied by a large half-unconscious shape. Crossing her arms, she shot Norah an annoyed look.

The figure moaned, and Stewart eyed him.

"He chased four martinis with six more martinis," the bartender explained. "When we cut him off, his card got declined, and he jumped into the fountain to try to collect the quarters in it. Eventually, he laid down in the water. It took our bouncer and three of our dishwashers to haul him onto dry land. The only thing he's said in the past two hours was 'Norah Wintry' over and over. I thought he was saying *more wineries,* but eventually, he sobered up enough and I realized it was a name."

Norah, assuming one of her clients was at the tail end of a bender, approached the vinyl bench cautiously. The man didn't look familiar.

In any case, drunken ranting was not the kind of word-of-mouth advertising First Arret was looking for.

"Maybe it's someone we rejected," Madge suggested.

They approached the figure slowly, and Norah gasped when she saw the face.

"Harry Bing?"

"You *do* know this guy." Stewart sounded relieved. The bartender was a small man with dark skin who looked pissed off about being saddled with a non-tip-generating morning crisis. "Does he have a family?"

"I hope not," Madge said.

Norah shook her head. "I don't *think* so."

"Oh. Well. Do you want to take him, or should we call the cops?"

Norah sighed. Harry Bing was an asshole, but he had close ties to Garton Saxon. Was there any chance those ties included love?

"We'll take him." Norah pulled out her blue gum eucalyptus wand.

"There is, um, just the small matter of the tab," Stewart said. Norah now understood why he had called her instead of the police. Cops were notoriously bad at picking up their arrestees' bar tabs. She grudgingly pulled out her wallet and handed him her card.

A few minutes later, they were on their way out of the bar.

"We came down here, and we're not even going to get a drink?" Madge asked, outraged. The top floor of Clifton's had an excellent not-so-secret tiki bar. "They make a scorpion bowl that's big enough to bathe in."

Norah grunted and kept up the antigrav spell under Bing as Madge shoved him along.

"When things slow down, I will buy you enough scorpion bowls to do laps in," Norah promised. She might take a dunk herself.

"Wintry," the floating, comatose body muttered. "Norah Wintry." The aggravation underlying the words made it more a curse than a cry for help.

Madge huffed as she gave Bing another shove. "We're going to regret this."

"I know." Norah sighed.

In the car, Norah activated her radio magic to see what Bing wanted. He was shedding a lot of emotion, but nothing she could understand. His feelings and desires were half-digested oatmeal, indecipherable even with her special powers.

"We can't take him back to the office," Madge said as they turned off the 101. "He's going to start puking soon. Unless he dies, but I don't think he's going to do us the courtesy."

The self-embalmed power agent moaned from the backseat. Madge had wanted to put him in the trunk. As they drove, Bing's face transformed from green to greener. The pixie might have a point.

"We'll take him to my place," Norah said with the enthusiasm of a rabbit welcoming a boa constrictor into its warren.

Norah loved doing magic, but today she was extra grateful to be a witch. She and Madge managed to undress, bathe, and dry Bing without having to see or touch him. Norah even managed to turn three martinis' worth of gin in his stomach into water, a move she decided to call the "Reverse Jesus."

They deposited him on Pepe's dog bed to sleep, and Norah felt a great affection for the little black-and-white goat when he kicked Bing in the shin every time he trotted by on self-appointed guard duty. She patted Pepe's haunch but whispered that he should knock it off. "You'll only give him one more thing to whine about when he wakes up." The goat gave her the evil eye, but the kicking stopped.

Madge left to meet a potential *Greenlight My Heart* producer at First Arret. "Don't call me unless you need help burying a body," she said, then flitted through the open window.

Norah sat on her couch checking emails. She paused every time Bing made an alarming noise. Occasionally, she turned up her radio magic to check on Bing, but all she could feel was his amorphous psychic sludge. Sifting through the emotions in the room, she realized that Bing's catastrophic mood was distressing her Oriceran hybrid houseplants. It had been a bad year for them.

"Vesta, water my plants," Norah said. The home assistant floated up, and small clouds appeared over the plants. As soft rain filtered through the room, Bing's moaning slackened.

Patting a dewy leaf on her grafted mint plant, Norah sang the first line of an old witch's lullaby. The green leaves perked up, and when she saw how much the plants were enjoying it, Norah felt obliged to finish.

"Zoomy zoomy zoomy broom
"To the stars and to the moon
"Sparkle sparkle sparkle wand
"Through the sky and then beyond."

A hacking cough echoed from Pepe's dog bed, and Bing opened one eye to a slit.

"You're pitchy," he grated through gin-fried vocal cords.

He was right, which annoyed Norah even more. *My plants never complain when I'm off-key.* "Save it for your clients."

Bing's eye closed, and silence enveloped the room. Norah, disgruntled, sang louder in a reedy falsetto. Bing's groan rose from a whisper to a discordant whine.

"Please stop," he said.

"I'll stop singing if you sit up and eat some toast," Norah replied. Bing buried his face in the bed, and Norah shrugged.

"Vesta, play the instrumental track for *Achy Breaky Heart*. I hope you like karaoke, Bing," she said.

"Joke's on you," Bing said, voice muffled. "I like *Achy Breaky Heart*."

"Not the way I sing it," Norah said cheerfully as the opening bars played.

She did her best impression of a dying hyena. Two verses in, Bing got on his knees and crawled over to the sofa, then flung himself on top of it with a pained expression.

"I won't see Billy Ray Cyrus disrespected like this," he moaned. "Bring me the toast."

"You're an agent. Aren't you supposed to have better taste?" Norah asked.

"You're the one who's failing to appreciate a national treasure. Besides, I don't rep musicians," Bing called as she went to get the bread out of her freezer.

When he had choked down three bites of toast slathered with Stan's excellent homemade grapefruit marmalade, Bing raised himself to an approximately upright position.

"Where's the porky pixie?" he asked blearily.

Norah sucked in her breath and nodded at Pepe, who trotted over, turned his back to Bing, and kicked the agent in the shin with the sharpest part of one hoof. Bing emitted a satisfying bellow of agony and, as a bonus, woke up a little.

"If you're rude to Madge again," Norah said, her voice low, "I will turn the rest of your blood to gin and drop you into the nearest manhole. Do you understand?"

Bing rubbed his shin in silence. Norah shook her head at Pepe, who was winding up for another kick. The goat trotted over to his dog bed, sniffed it, wrinkled his nose in distaste, pulled an argyle blanket off the back of Norah's sofa, and made himself a small nest in the opposite corner.

"I'll get you a new bed that doesn't smell like a fraternity toilet," she said, glaring at Bing. "I paid your bill at Clifton's, by the way. It was astonishing. I've seen rock stars do less damage."

"Do you expect me to pretend I'm going to pay you back?" Bing said. "You can send someone to break my kneecaps, but unless they contain hidden reservoirs of gold I don't know about, it won't help." Bing heaved, and Norah handed him a trash can. He managed to avoid puking by stuffing more toast into his face.

Norah shook her head. "I'm not sending anyone to break your kneecaps, but I do expect you to give me information about Garton Saxon's ex-wives."

Bing choked so hard that a bite of toast shot across the room and landed near Pepe's feet. The goat sniffed the bread, then kicked it under the nearest plant table. Apparently, Bing's saliva was a bridge too far for even the least discerning scavenger.

"As much as I'd love to have my eyeballs covered in sweet and sour sauce and served on art deco silver toothpicks, I will not be betraying Garton Saxon at this time. Wherever he is," Bing replied.

"Do you love him?" Norah asked.

Pepe snorted. Bing looked like he didn't understand the question.

"Ugh. Come with me," Norah said and hauled Bing to his feet. He wobbled briefly, then tumbled to the floor. Pepe raised the pointiest edge of his hoof and looked hopefully at Norah. She shook her head, helped Bing to his feet, and walked him carefully to her back bedroom. He took one look at the oil painting and started screaming.

"It's horrible," he said, cowering behind her.

"Yes," Norah agreed and spun him to face Saxon's crystal coffin. That inspired more screaming.

"Kiss him," Norah instructed, pushing Bing toward the statue.

Bing's expression twisted, and sweat that smelled like gut-rot moonshine beaded on his forehead. "What kind of twisted game are you playing, Wintry?"

"It's a witch thing. Just do it," she said, hoisting the crystal lid of the coffin. As Bing leaned over, a bead of sweat dripped onto Saxon's stiff form.

"We're not trying to hurt him. We just want to wake him up," Norah explained.

Bing recoiled. "Wake him up? Wake *him* up? Do you also want to release a bunch of puckish Siberian tigers into a children's playground?"

The beads of sweat turned to rivulets as Bing leaned over and pressed the tight line of his lips against Saxon's smooth forehead.

Unsurprisingly, nothing happened.

"If you tell me everything you know about Garton Saxon's exes, I will introduce you to the world's most comfortable mattress," Norah said. Carrot first, then the stick.

"Muriel Jacobs. Lives in Pasadena. Saxon sent money, I think. I'll give you the address. The rest are dead, mostly under mysterious circumstances."

Norah was grateful to have a name.

Muriel Jacobs, I hope you have terrible taste in men.

CHAPTER TWELVE

Norah's ability to take ridiculous things seriously was her secret power, but the risqué puppet show pushed her to her limits. The act featured a wooden marionette performing classic burlesque. The clothes were all wooden, too, less bump-and-grind than splinter-and-sand.

She fidgeted in her seat as Frondle, leaning toward the action, squeezed her hand.

"I'm learning a lot about human anatomy!" he said cheerfully. "Elves don't have that floppy bit," he whispered, pointing at an embarrassingly accurate piece of carved wood. A woman sitting behind them shushed him.

Castor had generously provided Frondle with two front-row tickets, dead-center. When Frondle had escorted her to the seats, she wondered what the elf had done to his roommate to deserve this.

The marionette onstage fluttered a large feathered fan to the side. Frondle kept looking at her. She thought he might be checking to see which of the various activities presented before them might interest her, so she kept her face neutral. When she turned to smile encouragingly at the light elf, a balsa wood bra hit her in the face.

"Ow," she said softly and was shushed again. She rubbed her cheek and tried not to make eye contact with the puppeteer. The number ended, and Norah casually opened her purse to peek at the time on her phone. She learned two things. One, they had been at the show for fourteen minutes, and two, in those fourteen minutes, her mother had called her seven times.

Anxiety at the prospect of an emergency battled with her joy at the prospect of a legitimate reason to leave. She ran out of the theater, ignoring the offended protests of the serial shusher.

"Norah?" Petra asked after the first ring.

"Where are you? Is Dad okay?"

"The family's fine, but there's been another attack on an old colleague. Do you remember Jeronda Cole?"

Norah vaguely remembered a wispy woman who kept candied fruit in her purse.

Petra continued, "Someone attacked us while we were walking in Griffith. We're taking her to your apartment. I just wanted to warn you."

"Someone attacked you? Are you okay?" Norah asked, but Petra had hung up.

Frondle flew out from the theater, doors flapping behind him. "Is everything all right?"

"No," Norah said. "I'm sorry, but I have to go. There was another attack. My mom's at my apartment. You don't have to come."

She hoped he would. Dressed from head to toe in white linen, he looked like an extremely sexy meringue, and she didn't want the night to end. Additionally, "Never leave a man behind" applied to risqué puppet shows even more than it did to warfare.

She cursed the traffic on the way back from Highland Park, and when they finally pulled into the parking lot, she burst out of the car at a run. Frondle loped behind her as she raced up the stairs to her apartment.

Stan met her at the door.

"Norah. Hello, Frondle. Thanks for coming. I'm hoping you can convince your mom to let me take a look at her arm."

"Her arm? She said everyone was fine."

Norah pushed past him into the living room. A small blanket-covered figure was lying on the sofa. Norah hoped the sofa didn't still smell like Harry Bing. Petra was kneeling on the floor and coaxing pale green magic into the body with her wand, but something was wrong.

She was working left-handed. "Mom?"

Petra turned, which revealed the right side of her body. The tattered edges of her linen shirt smoldered. An angry red burn forked across her skin, laced with the bruise-colored magic of a curse.

"You said you were fine," Norah growled.

"I *am* fine. Don't worry. The curse is blocked at my shoulder. I'll get to it once Jeronda is out of the woods. Will you help me? I could use another wand."

Norah crouched beside her mother, and her hand flew to her mouth. "Oh, my God."

Below the wisps of silvery hair, Jeronda had shriveled to half her size.

"She needs blood," Petra said. "We were hiking. We always do the same trail when I come out to visit. Jeronda was ahead of me and hit a magical trap. It made her blood… Well, it made it disappear."

"What?" Norah shivered. The room seemed dark, and she stood to turn on a reading lamp.

"It was horrible, like seeing the water let out of a balloon," Petra said. "When I leaned down to check on her, someone hit me from the side with a curse."

"How is she still alive?" Norah asked.

Petra made a peevish noise without looking away from her work. "I know it's easy to forget, Norah, but in addition to being a lightning-fast diaper changer, I'm an extremely powerful witch. Much like an excellent Japanese whisky, I've only gotten better." Irritation only showed up in Petra's voice when she was in serious pain. She was a powerful witch, but she was also afraid.

Pulling out her wand, Norah knelt beside her mother and inspected the body. Jeronda appeared to be deflated rather than damaged.

Norah drew the outline of an oval in the air, then shrunk it to the micro-scale and sent it spinning into Jeronda's arteries. She was proud of this one. Each time the spell replicated a blood cell, it replicated too, initiating exponential growth. Petra, who had been manufacturing blood out of thin air one drop at a time, raised an eyebrow at Norah as the deathly gray skin on Jeronda's face flushed.

"Neat trick," Petra remarked. "You'll have to teach me that one."

Norah took her mom's hand. "Let me work on your arm, and I'd be happy to."

"We should keep working on Jeronda," Petra protested, but the witch's color continued to improve. The deep wrinkles in her skin were smoothing out, and she sank deeper into the couch cushions as her blood volume increased.

"Mom, your arm is cursed and barbecued like the world's most dangerous brisket. Please let me look at it. We'll keep an eye on Jeronda, I swear."

She shot a spidery blue spell into her mother's arm. The curse crackled and fled from the magic. Petra let out a cry of pain, then bit her lip so hard she drew blood.

"Sorry," Norah said. She changed tactics to weave blue magic at the borders of the curse. Close, but not close enough to send the dark magic skittering away. Slowly, she worked her way around the curse. It was like doing crochet around a tree branch. The finished product was a forking tube of healing blue around her mom's arm.

"This might hurt," she told her mom. Petra squeezed her hand and nodded.

Norah shot anticurse magic into the tube, then sealed it.

"Argghhh," Petra moaned as the blue magic sank into her arm and acrid magical smoke rose. After a minute, the smoke disappeared. With nowhere to run, the curse had imploded. Petra touched the raw skin on her elbow, wincing. She now had only a normal burn. Stan approached with a wooden container of salve.

"Oriceran aloe," he said. "I pretty well denuded your plant, Norah. I'll get you a new one, but you might want to apologize to the others."

"It's fine," Norah said faintly, relieved to see her mother's pained expression relax as Stan coated her arm with the salve. She touched the sunburst tattoo on her wrist, relieved that the matching design on her mother's arm hadn't been touched by the burn.

Petra plastered a smile on her face as Stan tended to the worst part of the burn, and something inside Norah cracked. She ran to the bathroom, prepared to throw up the burrito Frondle had bought her two hours ago. Instead, she breathed hard and splashed cold water on her face.

A moment later, there was a knock on the door. Frondle stood there with concern on his face.

"Are you all right?" he asked.

"No. I'm not all right. I'm furious." Norah braced both arms on the sink, water dripping from her face. "I want Saxon awake and talking. I want Dark Hound shut down, and I want the person behind it locked up in the smallest, darkest hole on Earth or Oriceran."

Frondle took Norah's hand and grasped it. "We will find these villains, and we will introduce them to this small dark hole. You have my full support."

"Thanks, Frondle," Norah said. His blue eyes were tinged with a serious gray, and he looked so wonderful that she wanted to kiss him. His lips looked very soft and warm.

Unfortunately, snot was dripping down her nose, which always happened when she did difficult magic. She didn't think he was going anywhere. At least, as long as he didn't see the incredible volume of mucous she was about to blow out of her nose.

"Can you give me a minute?" she asked.

Closing the door, she cast a cone of silence above herself and expelled a kiddie pool's worth of gunk from her sinuses. When she opened the door again, she jumped. Frondle hadn't moved from his spot just outside.

"Norah, I have decided. I will swear an oath to take down Dark Hound!"

Norah could get behind that. "That's a great idea. I wanna swear an oath, too. Ooh, my first oath! Do we need a Bible? I'm not religious. Wait!"

Norah ran into her bedroom and pulled a book from the shelf. Returning, she brandished it at Frondle. It was a beautiful leather-bound copy of *Pride and Prejudice* with a peacock embossed in rich sunflower yellow on the cover. Norah's late grandmother had given it to her when she graduated from college.

"It's not a first edition, but it is over a hundred years old," Norah explained. "Have you read *Pride and Prejudice*? You should. Not this copy, though. You can get it from the library." She felt amped up, as if she were running downhill.

Frondle nodded solemnly. "I am unfamiliar with Earth oath customs, but I trust in your passion."

He pulled her out into the living room. "Stan? Do you have an elven sword?" the light elf asked.

Stan raised an eyebrow at their sweaty faces and bright eyes. After a long pause, he said, "Wait here."

When he returned five minutes later, he carried a scimitar. The silver metal was practically glowing. Norah was tempted to turn off the lights and find out. The handle was carved from some kind of Oriceran wood. The black-and-white rings were close together, like layers of paint. The blade was unadorned. It looked old and dangerously sharp. Frondle drew in his breath. The curved blade reflected in his astonished eyes.

"Stan," he whispered.

An unusual expression crossed Stan's face.

Is Stan smug? Some current of light elf understanding passed between the two men, and Frondle, awed, lifted the blade as if it were a fragile newborn. After a moment of admiration, Frondle grasped the hilt, sank to one knee, and plunged the tip of the blade into the wooden floor. The silver metal, harder than steel, sank in a full inch. Norah, who had long abandoned all hope for her security deposit, winced. Frondle looked dashing, and warmth blossomed within her.

"I, Frondle, swear on my honor as a light elf to work tirelessly until the foul website Dark Hound has been destroyed. I will walk no other paths and forgo all pleasure until my word is redeemed."

The sword *was* glowing. So was Frondle. Soft light flowed into him from the blade. He touched his forehead to the hilt, and light exploded outward like a small galaxy. Norah gasped at the drama and uneasily ran her hand across the cover of *Pride and Prejudice*.

Frondle looked up at her through pale lashes. She sank to one knee beside him and placed a hand on her book.

"I, Norah Wintry, swear upon my honor as a witch that I will do everything in my power to take down Dark Hound. If I fail in my task, let my wand be splintered, and, uh, may all my days be bad hair days. This, I swear." She kissed her book.

If I'd known I would be swearing a sacred oath, I would have hired Sid to do some punch-ups.

It was the thought that counted. As Norah and Frondle scrambled to their feet, Stan looked on inscrutably.

Norah turned to her partner-in-oath. "I need to track down one of Saxon's ex-wives. Will you help?"

"I will," Frondle said, then reverently handed the sword back to Stan and gave Norah a shy smile. "My bow and sword are yours. Whatever you need."

With that, he swept out of the room, long blond hair flying. "Text me!" he cried over his shoulder.

"How is he getting home?" Petra asked, eyeing the strong muscles of Frondle's retreating back.

"He usually runs," Norah replied.

"What an athletic young elf." Petra sounded impressed.

Stan emitted a noise that sounded like laughter.

"What?" Norah asked.

"Nothing. The oath surprised me. I thought you two were, you know, *interested*."

Norah flushed and crossed her arms. "We are. I think we are. What do you mean?"

Stan's eyes sparkled. "You remember the part of the oath about forgoing all pleasure? *All* means, well, *all*." He had the decency not to waggle his eyebrows. Petra suddenly became interested in making tea in the kitchen.

"Oh," Norah said. The blossom of warmth inside her chilled. "I... Hmmm."

Damn it, Wintry. Stupid oath-taking witch.

Stan grinned. "That's all right. Consider it a motivating factor. However, you should know that elves take their oaths very seriously." He looked outside. It was fully dark.

"Minnie's coming over. Call me if Jeronda takes a turn or if your mom's arm acts up."

"I will. Thanks."

The blade of the elven sword glinted as Stan carried it out the door.

CHAPTER THIRTEEN

The tattooed barista shoved Quint out the door of the café.

"*Please* don't bring him back until he's prepared to play something other than Leonard Cohen," she said. "I love the High Priest of Pathos as much as the next girl, but if I have to listen to *Hallelujah* one more time, I'm going to stick my head in the bean roaster. It's bumming out the customers too. I'd fire him if he wasn't my boss."

Frondle looked at Quint. The normally cheerful wizard looked seedy today, with shadowy stubble and dark undereye circles as if he'd been living in a cave. Had Norah asked him to bring Quint along just to get him out of the house? Maybe, although a wizard might come in handy.

"Who's Leonard Cohen?" Frondle asked, raising an eyebrow at the barista. He was still getting a handle on Earth music.

She looked disgusted. Without breaking eye contact, she closed the door in his face.

"Will you drive?" Quint asked, shoulders slumped. The lovesick café owner was more lump than man at this point.

"I don't know how, and I don't have a car," Frondle replied brightly. One of these days, he would have to learn. He might have to pretend to drive a car in a movie someday.

Quint, groaning, took Frondle through the alley to a silver sedan that was crammed full of In-N-Out wrappers. Frondle fluffed them into a nest and settled into his seat. Quint didn't even apologize, just plugged in his aux cord, started the engine, and hit a button on his phone.

Frondle read the playlist's title. *"Music for crying on leg day.* Is leg day a somber American holiday?"

"In West Hollywood, it is," Quint responded.

Frondle was not sure if he was joking. Probably not. American holidays were confusing, cobbled together from different religious traditions and rebooted in forms that maximized merchandise sales. He'd made flashcards of the major figures. There was the chimeric rabbit that laid eggs for the long-haired sandal enthusiast, the dead bird of gratitude, the pumpkin-men with fire for brains, and the red-and-white-suited grandfather who fulfilled children's toy-shopping orders.

"What day is Leg Day?" Frondle asked, opening his calendar app.

"Thursdays and Mondays."

Frondle dutifully typed in the information.

Lovely but sad music filled the car, and Frondle listened intently. Traditional light elf music was beautiful but literal. Pretty songs about pretty forests—that sort of thing. The minor key of this American music wrenched his guts.

"This makes me feel happy about being sad," Frondle noted, awed. Quint chuckled.

"Yeah, Leonard Cohen will do that to you." He gave a long sigh. Clearly, Frondle had underestimated human lung capacity.

"You like being sad?" Frondle asked.

Quint snorted. "You sound like my ex. Not Hazel, the one before that. I mean, there were a few girls in between, but they didn't count." Another lengthy sigh. Was it bad for human lungs to be devoid of air? "Anyway. I don't *like* being sad. I *am* sad."

"Norah said a sexy fire elemental dumped you, and now you're wallowing."

Quint's eyes narrowed. He hit the accelerator so hard that Frondle's head bumped the top of the small car. "I don't like the word 'dumped.' It sounds negative when people accuse me of doing it. Besides, the thing with Hazel was mutual."

"You mutually agreed that she should dump you?" Frondle asked.

Quint pressed his lips together, appearing to listen intently to the music.

Frondle cleared his throat. "I have taken a holy elven oath and forsworn love until Dark Hound is destroyed."

It had been the noble thing to do, and he was good at doing the noble thing. When Norah had sworn her own oath, she had looked so fiercely beautiful that Frondle wondered if he'd made a mistake, but that was the purpose of an oath. It would keep them from getting distracted. They could think about romance after their swords had been slaked with the blood of their enemies.

"*You* could swear an elven oath," Frondle suggested. A distraction would be good for the wizard.

Quint emitted a noise similar to one that might be made by a duck in the depths of ennui.

"Instead of sadness, you could have a driving purpose," Frondle explained.

"Now you sound like my mom," Quint grumbled. Everything Frondle said seemed to annoy him, so the light elf decided to be quiet and listen to Leonard Cohen.

By the time they got to Ojai, they had made their way through *I'm Your Man* and *Songs of Love and Hate.* Quint responded better to the songs of hate than the songs of love.

When they pulled up at the retirement community, Frondle was twitching with unused energy. "Should we go for a run?"

Quint looked at his skinny jeans and shook his head.

"Let's go find this Muriel and see if she's still carrying a torch for the old elf."

Muriel Jacobs, who had been married to Saxon in the 1970s, now lived in a pleasant orange-tree-lined retirement community outside of Ojai.

Quint kneeled and put a hand on the ground. "At least this place is chock-full of power," he muttered.

"That'll be the energy vortex," a man's voice said behind them. A leathery, shirtless man in tie-dye shorts who was riding a bicycle skidded to a stop beside them.

"You caught it on a good day. The vortex is strong." The man hopped off his bike and walked it up the stairs into the Sunbird Meadows courtyard.

A resident! "You don't know Muriel, do you?" Frondle asked.

The man came to a dead stop in the middle of the stairs, turned, and carefully inspected Frondle's pointy ears.

"What's your name?" the man asked, eyes narrowed. He put his bicycle between himself and them. It might be prejudice, but Frondle didn't think so. Usually, people who didn't like elves were rude from the start.

When Frondle introduced himself, the man relaxed and waved them inside, introducing himself as "Bob." As they walked through the citrus trees, Frondle pulled an orange off a tall branch and bit through the rind, savoring the scented oils.

"You be careful," Bob said. "If you keep demonstrating your ability to reach the highest branches, you're likely to be roped into manual labor."

"We won't be here that long," Quint said peevishly.

Bob stopped at a door with a festive summer wreath and knocked three times. His tanned face lit up when he saw the woman who opened the door.

She smiled just as broadly, her bright face framed by long hair dyed black and twisted into a knot. Her silky top and matching wide trousers fluttered in the warm afternoon breeze. Like Bob, her smile dimmed when she saw Frondle.

"Hello," she said. Something passed between the two older people. Not prejudice since there was no curl of the lip or twinkle of distaste. What he was seeing was fear.

The woman glanced inside at a pleasant sitting room decorated by someone who'd had great taste in the seventies. It had shag carpeting and argyle blankets thrown over the sofa. Eyes on Frondle's ears, Muriel stepped outside and closed the door behind her.

"How can I help you?"

"Might I impose on you for a few minutes of your time, madam?" Frondle requested, dropping into a shallow bow. Some humans, especially in America, hated formal bows, but old ladies usually liked them. Instead of smiling indulgently, Muriel cringed.

She waved them to some cushioned chairs on a shaded patio. Frondle sat very straight-backed in his. Quint slumped into his despite Muriel's disapproving glance at his posture.

"We're here to ask about your ex-husband," Frondle began.

Her face grew remote.

"You mean Jerry? He passed two years ago."

She twisted the wedding ring on her left hand, which Bob patted.

Quint leaned forward. "We're here about Garton Saxon." The wind whistled eerily between two of the nearby brick buildings, and a few leaves floated down off the trees in the courtyard.

"Is he dead?" Muriel asked, her steely expression softened by an eager flicker.

"Not exactly," Quint replied.

Muriel shrank back in her chair. "I hate that that bastard is going to outlive me, but hope springs eternal. Why are you here?"

"Can you tell us a little bit about your relationship with Saxon?" Frondle asked.

Bob stood and stepped between them and Muriel.

"If you two want to reopen old wounds, you'd better explain yourselves." He poked Frondle in the chest with a leathery finger. It was a lovely formal gesture of protection.

"Of course, sir," Frondle replied. "I have sworn an elven oath to—"

"Write a biography about Saxon," Quint interjected, shooting Frondle a *follow-my-lead* look. "As I'm sure you two know, Frondle is a famous elven investigative...poet."

"I've never heard of an investigative poet." Muriel's voice was harsh.

Bob looked interested. "I've dabbled with the odd canto myself," he said, producing a ratty Moleskine from one pocket. Muriel sighed. Frondle guessed that she had been the primary target of Bob's poetry.

"It's like journalism but rhyming," Quint explained. "It's an Oriceran thing. They're mad about poetry."

"Tough luck. There are only so many words that rhyme with 'bastard,'" Muriel said.

Frondle nodded, English vocabulary filtering through his brain. He would support Quint. "There are a few, Madam. Bastard. Plastered. Mastered. Vast herd. Rat turd."

Muriel's eyes narrowed. "You might be onto something with that one."

"It's not a perfect rhyme," Frondle replied apologetically. He began to fit lines together in his head. "It's a slant rhyme, but it still counts. Saxon the bastard, a flaxen-haired rat turd," Frondle recited, voice booming in a classic light elf intonation. That made Muriel laugh, a lilting sound that brightened everything in the courtyard, including Bob's face.

"Frondle here wants the truth," Quint continued.

Frondle had been bad at lying until someone had explained to him that it was just like acting. "The truth is a dark mistress, but I wouldn't trade her for another," he said, digging into the juicy role. Finally, his improv classes were paying off.

"I'll talk to you." Muriel's face got more serious. "But off-the-record. I hate to deprive the world of 'flaxen-haired rat turd,' but you'll understand soon why I have to stay quiet."

Frondle bowed his head gravely. "Of course, madam. Your generous counsel shall not leave this orchard."

Muriel nodded. "I remember our wedding like it was yesterday. I was twenty-three. I wore yellow silk with daffodils in my hair, and we walked barefoot along the beach."

Quint's eyes peered into the middle distance at this image, and he emitted another low sigh, like a leaking tire. Presumably, he was imagining a similar event with Hazel in the lead role.

"How long were you married?" Frondle asked. Then, to hammer his role home, he muttered, "varied, carried, harried."

"'Harried' is right," Muriel said. "After he brought me home, he changed. I'd been doing a little acting. Nothing major, but I was the Westman's Beer girl. I was on a billboard in Santa Monica. I have a photo somewhere."

"Motto, big toe, grotto," Frondle chanted.

"No-go!" Bob chipped in, scribbling an inspired line in his notebook. Muriel crossed her arms, and Quint shot

Frondle a warning look. What? Was he not creating enough rhymes?

"Grotto doesn't scan, dear," Muriel offered. "Anyway, he didn't want me acting. He said it was a profession for sickos."

Frondle started to protest but then remembered he was supposed to be an investigative poet, not an actor. *Hmph. Would a* sicko *pretend to be an investigative poet?*

"Soon, I didn't have any friends, but I still loved him."

Quint leaned forward.

Though Muriel looked strong, Frondle heard a quaver in her voice. "He didn't want me working, and then he didn't want me seeing my friends or calling my family. He said they were too involved in my life. Once he'd cut me off from everyone and everything and destroyed my career, he threw me over. Told me he was leaving me for another woman. Poor thing, she's dead now."

"It seems like a lot of Saxon's ex-wives ended up dead," Quint stated.

"Believe me, I know," Muriel said darkly. "You know what the greatest shame of my life is? When Tillie died—she was the one he replaced me with—I begged him to take me back. I thought I had a chance."

Quint's expression brightened. He understood that. "Are there any other ex-wives?"

"Not in the land of the living. I'm it, and I intend to stay that way. That's why I can't have you go blabbing about all this in some Oriceran recitation hall."

"Why are you still alive when all others have passed?" Frondle asked.

Muriel clasped her hands and sat up straight as if facing a truth she hated. "Because I wanted him so badly, and I was in so much pain. If I'd been dead, he wouldn't have had that."

Her voice was quiet, and Bob's face had turned to marble. He wrapped a hand around hers and drew her close.

"I knew he was an elf," Muriel continued. "To be honest, it was part of the appeal. I felt like I'd been chosen for something bigger than this Earth, transported to a world beyond my own. I was special.

"Hah. Especially stupid is more like it. I saw him reinvent himself many times in Hollywood. When another one of his exes died in the late eighties, I wanted to tell someone, but what would they have done with '*My ex is an elf with magical powers, and I think he's murdering his wives*'? It would've been a padded room and three square meals of pills a day for me."

Bob's hand squeezed hers. "You *are* special, dear."

"That's right," Muriel agreed, smiling. "To be honest, Oriceran is dreadful. I've been there, now that it's opened. Can't stand those singing trees. Terrible racket."

Frondle chuckled. "Springtime *can* be operatic."

Muriel shivered. "Anyway, I did a little psychoanalysis in the eighties up in Esalen. I finally got over him, *and* I figured out why Saxon had kept me alive. It wasn't hard to keep up the pretense. Twice a year, I send him an unhinged letter begging him to come back to me. He writes back, makes false promises, and sends small gifts. I burn the letters, but I keep the cash. I live happily above an energy vortex. It's quite strong today, Bobby."

Bob nodded enthusiastically. "It certainly is."

"If he found out I'm not still pining for him, I'd likely meet an unhappy accident. Once I'm gone, it won't matter, I suppose."

"That won't be for twenty, thirty years," Bob countered cheerfully.

Frondle tented his fingers, face grim. The story offended his elvish sense of right and wrong. Saxon had squandered this woman's love, and he guessed she'd rather kiss a volcano caldera bubbling with magma than her ex-husband.

When Frondle rose, Quint shot him a confused look, but the light elf ignored him and bowed again. "I apologize on behalf of my countryman, and I thank you for your time. Should you ever have need of an Oriceran aide, I am at your service."

He pulled a card out of his pocket and handed it to Muriel. She stared at the headshot, which featured a shirtless Frondle in a cowboy hat pointing at something off-camera.

"You're an actor?" she asked.

Quint made a frustrated noise. "Investigative poetry is his day job. Let's go." He pulled the elf away, leaves rustling under their feet as he hustled him back to the car.

"You almost broke our cover," Quint complained. "Lucky for you, it doesn't matter. I have an idea."

CHAPTER FOURTEEN

"It's no use," Frondle said. "Clearly, any affection for Garton Saxon has drained from this woman's heart. For excellent reasons," he added.

"That's true," Quint agreed. "But she used to love him. I recognized that look in her eyes. It's the same one I've seen in Hazel's—empty death where once there was passion." He kicked a nearby rock, then made a small noise of pain, having kicked it harder than he'd meant to. Frondle took a dim view of this chain of events.

Quint continued, "But that's where I got this idea. I've sort of been looking into love spells."

Frondle was so shocked that he reached for the hilt of his sword before realizing he wasn't wearing one. "Love spells? Quint!"

"I know. It was a stupid internet rabbit hole. I would never cast one. I was thinking about how I don't want to make her love me *now*. I want to go back in time to when she *did* love me. I started looking into time travel instead."

Frondle grabbed Quint by the collar. "Those are serious

crimes against the natural order. Depending on your school of thought, love magic is worse than death magic, and time magic is worse than both. You could end the universe!"

"My universe is as good as dead now," Quint stated dramatically. Frondle wished Pepe was here to kick him but settled for shaking Quint like a rag doll.

"Anyway," Quint continued. "Time travel magic is dangerous and also a huge hassle. Like, a lot of work. I don't want to spend the next two years hunting chronocerouses for their horns. *But,* I found a spell that can transport someone back to an earlier point in their memories. If we cast it on Muriel, she'll think it's 1972 again."

Frondle frowned. Garton Saxon had not been a force for good, and Frondle did not want to do anything to make her love the evil elf again since she'd been through too much. But with the lives of every ex-Silver Griffin at stake, the price for moral clarity might be too high.

"Is it permanent?" Frondle asked. "I will not send that woman back into Garton Saxon's emotional clutches for all eternity."

"It's temporary. The spell takes a huge amount of energy to maintain, and it wears off almost immediately. I..." Quint's voice trailed off, and he looked ashamed.

"What?" Frondle demanded.

"I hired an ErrandBoy to practice on. I told him what I was trying to do, and he agreed. Apparently, it's way better than doing dirty laundry or whatever people hire them for. Nice guy."

Frondle frowned. Despite Quint's protests, he had

clearly done more than a little magical googling. "You're wading in deep waters, Quintilius."

Quint cringed at the use of his full name. "Whatever. He said he enjoyed re-living his college years."

"I do not think Muriel will feel the same way. It is wrong to change people's minds against their will," Frondle stated.

"We're not going to change her mind. We're just going to take it back a few years, and only for a few minutes," Quint corrected. "Maybe *this* is why Hazel dumped me. The universe knew I would need this knowledge at this moment to save lives."

"I do not believe the universe is deeply concerned with your love life," Frondle argued.

Quint waved that away. "Look, are we going to give this little old lady a *tiny* shove down Memory Lane, or should we just let my parents die?"

A new edge rode Quint's voice. It was possible, Frondle realized, that Quint's unrequited romance was a way to distract himself from the dangers facing his family. Perhaps he could bring that energy to a future monologue. Human beings were interesting even when they were being oddly obtuse. "I will help you with the spell. What do we need?"

As it turned out, Quint's plan consisted of waiting until Bob was gone and breaking into Muriel's apartment the old-fashioned way. Quint dropped his car off a few blocks down the road, and they picked their way back into a grapefruit orchard behind the apartment building.

Quint grunted as he crunched through the undergrowth. "How do you walk so quietly?"

Frondle, who flitted under the trees as quietly as a moth, shrugged. "How do you walk so loudly? It's very impressive." Finding a grapefruit tree with a good vantage point, he sprang lightly into the branches as Quint struggled up. He pulled out his wand and twined magic around the branches to make himself a hammock.

"I hope you appreciate Muriel's good example," Frondle said. "If she could overcome her unrequited love, you also might."

Quint grunted. "Okay, buddy. She was hung up on an *evil murderer*. I'm hung up on the most beautiful woman in the world, and she's a good person. It's different."

"Maybe she's a murderer too!" Frondle exclaimed. "You don't know her very well." He'd meant this statement to bolster Quint, but the young man responded with aggravated silence.

The weather was hot, and the tree smelled citrus-y. Frondle found himself napping in the dappled light between the branches.

When Quint shook him awake, it was dark. "I think Muriel went to bed," he stated.

Frondle peered through the branches. Muriel's apartment window was now a matte-gray square. He leapt to the ground and helped Quint down, trying to make less noise than, say, a herd of chronocerouses.

They paused at the fragrant border of the orchard.

"Can you make a small hole in that window?" Quint whispered. "So I can shoot in a confounding spell."

Frondle nodded and put his hands together. Drawing power from a string of fairy lights around Muriel's upstairs neighbor's window, he superheated a coin-sized circle of glass until it dripped away.

Quint brought out his white pine wand, and a thread of pale green magic danced through the hole and disappeared into the darkness behind. "That should put her to sleep for ten minutes or so," he whispered.

Frondle drew out a little more power and moved his hands slowly, gradually expanding the small circle until it was big enough to climb through. The glass was viscous and red-hot at the edges. When it was cool, he wove a rope of white light and anchored it to the floor of the room beyond. Quint grasped the rope and managed to haul himself into Muriel's room. Frondle followed and landed lightly in the unlit room.

He felt uncomfortably weak in the dark and quickly identified the location of every light switch in the room. Quint drew a series of twisting runes in the air. They hung, glowing, as he added lines and whorls.

Quint had practiced more than once. Frondle would have to keep an eye on him in Los Angeles, but for now, he was grateful for the wizard's confidence. Quint kept up a finger-aching pace with his wand, and soon the runes in the air twisted into curves that echoed the folds of a human brain. It was an impressive working.

At a whisper of noise from the living room, Frondle paused. Did Muriel have a companion dog like many other humans? As he turned to sniff the air, a white beard flashed in the doorway, and there was an all-consuming noise.

It would be wrong to describe the subsequent explosion as a flash. Flashes involved light, so Frondle was comfortable with them. This was an explosion of darkness, a void that consumed the room. Frondle reached out to access his power, but he was surrounded by a sucking black pool that sapped his strength and dropped him to his knees.

A few feet away, Quint rolled across the floor, clutching his head. His spell melted into mother-of-pearl drops. He had lost his wand, and as he scrambled for it, there was a shout, and a lithe figure whacked him on the head with a bicycle pump.

As Frondle crawled through the sticky darkness to help the wizard, there was another shout, this time female, and a table lamp ricocheted off his head. *A worthy throw,* he thought as everything went black.

When Frondle woke up, he felt drained. Worse than useless. Cold circles on his wrists told him why: black-hole onyx. Matching shackles glittered on his ankles.

Quint was tied to a wooden dining chair beside him, wandless and gagged. On the sofa in front of them sat Muriel and Bob, hands clasped. Muriel was running Quint's wand through her fingers, ignoring the outrage in the young wizard's eyes. Bob was fiddling with Quint's car keys and had the vehicle's registration in his hand.

"Would you care to tell me why my home has been invaded by a barista and an aspiring actor?"

"Aspiring? Madame, I have appeared in a national antacid commercial. My latest residual check is in my wallet," Frondle said primly despite his splitting headache. If they were going to insult him, they could at least be accurate. Norah had said that a national commercial was a very impressive achievement for a newcomer, and she wouldn't lie.

Muriel, giving in to curiosity, retrieved Frondle's wallet,

flipped through his juice shop punch cards, and pulled out a small check.

"Eight dollars and twenty-three cents," she read. Bob snickered.

"I know it's not *much*, but I get them every month," Frondle replied stiffly.

Quint made a noise of agreement, then gave a muffled protest. Frondle suspected it was along the lines of "*I'm not a barista. I'm a culinary entrepreneur.*"

Muriel's smile didn't reach her eyes. "Well, in that case, tell me why a working actor and a food services entrepreneur have broken into my home. While you're at it, tell me why you have a statue of Garton Saxon in your trunk."

"Where did you get black-hole onyx?" Frondle asked, jangling the cuffs on his wrists.

Bob leaned back and patted Muriel's hand. "When your lady love has a violent magical ex, you take certain precautions. Had to cash out my 401K, but it was worth it. Anyway, why am I answering questions? That is your job."

Frondle rubbed his wrists. Without his magic, he felt unbalanced, as if he were trying to hop around on one leg. He was still strong and might be able to fight these people, but considering the fiery looks in their eyes, victory wasn't guaranteed.

Frondle paused. "I will tell you the truth. That is not a statue of Garton Saxon in the back of the car. That *is* Garton Saxon, struck by a Sleeping Beauty arrow. He can only be awakened with true love's kiss. We wish to wake him up."

Muriel's expression shifted from disbelief to dismay. Bob stood.

"Where are you going?" Muriel asked.

"I'm going to drive that elf out into the Sespe Wilderness, bash his head in with a rock, and leave his corpse for an extremely unfortunate bear to choke down."

Frondle gasped, and Quint made a noise of protest.

"Please, you *can't*." The light elf was clearly distressed.

"Why not?" Muriel's voice was shot through with the steely anger of a woman who'd been thriving for decades despite fear.

Without going into detail, he explained their run-in with Saxon, the Silver Griffin murders, and the threat from Dark Hound. At this, Bob pulled out an aging laptop and navigated to the site, tutting as Frondle pointed out Norah's parents.

Muriel leaned back.

"What was your plan?" Muriel asked. "You'd hardly get true love out of these withered old lips."

"Don't sell yourself short, dear. I do all right," Bob countered. Muriel waved this away affectionately, and Quint and Frondle exchanged looks.

"We were going to time-shift your memories," Quint explained. "So you'd think it was 1972."

Bob frowned deeply.

"It would have been temporary," Frondle added, although it seemed a weak excuse. Muriel stood and ripped the gag off Quint's face. He coughed and breathed deeply, muttering a faint "Thanks."

"It wouldn't have done you any good," Muriel stated.

"What I felt for Saxon wasn't love. It was obsession. I loved that jerk about as much as a tapeworm loves its host."

Frondle was intrigued. If you knocked someone out with a Sleeping Beauty arrow, could they be revived with a kiss from their tapeworm? Did a tapeworm have a mouth? Several scenarios that would allow him to test his hypothesis arose in his mind, but he pushed them away.

"Have you tried his mother?" Muriel asked. "She lives in Palm Springs."

"Muriel," Bob cautioned. "Don't help these people."

She shook her head and looked Bob in the eyes. "I know what it's like to live under constant threat. I won't have it for anyone else. However..."

She pulled a notepad off the bedside table and wrote something. "Here's Glesselda's address. That's my phone number and Bob's email. He loves his email and checks it every day. If Saxon wakes up, tell us right away. I've survived before, and I'll survive again, but I have to have a little warning."

Admiration welled from Bob's eyes.

Frondle nodded. "Perhaps a light elf's word means little to you, lady, but I swear to do everything in my power to keep you from harm."

He looked at the address. Several very athletic men had invited him to pool parties in Palm Springs, but he had never gone. Perhaps he wasn't the right elf to go on this particular journey.

Inspiration dawning, Frondle dialed a number. "Petra? I wonder if I might impose on you for assistance."

CHAPTER FIFTEEN

The raw burns on Petra's arm had turned shiny pink as they healed, and they itched like a bitch. Jackie had insisted on driving, which left Petra without any distractions aside from complaining about traffic.

Jackie rolled to yet another stop, cursing. Leaving Los Angeles on Friday at rush hour had been a huge mistake. Petra had made the trip to Palm Springs in under two hours in the past, but today it would be more like four. A fiery itch crawled up her arm, and she gripped the armrests.

"We should have taken brooms," Petra said.

"I swore after the last set of splinters that I was done, but I think you are right," Jackie said.

They sat in traffic in silence for another few minutes, the hot afternoon sun blazing through the glass.

"How many people would your kids have to murder before you stopped loving them?" Jackie asked.

Petra glanced in the rearview mirror at Garton Saxon's frozen face. Unable to shove him into the trunk without breaking off his legs—Jackie had objected to this expediency, although Petra considered it fully reasonable—they had laid him diagonally across the back seat.

"I've killed fifteen people, and my mother never stopped loving me," Petra said quietly. "Although she did imply that I'd be more lethal if I dropped a few pounds."

"Nana was a pretty hard bird," Jackie agreed.

"She lived in hard times. I'm not sure those people count, though. Not the way you mean. All fifteen were trying to kill me, often quite creatively. If we're talking self-defense, I don't think I have a ceiling. Let the bodies pile up," Petra stated angrily.

Jackie nodded. "Yes. If Leaf took out anyone who was trying to hurt him, I'd appreciate him saving me the trouble."

Petra considered the question. Her kids hadn't been sheltered, but the attack at Norah's apartment had been their first real taste of battle. It was nothing like the evil that Garton Saxon had done, however. "I suppose if we're talking Ted Bundy-style murders, then two."

"You'd give them one freebie?" Jackie asked, amused.

"I mean, I wouldn't approve, but children make mistakes," Petra replied. "Although Andrew's marrying you was *not* one of them."

Petra had always liked Jackie. Andrew had met her at an art installation. At the time, she'd been the go-to producer of custom neon signs in Los Angeles. Since Leaf was born, she only took one or two commissions a year.

Jackie, staring straight ahead, heaved.

Petra patted the younger witch's shoulder. "Morning sickness? Oh, dear. Would you like me to drive?"

"No. It's better if I do. I got carsick even when I wasn't pregnant."

Petra gave in and scratched the burn on her arm lightly, grazing it with her fingernails. Now she understood why Jackie had insisted.

"What do we know about this Glesselda woman other than that her son's a monster?" Petra poked the nearest part of Saxon's frozen body she could reach.

"Which means that *she's* a monster, or she was dealt a tough hand." Jackie looked nervous.

"Are you sure you're up for this, dear?" Petra said.

Jackie nodded. "Yes. Definitely. I'm happy to be useful."

Petra had nailed her guess on their travel time. The last glow of twilight had disappeared over the mountains when they rolled down a broad tree-lined street of downtown Palm Springs. Glesselda's apartment complex was a sunset-colored confection surrounding an ostentatious pool that glowed turquoise, lit by cheerful lights. In the hot desert night, women and men in colorful swimsuits and eccentric accessories dove into and climbed out of the water. Petra wished she'd brought a suit.

When they reached the address Frondle had sent them and knocked on the door, no one answered, so they plodded down the stairs to the pool.

Petra flung herself on a lounge chair next to a woman in her late sixties wearing a pink caftan. The group's youngster, apparently. The woman raised the brim of a straw hat and looked Petra up and down.

"Are you new, or are you one of Archie's rotation of girlfriends?" asked Pink Caftan. "If it's the latter, you'll forgive me for not learning your name. Only so much room in the old brain pan at my age."

"I guess you could say I'm new. I don't know Archie in any case. I'm Petra."

"Nice to meet you, Petra. I'm Darlene. That your daughter?" She tilted her head toward Jackie, who lingered on the shadowy edges of the courtyard.

"Daughter-in-law. Any chance you know where to find Glesselda?"

"If she's not at Marco's, she's at Biff's, or vice versa." This was said with the casual disdain of someone who pretended not to care about juicy gossip but always had some to share.

"Are those her sons?" Petra asked with a bright intentional obliviousness.

Darlene's reply was a resounding snort. "I don't care how wrinkle-free her elven skin is. She's older than all of us and way too old to be carrying on with multiple personal trainers. I'd tell those poor boys what the score is, except Glesselda charges us 1990s prices for rent. Keeps us quiet about her shenanigans. Nice lads. I expect they'll be fine in the long run."

"Sure." Petra digested that. "Hmm. Any idea where Marco and Biff live?"

"The apartment complexes on either side of this one. They're both in 201. I don't know how she swings it, but she says she's too old to remember multiple numbers."

"So, whose day is it?" Petra asked. She couldn't help but admire the elderly elf.

"Hah!" Darlene's laugh echoed across the concrete

surrounding the pool. "Unfortunately, I haven't been added to that shared calendar. They're both pretty close."

From the shadows, Jackie chuckled.

Petra waved an appreciative goodbye. "It's been a real pleasure, Darlene. Next time I'll bring a suit."

The apartment complex to the north of Glesselda's was similar, a large U-shape surrounding a pool, although its color scheme was ocean-blue.

"This woman is my hero," Jackie said as they climbed the staircase to the second floor. The knocker on the door was shaped like a fish's tail, and Petra rapped it sharply against the blue wood of the door.

A muscular young man in tight gym shorts answered the door, kettlebell in hand.

"Are you, um..." Petra was about to say "Marco" but realized it might be Biff. This was not the time to alert their target's boyfriends to her two-timing.

"Is Glesselda here?" Jackie said. The young man shook his head.

Petra smiled. "Okay. Sorry to bother you. We'll check with, uh, her phone."

"Her phone! Why didn't we think of that!" Jackie exclaimed, pulling Petra back down the walkway.

"Do you think that was Marco or Biff?" Petra whispered as they walked south past palm trees and waxy green landscaping.

"My money's on Biff," Petra replied.

"I'll take that bet," Jackie said, huffing up the stairs. "Five bucks?"

"Fine with me," Petra said. This knocker was a brass crab.

Possibly Marco's door was answered by an almost identical-looking fitness enthusiast in even smaller gym shorts. Petra thought that violated some physical law.

"Hello!" Petra said. "What's *your* name?"

Possibly Marco frowned. "What? You knocked on *my* door."

"Biff? Who is it?" a female voice cried from the depths of the apartment.

Petra removed a five-dollar bill from her purse and handed it to her daughter-in-law.

An elf in a diaphanous feather-trimmed robe swanned out of the bedroom. She looked about fifty in human years and had a vivid streak of pure white in her black hair. Petra had never seen an elf with gray hair. That meant Glesselda was very old. Considering her choice of companions, she was young at heart.

"Glesselda?" Petra asked. As she extended her hand, her forearm brushed the wand in her pocket. An elf this old would be stupendously powerful, and Petra wondered if she should have brought more backup to confront this mother of a monster.

"We're here to ask you about your son," Jackie added.

Glesselda's eyes narrowed. Before Petra could speak, an enormous hand made of shining light reached out from a bronze floor lamp in the corner, knocked Biff aside, and slammed the door in Petra's face.

"Damn." Petra kicked the Welcome to Muscletown mat outside the door. As she knocked again, "You have a son?" filtered through the door.

"What's Plan B?" Jackie asked. Petra reached for her wand and sent an exploratory burst of pale green magic toward the lock. It crackled, but half an inch from the metal, the magic disappeared. When Petra activated her magical sight to look for traces of the magic that had absorbed it, there was nothing.

"What the hell was that?" Jackie asked.

Petra shook her head. "That was some extremely powerful light elf magic."

"If she's so powerful, why is she spending her time lounging around a pool with muscular young men?" Petra stared at Jackie until the question sank in. "Fine. Now that I say it, I can see the appeal."

"Who's going to stop her?" Petra asked.

Over the next fifteen minutes, she sent a variety of spells at the door, including two of her own devising. She even borrowed Jackie's wand to try a dual-wield takedown. Nada. Zilch.

They needed more information.

Fortunately, Darlene was still by the pool. She had a clear glass mug shaped like a pineapple in one manicured hand, and the rum inside was rapidly disappearing through a long crazy straw.

"Petra! Welcome back!" Darlene said. "It's piña colada night. Would you care to indulge?"

"Possibly," Petra replied. "Although I was hoping you could give me the teensiest bit of information first. Aside from Marco and Biff, does Glesselda have any interests?"

"Like, knitting?" Darlene asked.

"Sure. Is there a book club, something like that? Anything outside the house?"

"There's bingo night," Darlene offered cautiously.

"When is that?"

"Monday night, but I don't like the shifty look in your eyes. Don't go messing with bingo night. It's a staple of the community."

"Thank you so much, Darlene," Petra replied. "I promise to treasure your bingo night as if it were my own."

CHAPTER SIXTEEN

"Everyone who knows Garton Saxon hates him," Madge said, breaking off a piece of a bath bomb that was nearly as tall as her and chucking it into the crockpot on the side table. The bath bomb fizzed, and the pixie kicked off her gold custom sneakers while giving Norah a warning look. "I don't care one way or the other, but I'm about to take this bath. Unless you want to see the full Madge, I'd close the curtains."

Norah rolled her eyes and pulled a large pink lampshade out from under the side table. She plopped it neatly over Madge's makeshift hot tub.

"Suit yourself!" Madge called, and there was a loud splash. Steam shot up from the lampshade, and after a moment, the pixie resumed speaking. "Anyway, if everyone who knows Saxon hates him, we have to find someone who doesn't know him."

"If they don't know him, how can they love him?" Norah asked. She strode over to the magical dominos game in the corner of the room, plucked up a small black tile, and added it to the growing explosion of pieces. The game was swiftly approaching critical overload.

"You don't have to know someone to love them. I love Marisa Tomei. Have you seen *My Cousin Vinny*? A masterpiece of American cinema."

"Garton Saxon isn't a household-name American treasure."

"Not to most people. That's why I created an account on the SilverLionFans forum. You're looking at Lioness420. I have identified three separate megafans of Saxon's work, and I have a bulletproof way to make one of them love him forever."

"What?"

"I posed as Saxon and offered one a teeny tiny cameo in *The Players*."

"What? What cameo?"

There was a lot of splashing.

"Madge! What did you do?"

"I'm sure Sid can write one measly little cameo. Like, a stranger coming to the door who gets eaten by the beast."

"Are you willing to risk First Arret on it? Jackie and Mom might still find something."

"Pff. They're holed up in a hotel, waiting for the world's most powerful elf to go to bingo night. It's not like Bitta has to use the shot. Three takes, we promise her a meet-and-greet with Saxon, she kisses the statue, it's all done."

"Are you crazy? That will never work!" Norah protested. There was more splashing from inside the lampshade. "I believe in you!" the pixie shouted.

Two hours later, Sid was staring at her like she was the

craziest witch west of the Mississippi. "A *cameo*? We're four days into filming."

"I'm just the messenger," Norah said in her most confident Hollywood voice. "If you really want to tell Bitta she's wrong about what the second act needs, knock yourself out. Assuming you can make it through Celestia."

Sid turned the color of the marble statues in the fake palace gardens. In the distance, someone was crying. Not unheard of on a film set, but Norah hoped it was an actor rehearsing.

"Ugh. Celestia. That woman terrifies me," Sid confided. "I saw her split a hair in half lengthwise with that fancy knife she claims is for opening emotional portals."

"You know I've *actually* opened a portal," Norah said peevishly. "Using my razor-sharp skills, not some cheesy knife."

"Did you say cheese knife?" a sharp voice asked. Norah spun. Celestia was standing imperiously behind her, clad in purple velvet robes. Unable to stop herself, Norah brushed her fingers against one velvet sleeve and made a small noise of appreciation. "So soft," she whispered.

As the sleeve fell back into place, Norah realized Bitta was standing behind Celestia.

"If there was a cheese knife on set, it has been removed. I have ordered all dairy and wheat purged from Craft Services," Celestia stated.

Norah now understood the cries of sorrow in the background. Angelo couldn't have been happy about the menu changes.

"He wasn't pleased," Bitta added. "But Angelo's a team player."

"I need to talk to you." Norah dodged around Celestia to pull Bitta aside. Celestia trailed behind them, crystals clanking inside her purple robes. She hovered beatifically as Norah pulled Bitta onto a faux-marble bench and told her Marina wanted a cameo. She was lying through her teeth so hard she was afraid they would pop out.

Bitta was even less happy about the cameo than Sid had been.

"It has something to do with the financing," Norah said, sweat dripping off her forehead. "Marina was very insistent. Cut it in the edit if you hate it, but don't piss off our funder. Especially if you want the money for that fountain stunt you were telling me about yesterday. I know you want that."

Bitta's eyes turned watery and focused on some far-off aquatic dream. "Fine. We can do the cameo. Later today, when we're shooting the players' arrival."

Norah felt a huge wash of relief. "Thank you, Bitta."

As Norah turned away to call Madge with the good news, a hand pulled her into an alcove in the reconstructed chapel.

"Wha…" Norah began, then her side slammed into the plinth of a plaster saint. She rubbed it, annoyed.

Sid morosely fidgeted in the shadows. "I can't do it, Norah. I did so many edits already. You don't understand. I'm a fraud."

As Norah stuffed her phone in her pocket, prepared to tell Sid to suck it up, her finger brushed a small, hard nodule—the pilfered pink fairy. *Maybe it's time to deploy the big guns.*

"I will give you *one* dose," Norah said, dangling the

bubblegum-hued bean in front of his face, "if you shut up and write the stupid cameo."

Sid's eyes tracked the bean, hypnotized, and he held out his hand. When it dropped from her fingers, he scarfed it like he was starving.

Norah waited for the characteristic pink haze to swirl around Sid. His terrified, pale face didn't flush. Instead, it turned a sickly chartreuse. His eyes yellowed. Sid coughed, and a bubble of spit appeared in the corner of his mouth. He coughed again, and a hand pushed out of his mouth, and not the delicate manicured fingers of the cotton candy fairies.

These were long green fingers with needle-sharp nails that left scratches on Sid's lips as it crawled out. The fairy's skin was covered in tiny dull scales, and it unfurled tattered bat wings as it soared into the air, hovered for a moment, and dove for Sid's eyes.

The screenwriter put his arms up just in time, and the fairy raked its nails across his wrist. Blood seeped from the thin lines as the fairy screamed, "You're a fraud, and you'll never make it on your own!"

"I *am* a fraud," Sid whispered. He clawed at the scratches, which were now puffy pink welts.

"Oh, no. He has the greenies," someone behind Norah said. She turned to find Angelo, wanly holding a large plastic bowl of carrot shavings.

"What?" Norah asked.

"If you do too much pink fairy, a switch eventually flips. It prevents Genghis Khanian levels of confidence, but it's difficult to watch. Hm. Do you want any...I hesitate to call it food." Angelo held out the bowl of carrot shavings.

"I'm okay," Norah said, nauseated as another bubble of green phlegm appeared in the corner of Sid's mouth. "What do we do?"

Angelo shrugged. "You wait. That's all. It wears off eventually."

A new fairy with rusty scales and red eyes emerged from Sid's mouth. It high-fived the first fairy, and the two miniature monstrosities flew in opposite directions, pulling out strands of Sid's hair as they circled his head like a merry-go-round from hell.

Sid's eyes went wide, and he scrambled back and slid across the floor on his butt. A low whine of fear escaped his throat.

"You'll be okay, Sid," Norah assured him. He started to hyperventilate and brought his hand to his face. At first, she thought he was puking another fairy, but his finger indicated a spot above Norah's head. He was no longer looking at the monster fairies.

Norah followed the finger, then screamed. The six-legged, black-furred beast was behind her, so close she could feel its rank breath on her face.

Wait, breath? It's not supposed to breathe.

Slobber glistened on the beast's fangs and dripped down in a long rope. A globule fell to the concrete, splashing Norah's shoes.

By instinct, she turned her radio magic on at the lowest level, feeling stupid for doing so. The monster was just a puppet. A very realistic puppet, except...

Except it wasn't. A distinct sense of *wanting* emerged from it and flowed toward Norah in a confusing churn. The beast had desires.

The monster's eyes were different, too. Before, they had been glassy and fake. Now, they oozed lethal intelligence. They were as big as teacups and the color of grass, with very small pupils.

Norah scrambled back and tripped over Sid, then fell onto him as a green fairy screamed, "You're like half a pair of scissors. You can't do the job!!"

No time to mull over that one since the monster skittered toward her. It raised a foreleg before Norah could get out of its way and, with a mighty thrust, tossed her ten feet across the room.

Norah cast an antigrav cushion as she flew through the air but got the placement wrong and slammed into a marble arch. She desperately tried to suck in air but was unable to move as the beast reared back to take another swipe at her.

"Oh, no, you don't," someone said behind her.

It was Stellan, holding a huge axe. His beard, backlit by buttery yellow light, blew back in a gleaming wave as the monster bellowed. Its hurricane-force hot breath hit the dwarf in the face.

"I made you, and I can destroy you!" Stellan shouted, sprinting toward the beast.

It raised a furry leg to protect its body as Stellan's axe swung. The silver blade connected, and black blood splattered. Stellan touched his gorgeous silky beard, now matted into sad, sticky clumps. "My manly beard! My elegant chin curtain! I'll get you for this, monster!" he screamed.

The beast limped on its bad leg as it rose to its feet, injured but not out. It still had five good legs, and one of those slammed into Stellan's chest and knocked him to the ground. It trampled him as it stepped into the open space beside the set.

Norah, who had finally got her breath back, cast a stunning spell, but it harmlessly hit a window as the monster veered toward the building's perimeter. Norah sprinted toward it, ducking a chunk of flying masonry as she followed the beast toward Craft Services.

There, Angelo stood in front of his temporary kitchen with a Wüsthof chef's knife, prepared to defend his sad salads to the death. "Stay back!" he shouted at it.

The beast barely looked at him, but it clothes-lined him with an extended leg as it tore past.

As Angelo hit the ground, a large deep-red stain spread across his chest.

"No! Angelo!" Norah skidded to a stop beside the caterer. "Are you okay?"

Norah raised her wand to send a healing spell into his body, but he caught her arm.

Angelo whispered, "It's marinara." He coughed dramatically. "For putting on top of shredded zucchini. We will always remember it."

His hand loosened from her arm and fell as he quietly passed out.

"I've never known anybody more devoted to his food than you, Angelo," Norah murmured.

Another scream. Norah pulled away from Angelo and sprinted in the direction of the chaos as a spine-wrenching metallic shriek echoed around the building.

There were shouts and then silence as Norah reached the warehouse's loading dock. The monster had split the sliding metal door down the middle with laser-like precision, but it had been distracted from its escape by a challenger.

A shirtless Duncan, wearing the baggy striped breeches from his costume, raced onto the scene as the monster's mossy green eyes latched on him. He whipped out his wand and shot a stunning spell at the monster. To Norah's astonishment, the monster did not topple over like a rag doll. It leapt into the path of the spell, its mouth constricted in a puckered ring, and it sucked in air like a vacuum.

Not just air. Crackling sand-colored magic flowed out of Duncan's wand in a turbulent stream and vanished into the dark circle of the monster's throat.

The young wizard screamed in agony. Norah put her wand up, then lowered it in alarm. It wasn't just Duncan's spell the monster was sucking down. It was siphoning out his magical powers.

The final *slurp* was audible not through Norah's ears but through her magical senses. Duncan was still breathing, but he'd fallen to his hands and knees, hollowed by the beast's whirlwind consumption. His wand lay dark and useless on the ground next to him.

The monster's mouth opened again, exposing a fresh new row of teeth. Its body shuddered as it let out a burp.

Its black head tilted back, and it let out a triumphant scream. Then, in a flurry of legs and fur, the monster reared back and punched through the flap it had cut in the metal door. Flinging it aside with its new powers, it scrambled outside.

Norah raced past the weeping Duncan and followed it.

As she passed through the hole it had torn in the doors, the black fur caught on the edges of the metal brushed her arms. She could smell the last regurgitated-fish-sauce traces of the monster's breath as she slid through the gap into the sunlight.

In the distance, a black shape burst through a chain-link fence, long legs windmilling, and disappeared in a drainage ditch beyond. Norah came to a stop and gasped for air, her legs shaking.

Stellan, his callused fingers raking his ruined beard, emerged through the hole in the metal door, blocking the bright California sun from his eyes with a bloodstained hand.

"What the hell, Stellan?" Norah asked. "I thought we'd tightened security. Is someone on set doing this?"

Stellan shook his head. "It's not like the other day. That was someone making the monster's limbs move. It was a prank. Now…"

The monster wanted pain and destruction.

"It's alive," Norah finished.

Stellan nodded grimly. "Its eyes were different the other day."

"Different? Different how?" Norah demanded.

He shrugged helplessly, and she told him about the monster's intelligent green eyes. His expression grew harder. She pulled him over to where Duncan was crumpled on the concrete floor. Despite his muscles, he looked very small.

"Norah, my magic!" His voice was a low croak. "It's…it's gone."

He looked like he'd just had his heart pulled out of his

chest. He sat up and retrieved his wand, but it was black and dead in his hand.

"Are you injured? I mean, physically?" Norah asked.

Duncan shook his head.

"We'll find a way to fix this." She patted his shoulder.

The wand fell to the floor with a dull clatter. He covered his face with one hand and laughed. It sounded like a sob.

Stellan straightened with a growl. "I think it's time we paid a visit to my shop."

CHAPTER SEVENTEEN

The bingo hall was near Glesselda's apartment. Petra had spent the past two days lounging by the pool of their motel, watching *Golden Girls* reruns, and eating takeout Chinese food with Jackie. It was a pleasant way to spend twenty-four hours, but two days was pushing it.

Petra got antsy and started pacing the motel's hallways and making frequent trips for ice. The dry heat had, if nothing else, alleviated Jackie's morning sickness.

As the sun set, they put on their nicest outfits and headed to Zoolies, a bar on Arenas Road. It was busy, but they found the last two seats in the room. Petra ordered a Shirley Temple in support of Jackie until the younger woman begged her to cut loose.

"Please let me watch you drink a Cosmo," Jackie pleaded.

The room's mic clicked on with a crackle of static, and a loud announcer said, "Who's ready for drag bingo? Please welcome to the stage the high priestess of passion, the voluptuous vixen, Miss Bridget Troll!"

Petra let out a sharp gasp of appreciation when they saw their host. The Kilomea was over seven feet tall, although six inches of that was glittering gold and clear pink rubber heels. The rest of the drag queen's body was sheathed in a mesh made of Oriceran red opals. The shifting, glittering fabric hurt the eyes.

"I've never seen a Kilomea drag queen," Jackie whispered. Neither had Petra.

"Aren't you all precious!" the Kilomea exclaimed, voice deep but sweet like blackstrap molasses. She grasped the microphone with a velvet glove to uproarious cheers.

"Bring me my cage!" Miss Troll shouted, and a bingo cage was wheeled out.

They had each gotten a single bingo card, a measly supply relative to some of the players' stacks. As Miss Troll drew numbers and bantered with the audience, they halfheartedly marked their squares.

Glesselda arrived unaccompanied, having left Marco and Biff to a free evening of muscle-increasing activities. Wearing a gold brocade jumpsuit, she was impossible to miss. After keeping an eye on her for fifteen minutes, Petra wished she'd brought sunglasses. The molten sheen of the fabric jarred her eyes so badly that she thought it would give her a migraine.

"B-22!" Miss Troll called, adding, "I wish I could be twenty-two again, don't you?" Jackie stamped a square of her card amid the requisite laughter, then stared.

"Bingo!" the young witch cried, then clamped a hand over her mouth. An early win hadn't been a part of their plan, but it was too late. She stood as women with tables plastered with vast grids of bingo cards glared at her one measly card.

One of the glaring women was Glesselda, who watched Jackie with hawklike eyes as she shuffled up to collect her prize, a large novelty mug in the shape of Betty White's head. Glesselda turned and stared straight at Petra, red-hot anger in her eyes. She whispered something to a woman at a nearby table.

Suddenly, light swept down from overhead, knitting into a table-sized spatula that slid under Glesselda's abandoned bingo cards. The spatula carried the cards across the room and deposited them at a nearby table to a chorus of cheers. By the time Petra looked back from this new fan club, Glesselda was halfway to the door.

After half an instant of wondering what it looked like when Glesselda made pancakes, Petra ran after her.

"Wait!" she shouted.

The elf wound through the packed space, walking faster. Petra looked anxiously from Miss Troll to a pair of earth elementals in the corner who were watching the scene with intense interest.

"Screw it." Petra went for her wand. She was lucky her grip was firm because before she could raise it from her pocket, Glesselda twitched a red-manicured pinkie. A splintered shaft of light shot from the LED disco ball dangling from the ceiling, wrapped around one of Petra's ankles, and yanked her off her feet. She hung upside-down, struggling against the light-rope on her ankle and suddenly glad she'd worn pants.

Petra twitched her wand in a quick circle and slash to break the loop. When it snapped, she hit the floor, her shoulder encountering a sticky coating of old beer and crushed peanuts. The stab of pain was drowned by a wave of adrenaline.

Gold brocade glinted at the edge of the room, rushing toward the exit. Petra fired a quick-locking spell at the door, then pushed through a crowd of windbreaker-and-visor-clad bingo-hall denizens until she could see enough of Glesselda to decide what to do.

There! That gold brocade begged to be seen. When the elf reached for the door and found it locked, Petra felt smug satisfaction.

Until Glesselda's pointer finger, weighted down by a diamond the size of a small moon, twitched, and a key made of blazing light extended from her finger.

Before she could tap it against the doorknob, a stream of lemon-yellow magic snaked around the light elf's wrist and pulled her toward Petra.

"I've got your back!" Jackie called, breathing hard.

Petra shot a stunning spell at Glesselda, but it was deflected by a lazily cast disc of light.

Heavy fingers encased in velvet wrapped around Petra's arm where it had been burned, and she shrieked in pain. Miss Troll let go with a surprised intake of breath and trotted between them and Glesselda.

"Exactly what do you think you're doing?" the drag queen asked, her no-nonsense fighting stance made more terrifying by her platform stilettos.

Glesselda abandoned any pretense at subtlety and sent a bright fireball of light at the doorway. It blasted an elf-shaped escape hatch to the outside.

Seeing an opportunity, Jackie dove through the Kilomea's legs, arm outstretched, and slid on her side as a sunshine-colored stunning spell left her wand and hurtled toward Glesselda's retreating back.

Half an instant before it hit, Glesselda disappeared.

"What the fuck?" Jackie scrambled to her feet and headed to the door.

Petra darted around Miss Troll in the chaos and dove through the hole, scanning the street. Glesselda hadn't hidden or jumped, or made any other escape. She had winked out of existence, which meant she had cast an extremely powerful spell. Accessing her magical sight, Petra inspected the surroundings. There was nothing except...

She almost missed it. The pebble shone with a near-infinite density of magic, but it was so small and ordinary-looking that it was difficult to pick out of the environment.

"I'm calling the cops!" a deep voice said behind them. The burly wizard bouncer at the door tapped a wooden baseball bat threateningly on the ground. The bat crackled with rusty red magic.

"Is that his wand?" Jackie whispered. Petra nodded and backed away after scooping the pebble into her pocket. With one more glance at the baseball bat, they ran.

They were two blocks away before she pulled Jackie into an alley behind a metal garbage can and showed her the pebble.

"What is that?"

"A pocket of unreality, like in that dreadful painting Norah brought home from work," Petra said, shivering. She kept an eye on the entrance to the alley but didn't think anyone had followed them out of the bingo bar chaos. Breathing deeply, she explored the pebble with her magical sight, sending ropes of pale green spellwork around it. The magic inside the pebble was small and fine. Every time Petra's magic touched it, it constricted and shrank, the pebble tightening.

"I have an idea." Petra smiled. "If you're willing to drive."

The return trip to Los Angeles only took two hours, but Petra was tired by the time they pulled into Norah's parking lot. As her adrenaline receded, a bright pain in her shoulder emerged. The fall had aggravated her burned skin, and they didn't talk much as they trudged up the stairs to Norah's condo.

Frondle met them at the door, to Petra's consternation.

"She's visiting the prop shop. Another mishap on the set. Nothing serious, though," Frondle added, seeing Petra's anxiety.

"Would you mind grabbing Saxon from the car, dear? I don't have it in me," Petra requested. Frondle looked worried but nodded, and Jackie went with him to the car.

Petra made her way down the hall, humming a quick hello to Norah's plants. The green leaves bobbed cheerfully in response, but she didn't stop to chat. Instead, she strode over to the crystal coffin in front of the television, opened the lid, chucked the magical pebble inside, and closed it with a thud.

The results were near-instantaneous. Unable to untangle the magic inside the pebble, Petra had settled for negating it. As quickly as she'd disappeared, Glesselda fell out of her pocket of unreality, cursing. Glossy gold fabric filled the coffin like metal in a crucible. Hands waving wildly, the light elf strained to gather light from sources around the room, but it fizzled out the second it touched the black-hole onyx studs lining the sides. Abandoning that, she used what little light filtered through the crystal walls of the coffin to create an enormous fireball, but that, too, fizzled out when it hit the black-hole onyx.

"What have you done?" Glesselda demanded.

Petra stared at the light elf meditatively.

"I'm really sorry about this, Glesselda. We needed to talk to you. When I found your pebble, this seemed expedient."

Glesselda sputtered, and a mist of spit hit the crystal wall.

"What the—"

Frondle's voice grew alarmed when he saw the light elf writhing inside the frosty crystal container. Saxon's frozen body hit the tile floor with a thud. Glesselda, staring past Petra, stilled.

"Garty," the light elf called softly.

That was promising. Petra moved to give Glesselda a better view. "That's right. We have Saxon. He's all right, but he's been shot with a Sleeping Beauty arrow. We need you to wake him up."

Glesselda glared. "Why would I help you? You kidnapped me."

"That's an extreme way to put it, but a wonderful answer to your question. If you help us, we will un-kidnap you."

Glesselda pushed on the lid of the crystal coffin, but it was tightly secured. The locking mechanism was protected by extra strips of light-dampening black-hole onyx. "I have conditions."

"I can't make any promises, but I'm happy to hear you out," Petra replied.

"Garty has been very successful but also quite the troublemaker."

Frondle gave a ferocious scoff behind Petra's back.

Petra nodded. "Troublemaker is accurate, in a way. Like calling Jeffrey Dahmer a foodie." Jackie stifled a laugh.

"How do you know I won't just kill you the second I get out of this box?" Glesselda asked.

Petra shrugged. "If that was on the table, you would have done it already. If you were murderous, you'd be spending your retirement innovating in the world domination space, not alternating weeknights with athletic young men. That setup seems to have a lot of charms, which I suspect you'd be loath to lose."

Glesselda narrowed her eyes, annoyed by her enemy's bullseye. Then, her shoulders sagged, and she flung herself onto the floor of the coffin, crossing her arms. "I want a whirlwind tour of Los Angeles's finest entertainment, starting with Disneyland. With Garty lurking behind every 35mm camera in town, I've never been able to enjoy myself here."

"You want a southern California vacation?" Jackie asked, leaning over the coffin.

Glesselda brightened. "Exactly!"

"That can be arranged," Petra told her. "I suppose I should call Lincoln and tell him I'll be gone for a few more days."

CHAPTER EIGHTEEN

Norah eyed a nearby goose sunning on the grass near a low marble memorial bench. It hissed, and she took a step back.

"That thing looks like it wants to eat me," she whispered to Stellan.

He waved at the goose, which hissed even more evilly. "She's just saying hello."

Hollywood Forever's shady lawns were cool in the morning air and wet Norah's sneakers with dew. Before encountering the geese, they'd passed a large colony of feral cats. Norah wondered if the two groups ever had a showdown. The cemetery was the final resting place of Judy Garland, Johnny Ramone, and Mel Blanc, among other glitterati, with graves dating back to the early 1900s.

To the east of the complex, across a vast expanse of lawn, stone, and more than one muscular marble angel, was a murky pond with a mausoleum in the center. Shooing away geese, Stellan led Norah on a small walkway over the pond. Metal bands crossed the oxidized green of the bronze door, forming a grid. Stellan tapped the tiles in an elegant sequence, and a latch clicked.

The door sprang open, revealing a cool blue room tiled in a pigeon-blue and gold mosaic, with angels dancing at intervals on the walls. There was barely space to walk between the seven marble sarcophagi.

Stellan led Norah to the back of the space, where light trickled through a stained glass window onto a sarcophagus lid carved with a beautiful resting woman. She was smiling. Norah touched one fold of her flowing robes, sure it must be silk, but the marble was cold under her finger.

"Pardon me." Stellan poked two fingers into the woman's stone eyes.

With a loud scrape, the sarcophagus lid slid aside on a noiseless dwarven mechanism, revealing a narrow staircase of pale stone. The somber atmosphere of the cemetery and mausoleum vanished in the boisterous chatter that rose from the opening.

"Follow me." Stellan leapt dramatically into the side of the coffin. He had cut his beard short after the monster blood that had doused it had proved too sticky and persistent to remove and constantly touched the bristles.

The staircase shot down in a single stretch into a long tunnel, which ran a short distance under eerie, rippling light from a glass skylight in the ceiling. Norah realized the skylight was made of water. They were under the muddy pond.

Soon the tunnel opened out, and there was movement in the distance. The volume of the voices rose. To access this room, they had to pass through a set of monstrous jaws carved from the pale stone of the tunnel. The exact shape of the beast was swallowed by the surrounding stone, but Norah shivered as she stepped under concentric rows of serrated teeth. Two fangs jutted so low that Norah had to duck under them. Someone had slapped a pink sticky note on one.

Abandon all hope, ye who enter here.

"Nice," Norah said.

Stellan looked at the note and rolled his eyes. "They're good kids down here. Total weirdos, obviously, but good."

"Sounds about right," Norah said. A teardrop-shaped ruby the size of a chicken egg dangled from one fang. Norah sent it swinging with a tap of one fingernail, and magic crackled through her arm. Protective wards. "I love what you've done with the place."

The second they stepped into Stellan's monster prop workshop, an object hurtled at Stellan from a bench in the corner of the room. A moment before it struck his face, his hand shot up. Norah jumped as his fingers uncurled, holding the object out. It was a glistening eyeball, the iris flecked with glittering green and red veins spiderwebbing across the whites. It was the size of a fist, and it was wet.

Stellan squeezed it three times like a stress ball and rolled it around, looking at a white patch on the back.

He chucked it back at the table it had come from. "Gotta finish the back," he shouted. "In case the director decides at the last minute that he wants the eyes totally white. It's cheesy but popular."

"Got it," the young woman in the corner shouted. She had dark hair tied back with a black velvet ribbon, and her long-sleeved Bad Brains t-shirt was covered in paint.

"Welcome to hell," Stellan stated.

"It's nice," Norah said, trying to sound positive. It *was* nice, if a little goth for Norah's taste. The space was huge. Apparently, it was easier to find real estate in Los Angeles if you were willing to abandon the sun.

Stellan chuckled. "Oh, that wasn't an insult. That's what we call the workshop. Hell."

"Oh."

"Come meet my devils. All hands!" Stellan shouted. There was some good-natured grumbling as people carrying laser cutters, shears, bolts of fabric, carving tools, and silicone molds put down their work and collected in the large open space in the center of the room.

Eight people worked for Stellan: four dwarves, two witches, a dark elf, and a wood elf. He rattled off their names. The young woman with the eyeball was named Tabitha. Stellan explained what Norah had told him about the monster's changing eyes.

"Who was on eyeballs?" Stellan asked gruffly. Tabitha raised her hand.

"What did you put in and when?" Stellan continued.

"The first time or the second time?" the witch asked.

Stellan frowned. "What do you mean?"

"I put in glassy whites with red pupils. Exactly what was in the specs," the witch told him. "But then you said the client wanted something scarier."

"I said what?" Stellan asked sharply. Tabitha scratched the cobweb tattoo climbing up her neck, and a crackle of anxiety passed from person to person.

"You left me a voice message," Tabitha replied. "That the client wanted something more dramatic. It came by courier from the Czech Republic."

The blank confusion on Stellan's face turned to anger.

Norah walked over to Tabitha. "Do you still have the message?"

"I didn't keep it. I just put in the eyes you sent."

"Shit!" Stellan exclaimed.

"Did I screw up?" Tabitha asked. Stellan shook his head, though he looked like he wanted to scream yes.

Instead, he let out a deep breath. "When was this?"

"The day before the attack," Tabitha replied.

"You didn't tell me?" Now there was an elven-sword-sharp edge to his voice.

"I didn't want to..." Her voice trailed off and she pressed her mouth shut, face unreadable. Curious, Norah flipped her radio magic on. The room was alive with anxious emotion, but Norah couldn't sense any ill will.

She focused her attention on Tabitha. The young witch yearned to build terrifying monsters and confect gruesome special effects, but she didn't want to get Stellan in trouble. Norah understood.

"She didn't want to snitch on you," she told Stellan quietly.

Wary understanding flickered over Stellan's face. "You thought I was responsible for the attack?"

"No..." Tabitha told him, but Norah could tell from the bright anxiety crackling off of her that she was lying. "I mean, you said the money was shit. Then the first attack went viral, and I thought it was a tactic? I don't know."

"Okay. Your loyalty, while I appreciate it personally, has left us one step behind. The money *is* shit." Stellan eyed Norah. "But I didn't send that courier. Someone must have impersonated my voice. They could have done it with magic, but there's no shortage of actors looking for work in this town."

He turned to the other witch, a small blonde with colorless hair and dramatic red-and-black tattoos snaking down both arms.

"Were our security wards up that day?" he asked. The witch nodded.

"Go get them," Norah ordered. "I want to see that courier."

The blonde hurried away and returned moments later with the teardrop-sized ruby that had dangled from the entryway's fang. Scrambling through the storage shelves that lined every wall, she found a polished silver bowl inscribed with runes and tossed the ruby in.

Stellan pushed it into the open space in the center of the circle and added a few drops of a clear, oily substance from a shining copper flask in his pocket. As he stepped back, the ruby stood on end in the bowl, and wisps of red smoke emerged from its point. The wisps condensed into transparent ghost-like shapes.

"Show me the night before the attack," Stellan directed in a loud, clear voice. "I want to see the courier."

The mist swirled faster, then formed into a half-sized representation of the toothy entrance. Norah held her breath as the wisps coalesced into a human figure, package clutched in his hands. He had dark hair, bushy black eyebrows, and an angry expression. A familiar angry expression. In the magical replay, Tabitha met the angry man at the door. They talked, and she accepted a lunchbox-sized package.

Norah gasped. "I know that guy."

"An enemy?" Stellan asked gruffly.

"No. He's my boyf...my friend's roommate."

The man in the hallway was Castor, the guy she'd met at Frondle's.

"I've got to warn Frondle," she shouted, dialing his number as she sprinted out of the workshop. His phone went to voicemail.

You and your stupid elven "being present in the moment."

Driving south from Hollywood Forever into Koreatown at nine in the morning was horrible, and Norah's anxiety rose as she inched through traffic. She could have run to Frondle's faster.

She imagined his beautiful flaxen hair dangling from the slobbering jaws of a black-furred beast with mossy saucer eyes.

I could *run to Frondle's faster.*

Norah pulled into a yellow-painted loading zone, put on her hazards, and leapt out of the car. She sprinted the remaining distance to Frondle's apartment, dodging young Korean students with boba teas and shopkeepers opening for the day.

When she reached Frondle's building, Norah hit the lock on the front door with a blasting spell, flung it open, and ran upstairs. Frondle had warded the door into the apartment from the hallway with light elf magic, and her attempts to open the lock failed. She pounded on the door.

"Frondle!" she screamed.

He opened the door a moment later, confused. "Norah?" She let out the breath she'd been holding since she left Stellan's workshop. "What's going on?"

As he ushered her inside, Castor peered into the living

room from the hallway, bushy black eyebrows almost touching.

"Mr. Puppetmaster here is the one who's been fucking up my set." She pointed at Castor. "He tampered with Stellan's monster." She glared at the wizard.

Frondle's face looked pained. Norah guessed this might be his first taste of betrayal in his relatively short life. "Why, Castor?"

Castor looked from Frondle's hurt to Norah's anger, then opened his mouth. "Maybe you should ask Sid."

"Sid?"

Without answering, he spun and ran, arms pumping, toward the window at the end of the hallway. Retrieving a wand from his pocket, he shot out a spell, and the window slid up. Castor dove.

Norah threw a stunning spell, but the window snapped magically shut, and the crackling blue magic bounced off a residual protective ward Castor had thrown behind him. She reached the door, anxiety rising as she looked out. Half-obscured by the dusty glass, Castor was trotting down the alleyway. At least he wasn't a red puddle on the sidewalk.

"What did he mean, 'Ask Sid?'" Norah asked.

Frondle looked out the window.

"I don't know. We should ask Sid." He turned his high-wattage smile on Norah. "You came to rescue me. I am grateful." His arms swept around her in an embrace. Norah pulled back and met his icy blue eyes. There were faint flecks of gold just around the pupils, like a supernova. She leaned in, but the second before their lips touched, Frondle pushed her to the floor.

"Our honor!" he shouted.

The door to Ethan's room opened, and a ginger-haired head peeked out. "What's going on?" the hamster shifter asked, staring at Norah. She scrambled to her feet.

"It appears that Castor has become involved in nefarious deeds," Frondle said, face serious.

Ethan laughed. "Did he rejoin that mime collective? Those people were assholes." His voice got strained when he saw the looks on Norah's and Frondle's faces.

"I fear it is even more serious than mimes," Frondle said. "Do you have your car, Norah?"

"Oh, shit. That's a great question. Fancy a jog?"

They reached the street where she had double-parked just as a rusty blue tow rig was pulling up beside the Prius. A woman with short-cropped hair who looked like an aggressive bowling ball trundled out of the rig. Norah flung a quick prayer for forgiveness into the universe as she shot a stunning spell into the base of the woman's neck.

"Put her back in her rig," she said to Frondle and leapt into the driver's seat. As the light elf hauled the driver back in her car, the twin smells of onions and gochujang drifted into the car from a nearby bibimbap place, reminding Norah that she hadn't had breakfast. She shook her head. *Sid can buy me food while he explains himself.*

The instant Frondle closed the passenger door, Norah burned rubber driving away.

"Do you think someone will tow her?" Frondle stared at the frozen driver in her blue rig.

"Who watches the watcher?" Norah asked. As an Angeleno, seeing a tow truck get towed would give her a thrill.

Someday, Norah swore, she would work a job that

didn't require driving in Los Angeles rush hour traffic. Something relaxing, like an overnight shift at a cemetery or being a deep sea fisherman in a hurricane. However, today was not that day.

As she inched up the 101 toward Burbank, Frondle put a hand on her knee. His touch was electric.

"Is that allowed?" Norah asked breathlessly. Frondle's eyes grew serious.

"Is it distracting you from our honor-bound mission?" he asked. His fingers fluttered, and another jolt of electricity shot up her spine. If she'd been going more than three miles an hour, she might have driven off the road.

"Nope," she lied. Frondle's eyes narrowed suspiciously as he looked at her flushed face, then he removed the hand. Norah sighed.

"Has Castor ever said anything about Sid?" she asked.

"Nothing good. Once, Ethan brought him up in conversation. Castor got quiet and left the room. There were jokes about their relationship being like a bad divorce, although I do not think they were romantically involved."

"No," Norah agreed.

It took a minute to find the address Madge had tracked down from Sid's tax paperwork. His apartment complex in Burbank was as bland as he was, a labyrinth of identical clean gray hallways. A welcome mat outside the door said Welcome Mat, and Norah wasn't sure it was ironic. No one answered when she knocked, so she tried the handle. It was open.

Everything in the apartment was a putrid acidic green. At first, Norah thought it was an unfortunate decorating choice, but soon she realized that it was an optical illusion from a thin mist streaming out of the bathroom, along with indistinct high-pitched shrieking. She and Frondle exchanged worried looks, and she moved wand-first down the hallway.

When she pushed open the bathroom door, dense green fog spilled out, and the indistinct shrieking resolved into fervent insults of "Everyone at the potluck who said they liked your lemon tart was lying" and "Your body is too weird for clothes to ever fit you correctly." Wretched green fairies cut through the dense pea-soup haze, making occasional dives to swipe at the face of the figure curled up, fully clothed, in the bathtub.

"Sid?" Norah asked.

The screenwriter, face the color of glue, shrank away from her. "Get away from me!" It sounded more like a warning than a threat.

A large glass bowl of pink beans sat on the toilet. As Norah approached, Sid snatched it away and pulled it to his chest. His pale hand snaked into the bowl. A second after the pink bean went in his mouth, he coughed up another mean green fairy. "Your hair smells like salami," the fairy said and mooned Norah and Frondle, who made a small, offended noise.

"Why are you still eating those?" Norah asked.

"The fairies are the only ones who are telling me the truth," Sid growled, then his voice softened. "Besides, I deserve this."

"Does it have something to do with Castor?" Norah asked. A scaly green fairy straddled Sid's nose and casually ripped out one of his eyelashes.

"Stop that!" Norah exclaimed. She tried to take the bowl

from Sid, but he clutched it tighter, so she levitated all of the pink beans out of the bowl and into her jacket pocket.

"Can you help with the smoke?" Norah asked. Frondle nodded and began moving his hands in a wide circle. Soon, the green fog was a small, breezy tornado, which he funneled down into a fireball. The haze disappeared in its white-hot antiseptic light. One by one, Norah blasted the fairies out of the air, although it took her a second to find the one using Sid's little toe as a speed bag.

When the room was clear, she pulled Sid to his feet. "You need food."

"Food is for people who aren't terrible," Sid recited and sat back down.

"Put him in the car, Frondle," Norah instructed.

Fortunately, their party met no resistance in the hallway. Norah wasn't sure how she would explain why Frondle was carrying a kicking, protesting Sid over one shoulder.

Inside the car, child locks firmly engaged, Norah turned to the back seat.

"Here's what's going to happen. We're going to have a nice quiet drive to IHOP, and you're going to eat at least two pancakes with strawberry syrup. We're going to talk about what the hell is going on between you and Castor, and you are not going to repeat anything those horrible green fairies said to you."

"But—" Sid began, pulling on the door handle.

"If you deviate from that excellent morning plan in any way," Norah continued, "Frondle and I will go back to your apartment, steal your laptop, and send every professional contact you've ever met a photo of your butt."

Sid scoffed. "I've never taken a photo of my butt."

"I'll have Frondle draw one," Norah countered.

"I'm better at woodblock printing," Frondle told her thoughtfully.

"We'll figure it out. So, ask yourself, Sid...how excited are you about this widespread multimedia butt distribution?"

He stopped pulling on the door handle.

Two and a half pancakes later, Sid's color had improved. Norah ordered him hot cocoa, and, deciding that he was in good enough shape to interrogate, leaned in.

"What's the deal with you and Castor?"

"We, uh, used to be writing partners. It didn't go great."

"Was he controlling the monster when it attacked the set?"

Sid nodded miserably. Norah smiled to encourage him. "Okay, but why *this* project? Why now?"

Sid went paler, picked up the strawberry syrup, and poured it over his last pancake, apparently mesmerized by the goopy red stream. When he'd gone through half the bottle, Norah gently took it away.

Sid didn't look up. Finally, he opened his mouth, coughed, and in a small voice, said, "Castor wrote *The Players.*"

"What!?" Norah felt the urge to throw the syrup bottle at him.

"I mean, we co-wrote it before our, uh, creative differences. That's why I gave you the other scripts first, but Madge was so persistent. Send anything, she said. I don't get out-emailed often, but she wore me down."

What had the green fairy said to Sid yesterday? *You're a*

fraud, and you'll never make it on your own! It now made sense. Sid hadn't sent *The Players* right away, even though it met the brief perfectly. He'd sent three other scripts, including the sexy nun project. Norah's face got hot. Sid had made the worst possible choice.

"Why didn't you just tell me? We could have gotten Castor onboard. Gotten you both paid."

Sid made a derisive noise. "No way. He hates me. He would have tanked the project just to hurt me."

Norah was offended. Talking prima donnas off ledges was her bread and butter. Who was Sid to assume she would have failed? "Does anyone else know about this?"

Sid looked up. "When that scary lawyer brought me the paperwork, she asked probing questions. She seemed suspicious, but then the shoot started, and I thought everything would be okay."

Norah now understood why Castor had gone after the monster. It was a perfect choice for a disgruntled puppeteer.

"We scared Castor out of his apartment," she told Sid. "Where would he go to hide?"

"Probably to the puppet theater. He loves that place." Sid sounded derisive.

She looked at Frondle. "Will you come with me? Our last visit wasn't a barnburner."

Frondle smiled. "My sword is yours. Will Sid be safe, though? Perhaps we should take him home."

Sid cheered up at the prospect, but Norah shook her head. "He got us into this tangled web of marionette strings. He can get us out. Besides, we need someone to use as bait."

CHAPTER NINETEEN

The cheerfully painted facade of the Bob Baker Marionette Theater was gloomy in the dark. Norah had called her mother to invite her to join them, but Petra had sent a series of texts about taking a boat to Santa Catalina Island as part of something she called the Glesselda Spectacular Staycation, so it was just Norah, Frondle, and a cowering Sid. He'd coughed up what she thought was the last of the green fairies in the final stretch of the ride to Highland Park.

The windows of the building were dark in the middle of the day, and the door was secured with a sturdy magical ward. Castor wasn't taking any chances.

"Let's get up on the roof," Norah said. "No one thinks about roof security. Apparently."

Frondle moved his hands above his head in twining waves. Drawing from a nearby tungsten streetlamp, he wove a rope ladder made of light, hitching it over the edge of the building.

"Are you sure that's safe?" Norah asked, but he was

already up, scrambling over the lip of the building. The ladder was warm, and she held it steady as she pushed Sid up and followed behind.

By the time she plunked onto the gravel, Frondle had found an access hatch and was descending a rickety aluminum ladder into the building. *Roof security. Always gotta think about roof security.*

A few moments later, Sid and Frondle were standing in a workshop, illuminated by a small circle of light glowing in Frondle's hands.

"Where would Castor hole up?" Norah asked. Frondle frowned as he aimed the ball of light at the walls.

Harsh white lighting fell on a row of motionless clowns. Sid shrieked and stumbled over a discarded wooden puppet arm. Norah jumped.

"It's just the puppet storage," Frondle said, stepping closer. The marionettes were about three feet high, classic harlequins with black-and-white painted faces. The one in the center had red-checked pants and deep blue eyes. Its mouth was painted with a deep frown. As Frondle moved closer, the painted mouth flipped up into an eerie smile.

In a flurry of red plaid, the clown leapt onto Frondle's face, scratching at his eyes with splintery wooden hands. There was a flicker of blue movement, and Norah turned back to the clowns. The one on the far end, which had a blue bow and bright red circles for cheeks, was slinking forward, holding one of its strings like a garrote.

Sid grabbed a human-sized wooden puppet arm off the floor and swung it like a bat at the blue clown. The hand connected, and the clown flew back into the darkness.

Frondle detached the red clown from his face, then raised a net of protective golden light around them like a birdcage.

"I won't be able to keep this up for very long. It's too dark," he cautioned. Norah nodded.

Sid clutched the wooden arm to his chest like a stuffed animal. Norah's eyes widened in horror as the articulated fingers came to life and wrapped around Sid's neck. His shout of alarm was cut off in a gurgle as the chokehold tightened.

Norah, drawing on her internal energy, cast a magical well next to Sid's face to negate the spell. The diabolical fingers loosened, and the arm fell. Frondle lashed it to the concrete floor with glowing golden threads as Sid bent over, catching his breath.

Three more puppets emerged from the darkness. Norah had seen two of them during the sexy puppet show —naked three-foot-high marionettes. Revulsion slammed into Norah at their rigid indecency.

The third puppet was at least as tall as Norah, a bear riding a unicycle. It was meant to be operated by at least two people with a series of sticks. It had clearly been in storage and was half-covered in transparent plastic, which gave it a gloomy body-bag air. All three puppets were armed. The naked male puppet had a whittling knife, and the naked female puppet carried fabric shears. The bear swung a large wooden mallet over its head as the unicycle under its rear paws creak-creak-creaked forward.

The cage of golden light wasn't very big, and the puppet with the whittling knife stabbed between its shining gaps as Sid kicked at it.

They're made of wood. Think, Norah. Wand out, she sent a

stream of flames into the wooden puppet's body. The wood smoked and blackened but failed to ignite. *Shit. They must be fireproof.* If Stellan were here with his axe, these things would be kindling.

There was an idea. "Don't let them stab my ankles," Norah shouted to Sid, then poked her wand between the gaps in the cage. She forced her magic out into a foot-wide disk, then moved the wand rapidly back and forth to serrate the edges and sent it spinning toward the nearest nude puppet. Her makeshift saw hit the marionette between the legs. Sid and Frondle made noises of horror as splinters hit the cage.

"Don't get distracted," Norah shouted as she turned the saw on the bear, who was pounding on the golden cage, unicycle creaking beneath it.

The saw cut through the wheel of the unicycle, and the bear toppled to the floor. It then dragged itself forward using its front paws. Its paw swiped hard, and the golden light of the cage sputtered.

"Shit!" Frondle exclaimed. Norah spun the saw blade toward the final naked puppet, who was trying to snip the protective strands of light with its shears. Just as the spinning magical blade was about to turn it into sawdust, a voice screamed, "Stop!"

The puppet flew backward into the darkness as if pulled by a string. The wretched bear, which was still pulling itself across the floor, collapsed.

Castor stepped into the light, cradling the nude puppet in his arms like a freaky infant.

"Don't hurt my babies," he begged. The look in his eyes

was sorrowful as he stared at the puppet chunks on the floor near the cage.

"It's over, Castor," Norah replied. "Surrender now, or I'll turn this place into a woodchipper."

Castor put the puppet on a nearby table.

"Drop your wand and kick it toward us," Norah ordered. Just to be safe, she activated her radio magic. Three bright streams of emotion and intention hit her. Sid wanted to crawl into a dark hole for the rest of his natural life. Castor wanted this to be over. Frondle wanted...

Norah blushed and slammed the radio magic shut.

"Are you all right?" Frondle asked. She realized how close he was.

Never felt better!

Norah nodded rapidly, eyeing Castor as he dropped his wand and kicked it toward her. "You can let the cage go." The golden wires released, and she put a safe distance between her and her gorgeous light elf. It was important to stay focused.

"Explain yourself!" she told Castor.

The puppeteer walked over to the pieces of marionette lying on the floor. He shot a resentful look at her as he collected them. *Is that a severed puppet schlong in your pocket, or are you just happy to see me?*

Castor sniffed. "You know, I made these puppets by hand. It took a lot of specialty work."

"I'm sorry we neutered your marionette, but you gave it a knife and sent it to attack us. We'll call it even."

Castor delicately collected more pieces of wood from the floor.

"Leave it!" Norah exclaimed. "Explain yourself."

"Fine, but I want to sit down."

He led them into the darkened theater and turned on the lights. They pulled chairs into a small circle. Castor turned a pointed glare on Sid, then explained.

"Sid and I wrote *The Players* together, and I was pissed about being cut out of the deal."

"So, you wanted revenge?"

"Hey, I'm not the one who started this. You screwed *me* over."

"The monster was flinging chunks of marble. Someone could have gotten hurt," Norah countered. Castor's face scrunched. Frondle was intimidatingly grave.

"I tried to play nice. I called Silver Lion to ask about getting paid for my work. They sent a courier to the puppet theater with a terrifying lawyer that came out of an envelope. Freaky."

"You've met Cyprine!" Norah replied cheerfully. She didn't think it was a happy memory for Castor.

"Anyway, she said that if I made a fuss, I might get a little money, but only the sleaziest lawyers would get into a fight with Silver Lion. Even if I won, I'd never work again. She said she'd make sure I got fired from the puppet theater unless I signed a release saying I didn't write the script, even though I did. It was like the death by a thousand paper cuts from legal documents."

Norah sighed. She felt sorry for Castor, which was not convenient. "Go on." No point in dropping the intimidation act now.

" Obviously, I was pissed. I don't know anyone on Earth who'd be happy about getting thrown over two barrels in a row, so I decided to get onto the roof and do a little destructive puppeteering. That building is not secure, by the way."

Norah made a noncommittal noise.

"I thought I would inconvenience everyone, and that would be the end of it," Castor continued. "Then the whole thing went viral, which made me even angrier. Apparently, I only exist to help that horny-for-emails freak succeed in Hollywood. You know why we stopped writing together?"

"The volume of emails?" Norah asked blandly.

"Hah. Not that I haven't gotten my fair share, but no. He wanted to go solo. Said he didn't enjoy collaboration. He thought he'd be stronger without me as a weight around his ankle. That's not a metaphor, understand. Those were the words he used. Now his only measurable success is because of something *we* wrote together, which is a delicious irony."

"Okay. What did you do next?" Norah demanded.

Resigned, Castor closed his eyes. "Have you heard about the Wicked Armada?" Norah shook her head. Castor continued, "Once a month, a group of boats moors just off of Catalina Island. Used to be hippies with weed, then it was *traficantes* with coke. Now it's witches with potions. I mean, you can still buy drugs out there, but that's just scratching the surface. Curses. Magical artifacts. Stolen art, Earth and Oriceran. Any hideous thing your heart desires is available."

"For a price," Norah added.

"Yeah. It's not a charity service," Castor agreed. "Anyway, I met this guy named Chunk a couple years ago. He gave me some pink fairy and told me about the market."

"Chunk strikes again," Norah whispered.

"It was a disaster. I'd never been on a boat before, and I puked all over a bunch of Kilomea rock chocolate. Plus, the curses were all too expensive and waaayyy too scary. I hate Sid's fucking guts, but I don't want those guts turned into sand vipers, you know?"

Norah, who was even angrier at Sid than she was at Castor, was briefly cheered by the image. *Is that curse in pill form, and are there any left?*

"Then this crone came out of the bilge of the boat I was on. She smelled like kelp after two days on the beach, and she showed me these two eyes."

"What kind of eyes?" Norah asked.

"They looked real, although not like anything I'd seen before. Baseball-sized eyes the color of algae with pinprick black pupils, glistening like they'd just been plucked out of someone's face. The crone said they would bring a puppet to life. She sold them for a song, too."

"Jesus, Castor, have you never read a single fairytale? Did she throw in a monkey's paw while she was at it? Maybe a spindle or a tasty red apple?"

"I'm sorry, okay? It was a mistake."

Norah grabbed Castor's collar. "What are their powers? Where did they come from? Originally, before the Bad Boat."

"Wicked Armada," Castor corrected peevishly. "The crone said they had belonged to a giant's cursed marionette."

"And that made you think, 'Yay, hooray! Can't wait to keep these cursed puppet eyes in my bedroom next to the place where I sleep.'"

"I was just coming up in the puppet scene, and I thought

I might need an edge. I've been writing a one-man show for two years, and I was going to use them in that."

"Sure," Norah said. "Every time I go to a one-man show, I think, 'Hmm, needs more curses.'"

"I was going to revolutionize the one-man-marionette game," Castor stated defensively.

"I admit, at the present moment, I *would* enjoy seeing a marionette come to life and eat your face."

"So, you think it's a good idea?" Castor asked, refusing to back down.

"When's the next Wicked Armada?" Norah countered.

"Uh, I guess it's tonight. It's Tuesday, right?"

"Oh! Happy Leg Day, everybody!" Frondle chirped. Castor looked confused, and Norah shook her head.

"You have to stop spending time with Quint," she said, then ignored him to wave her wand menacingly at Castor.

Castor gulped. "I haven't talked to Chunk in years. I should have eaten that stupid business card, but I was on an all-potato diet."

Norah fixed Sid with a glare. "You're an artist." She glanced at the wreckage. "Draw me a sketch of those eyes as best you can remember. We're going to the Wicked Market."

"Where are we going to get a boat?" Frondle asked.

Celestia stood morosely on the prow of *The Hierophant*, hair and robes streaming dramatically behind her. Frondle was next to her, pulling energy from the stars to light their way.

Lolling on an antigrav beanbag he'd summoned, Chunk watched the pair appreciatively. "For someone who put up such a fuss, Celestia makes quite the pretty picture."

Norah glared at the wizard, who was wearing head-to-toe brown leather today. He looked rakishly handsome, like a cowboy on the seas.

"She doesn't seem to like magic much," Norah remarked, although she refrained from pointing this irony out to the astrologer.

"Also, her concerns about the seaworthiness of this boat appear to have been reasonabl—" A wave of seawater coming over the hull cut off the end of the statement. Norah and Chunk bailed it out with their wands, levitating bucket-sized globules into the air and dumping them back into the ocean. Cold and damp, she looked covetously at Chunk's leather, which appeared to repel water.

Castor had bowed out of seafaring, pleading motion sickness, so Norah had installed him in her home with Pepe as his warden and Sid's company as his punishment.

Her stomach rolled as another wave crashed over the gunwales. Norah leaned out over the churning ocean, hoping she might puke.

"You want something for your stomach?" Chunk asked, removing water from the boat with a lazy spiral of his wand. He made it dance from starboard to port like a Bellagio fountain. When he was done, he opened his coat to reveal a selection of pill bottles, vials, and one alarmingly large syringe. *I didn't realize syringes could have serrated tips.*

Shuddering, she shook her head.

"Why did you sell Sid more pink fairy?" she asked.

Chunk looked at her like she was a stupid child. "For the same reason I'm taking you out to the Wicked Armada. You paid me."

"A money-motivated drug dealer. How original," Norah commented.

"You're the one in the creative business," Chunk said. "Not me."

The moon silvered the waves with arcs of shifting light. It was pretty when it wasn't making her puke. She patted her pocket, where Castor's sketch of the cursed marionette eyes was neatly folded in a waterproof plastic bag inside the pocket of her silk joggers. Castor had done a good job. The drawing matched her memory.

The monster, according to Katie, hadn't been spotted since it had escaped the set a few days ago. The production moved forward without it in an act of will by Oleander, who had shuffled the schedule to put all the monster shots at the end. Even if Norah managed to track down the monster tonight, they'd be cutting it close. Her pleas for a few extra days of shooting had fallen on deaf ears. Marina, who took a dim view of anything other than enthusiastic success, had said, "I don't care if you have to put a gnome in a gorilla suit. Finish the fucking film."

Norah hoped it wouldn't come to that.

The Pacific was calmer farther out. After another hour of bailing and almost-vomiting, they approached a cove protected by dark, out-thrusting rocks.

The water here was still. Magically still. Even under a cool ocean breeze, it was as smooth as black glass. Norah shivered as *The Hierophant* cut toward a small collection of lights without causing a wake.

The Wicked Armada was surprisingly festive for an evil swap meet. Boats clustered together in the motionless water, with walkways between them cobbled together from planks, magic, shadow, and light. The boats surrounded three huge square rafts, sixty feet on a side, that Norah guessed were permanent fixtures here. Stalls dotted the wet wood under the sparkling night sky. There was a great deal of hushed commotion on these various platforms.

"It's quiet," Norah remarked. "I expected someone to be shouting 'Poison apples! Get your poison apples!'"

Chunk smirked. "Not exactly."

The boat bumped softly against the rubber of a Zodiac that was connected to one of these central platforms by a light elf bridge glowing with power.

Chunk secured their boat with a rope and hopped lightly onto the Zodiac.

"Have fun. Don't eat anything you haven't paid a lot of money for," he cautioned. Appearing to consider this sufficient warning about the dangers of the floating marketplace, he strode up the glowing bridge and disappeared among the stalls.

Norah walked up to Frondle. "You don't have to come with me."

Frondle waved that away. "I am honor-bound to help you. Besides, Stan loaned me his sword."

He pushed aside the edge of his flowing sky-blue cloak to reveal the glinting edge of Stan's precious scimitar. This made Norah more, rather than less, concerned about the dangers they might face. She didn't think Stan would have loaned him a weapon that valuable for less than a potentially fatal threat.

The planks of the light elf bridge swayed under Norah's feet, casting an incongruously pleasant glow as she thudded onto the raft platform beyond.

The first stall she encountered was, alarmingly, made of paper treated with some kind of magic that kept it standing in the damp ocean air. Then she realized the paper was covered with cramped arcane writing that she couldn't quite read. The caked brown of the words made her suspect they were written in blood. Inside the stall, slips of paper half an inch wide hung from small clips. Norah squinted at the one nearest the door.

Oopsie, where did your skin go? the paper said. A cold shiver went down Norah's spine, and she cast a quick spell to dry her clothes from the boat ride.

"See anything you like, dear?" a sweet voice called from inside the stall. An old woman in a floral dress and a crocheted scarf looked up from a small wooden desk, where she was scribbling on a piece of paper with a quill. Norah's mouth opened in shock as the woman picked up a small knife, pricked her finger, and dipped the quill in the blood.

"Misfortune cookies," Frondle whispered into Norah's ear, pulling her away.

She waved at the old woman and muttered a vague excuse. "You don't think she was the crone, do you?"

"I'm not convinced the crone was an old woman," Frondle replied. "It's a favored disguise among criminal magicals."

Norah's mother would probably have some choice words to say about that.

They passed another stand, this one constructed from strips of black velvet stuck together with a musky brown pitch. The construction was shaped like a swallow's nest, and its lightless entrance repelled Norah.

"We don't have to go into every one, right?" she asked.

"I hope not," Frondle said. "Let's ask around."

The next stall was brightly lit and looked ordinary. A brick oven on one side of the stall warmed the immediate surroundings, and Norah was drawn forward.

"Meat pie?" a cheerful, round-faced man asked, proffering a silver tray of flaky golden pastries. They smelled amazing, but Norah noticed a dripping hunk of unidentifiable meat hanging from a hook at the back of the stall.

"No, thank you." She took a deep breath. "Maybe you can give me some information. Do you know anything about an older woman selling haunted marionette eyes?" She pulled the sketch out of her pocket and showed it to the man. His eyes skimmed it, and his smile turned into a mask.

"Sorry. If it's not edible, it's out of my bailiwick." He turned to a tall light elf who was looking at the tray of pastries with eager anticipation.

The smell of fragrant herbs mingled with the scent of saltwater in the air. Nearby, a spiral metal staircase shot two stories up into the night sky. Small wire shelves at the sides held glass bottles of every shape, and bundles of herbs were tied to the banisters with colorful ribbons at random intervals. Next to the stairs, a medium-height barrel-chested man was smelling a bundle of small blue flowers. A familiar man.

"Angelo?" Norah asked.

Angelo looked over. Norah thought she saw a brief flicker of panic, but the expression melted as she approached.

"Norah! So good to see you!" Angelo greeted her. "Please do not judge me harshly for my walk on the wild side. An artist must be non-judgmental about his raw materials."

The smell of onions and meat wafted from the meat pie stall, and Norah wondered if whoever had provided the meat for the dish would agree with that statement.

"Then again, you are being naughty yourself," Angelo said, nodding at Frondle. "Ambitious people must always step on a few heads as they climb the ladder of success." He leaned in with a glint in his eye.

"We're not shopping," Norah corrected. "We're... Well, what do you know about cursed puppets?"

She showed Angelo the drawing and outlined their mission. "Have you seen any crones?"

Angelo looked hesitantly at the platform, from a wart-stricken woman in a black hood to a withered dark elf with white hair and a barbed crossbow to a witch in an unfashionably pointed hat.

"One or two," Angelo said. "Ask Lami if you can find her. She knows everyone."

An enormous man, almost as wide as he was tall, made a horrible racket coming down the metal stairs. Angelo moved aside.

"Quit wasting time, Angelo. Your mother's waiting," the

man snapped. His hair was white, and Angelo looked at them apologetically as the man hustled him away.

"Who was that?" Frondle asked.

"Domenico Consoli," Norah said. "The great Consoli patriarch." She'd heard stories about the elder Consoli, but they'd never met. She stared at the retreating sturdy backs. As they clambered down a rope bridge that appeared to be made of twining darkness, she saw a flash of board-straight hair as white as a winter sky. Angelo's dark elf mother?

"We should split up," Norah told Frondle. "Cover more territory. I'll finish the rest of this raft and that yacht, and you do the other one. Meet back up in, say, forty-five minutes?"

Frondle trotted away. Norah resisted the urge to climb the spiral staircase and look at the herbs. Above her, dark tentacles writhed in one of the jars, and she shivered, hand dropping from the metal rail.

A muted commercial chatter had risen up along the raft, and Norah began a circuit around the perimeter. Near the edge, illuminated by orange lights, a van-sized device made of foot-thick metal and glass dripped saltwater onto the boards of the raft. Norah approached and found that it was a submersible. A hand-lettered sign that said VLAD the Un-paler hung over a bar stool, where a bored-looking woman perched. Norah thought she was a vampire, but her skin was nut-brown.

"What is this?" Norah asked.

The vampire didn't look up from her phone. "Vamps only."

"It's a tanning service," a voice beside her said. A beautiful vampire with raven hair and elegantly arched black eyebrows swept her hand over the submersible, looking amused. "Vampires tan just like humans, only our...let's call it a smoke point is much lower. It's too risky to tan on the surface, but VLAD—that stands for Vehicle For Lower Aquatic Destinations, by the way—takes vamps down into the ocean to where there's the faintest glow of sunlight, and *boom.* Vampire tan. Night surfing is popular in Malibu, but even in the dark, no one wants to hang ten looking like a bleached egg."

Faint outlines of blue veins were visible under the woman's near-translucent skin.

"I take it you haven't indulged in this procedure," Norah said.

The woman laughed, a beautiful bell-like noise. "What can I say? I'm a traditionalist."

She was wearing high-waisted slim-legged pants and a long-sleeved cropped black shirt, both black velvet.

"At least you've given up those horrible neck ruffles," Norah said. The woman groaned.

"I know. Shape up, people. We're immortal bloodsuckers, not fangirls at an Anne Rice convention. I'm Lami, by the way."

Norah introduced herself, and they shook hands. "Angelo said I should talk to you." She pulled the drawing out of her pocket and held it out. "You haven't seen these haunted eyeballs, have you? A crone sold them to my friend, although she might not have been a crone."

Lami passed a pale hand heavy with stone rings over the paper. Her pitch-black eyelashes fluttered as her eyes widened in surprise. "Let me guess. They were dirt cheap."

Norah nodded, and Lami frowned.

"That's probably Ronni. She actually *is* a crone, you'll be shocked to learn. Don't tell her I called her that. She claims her grandfather is a trickster god. No one believes her, although she does her best to live up to the claim."

"That sounds right," Norah mused.

"To be honest, we've been trying to get rid of her for years. I know we're called the Wicked Armada, but people won't come here if their new glass lily eats the family hamster. For example."

Norah cringed but felt a surge of excitement. "Do you know where she is?"

"Follow me." The woman spun dramatically. Swaying, she led Norah into a tall, narrow, black tent barely big enough to fit a kitchen table. Inside, candlelight flickered over a chaise lounge upholstered in rich blue needlepoint.

"Sit down," Lami said. Norah complied. The upholstery was luxurious, and Lami fixed her with a probing stare. The woman's black irises were flecked here and there with deep blue.

"That's right, relax," Lami said. Norah felt a tension she hadn't realized she was holding pour out onto the cushions beneath her. She melted into the blue fabric.

"Don't move." With a faint smile, Lami slid out of the tent.

Norah couldn't move. She didn't want to. She wanted to wait right here for the beautiful black-haired Lami to return. A moment later, a melodious voice filtered through the curtain.

"Midnight snack! Get your midnight snack!"

What kind of snack was Lami selling? There was no

kitchen equipment inside the tent, just cushions and the lounge.

"Fifty to sip, two hundred to drain. Midnight snack for sale!"

Oh, shit. If you couldn't see the snack, you *were* the snack. Norah didn't want to be drained of all her blood, but this desire was remote and much less powerful than the compulsion to slump onto her seat and slip into a delicious nap.

"Lami, you little shit, knock it the fuck off," someone said. A moment later, the curtain was thrown open. The candlelight illuminated a very old face with an enormous wart between the eyes. Norah sucked in her breath in dismay. A wart on a witch was as bad as a neck ruffle on a vampire. Such a cliché.

She grunted in protest as the woman strode over, waved a hand over Norah's unfocused eyes, and dug long nails into her shoulders and shook her for a good thirty seconds.

Norah's will to live returned, and she pushed the witch away. "Knock it off."

The woman stepped back, nodding in approval. "Now that you're awake, show me these marionette eyes you've been flashing to every ne'er-do-well on this cursed flotilla."

Norah handed over the drawing. The witch barely looked at it before nodding and stuffing it in the pocket of —Norah rolled her eyes—her *broomstick* skirt.

"Hey!" Norah said. "I need that."

"Not anymore, you don't. Tell me everything that's happened so far with the eyes." The witch plopped down cross-legged on the floor and pulled a worn notebook out of a cloth bag. She flipped through a series of neatly-written notes to a blank page, wrote the date, and stared expectantly at Norah.

"Who are you?" Norah asked.

"The name's Geronima Ruggle, but you can call me Ronni."

"If you sold the eyes to Castor, why are you interrogating me? I should be interrogating you!"

"Tell me what happened, and I'll tell you what I know about the eyes. Take the deal or leave it. Not to twist the knife, but I just saved you from becoming street food."

Norah grudgingly accepted this and described what she'd seen during the monster's second attack. Ronni took notes at lightning speed, occasionally pausing to ask Norah detailed questions about how the monster had moved and when it had escaped. When Norah finished, Ronni spent a few minutes rifling through her notebook, wrote two more lines of notes in a small, neat script, and scratched her wart meditatively.

"This is all useful, so thank you."

"What is this about?" Norah asked.

"I'm an antiquities researcher," Ronni explained.

"For who? UCLA?"

Ronni's nose twitched in distaste. "Not likely. Those paperwork-obsessed dweebs don't have what it takes for real research. I'm, uh, independent."

"You sold Castor those eyes for research?"

"'Sold' is an overstatement. I gave the things to him, but yes. I got those eyes in a wreck dive off the coast of Egypt. We pulled up a whole felucca of interesting stuff, half-preserved by the water chemistry and half-preserved by magic. I was never able to figure out what the eyes *did*. I thought when that angry young man touched them that they might, say, scoop out his retinas, install themselves, and take over his personality, but no. It seems they needed a manufactured body."

Norah grew increasingly outraged as the witch calmly rattled off this explanation.

"You sold someone an artifact you thought would *scoop out their retinas*?! That's not okay, Ronni." Norah placed an anticipatory hand on her wand.

"You sound just like the assholes at the American-Oriceran Archaeology Society. Apparently, interesting work isn't a 'good fit' for their annual conference."

Ronni dug the tip of her pen into her notebook so hard it punctured the paper. "I just finished translating one of the scrolls we found in a cartouche near the eyes. Apparently, the monster that's wearing the eyes is a magic eater. Makes it hard to kill because when you get too close, poof! Your wand's as useful as a chopstick. Very cool."

Not to me! Norah sighed. "How can you fight this magic-eating monster?"

"I'll tell you on one condition. If you hunt the thing, I want to tag along. I'd love to measure the beast's power after it eats some magic. I'd *really* love to see it kill someone, so, you know, see what you can do! Here's my number."

Ronni handed Norah an eggshell-colored card that said, Geronima Ruggle, Independent Archaeologist.

Norah groaned. "Fine. When the time comes, I'll call you. As long as you're not going to help the monster."

Ronni looked offended. "I'd never interfere with an

artifact in its natural environment. What kind of scientist do you think I am?"

"An amoral one?"

"Hmph. You have my card. My broom can do zero to eighty in under five seconds. I can be anywhere in Los Angeles in ten minutes."

Of course she has a broom. Gives witches a bad name. "Where do you put your black cat?" Norah muttered peevishly. Ronni's head snapped up.

"He has a basket, thank you very much. To answer your question about killing it, according to what we found on the cartouche, the monster can only be defeated by a pure soul."

The flickering light of the candles deepened the lines on the woman's face, casting her half into shadow. Norah felt itchy and anxious and protested, "This is Los Angeles! Where am I supposed to find a *pure soul*?"

"Mail-order catalog? That's your problem. I look forward to your call!"

As Ronni clambered to her feet, footsteps pounded on the raft outside. Norah's grip on her wand tightened when she heard a mighty whoop. The tip of a glowing blade sliced through the cloth tent. Shining like the dawn sun, Frondle burst through the slit, wielding Stan's sword in one hand and a wooden stake in the other.

"Off, foul bloodsucker!" he bellowed. Ronni stepped nimbly out of range of both weapons.

Searching Norah's neck and finding it encouragingly un-punctured, Frondle glanced nervously at the damage he'd done to the tent.

"I heard you'd joined one of the food stalls on the wrong end," he explained.

Norah smiled, warmth spreading out from the pit of her stomach. "I worked it out." A white face peered through the slit behind Frondle, and Norah pointed at it.

"It was wrong to try to sell my blood, Lami."

The vampire strode in, looking at the slash in her tent with a calculating gaze.

"You said Angelo sent you. Hmm. Anyway, you destroyed my tent," she told Frondle, pointing a sharp red nail at him. He avoided her gaze.

"You tried to eat me," Norah countered.

"As you might remember, little witch, this place is called the Wicked Armada, *not* the Nice Happy Armada Where Good Things Happen." She ran a long finger over the torn fabric, and Norah felt a faint compulsion to throw herself at the vampire's feet in supplication. *Keep it together, Wintry.*

"We'll call it even." Norah grabbed Frondle's arm, the lean muscles warm beneath his skin as she pulled him away.

Norah's phone beeped with a message from Chunk. *Spending the night. Head home without me.* Staying together, they trekked back to Celestia and found her sleeping on her self-appointed watch. Embarrassed, she seemed happy to unhitch the boat and leave.

Norah and Frondle rode back on the balcony above the vessel's small cabin. The sea was calmer, and they only had to bail water out of the bottom once or twice. When Norah shivered in the night air, Frondle swept his sky-blue coat off his shoulders and draped it around her. Starlight sparkled from the curved blade at his side.

"Thanks for coming to rescue me from Lami." She snuggled against him. "If anyone eats me, I want it to be a fancy three-course meal."

Frondle put his arm around her. "I cannot aid your sworn mission if you freeze to death on this boat." He was looking past her, and he didn't seem to be talking to her. *Is he bargaining with his honor?*

The little balcony was suddenly warm, and a salty breeze ruffled Frondle's moonlit hair. Norah turned her face up to his, and his eyes were stormy.

"Nor—" Frondle began.

She cut him off with a kiss, and their lips melted together. When the position strained her neck, she swung her leg over the bench and straddled his lap. His long hands slid up her back under her shirt. They kissed for a long minute, warming each other in the cool air.

Just as Norah was about to suggest that Frondle might be more comfortable without his pants, he made a strained noise and slid out from under her. She hit the rough wooden bench with a thud, then looked on in horror as he unslung his sword belt and, in a single smooth motion, swan-dived into the churning waves.

"Frondle!" Norah shouted. Cursing, she raced down the creaky wooden ladder onto the deck. A splinter dug into her hand, and a drop of blood welled from her finger.

By the time she reached the rail, Frondle was fifty feet away. Arms moving in a sturdy freestyle stroke, he was swimming toward the shore, which was a faint dark line in the distance. Were elves strong swimmers? They were at least five miles off the coast, but he buzzed through the waves like a sexy motorboat.

Norah burst into the cabin, where Celestia was steering the boat from a small windowed compartment at the bow.

"Elf overboard!" Norah shouted.

Celestia cut the engine and joined Norah at the rail, but the dot of Frondle's body had disappeared among the waves.

"What did you do to him?" Celestia cried.

"I kissed him," Norah said miserably.

"Should we call the Coast Guard?" Celestia asked, looking more annoyed than worried.

Frondle was impulsive, overeager, and occasionally naïve, but he didn't have a death wish. Based on what Norah knew about his athleticism, he'd be okay.

"I hope his phone has a waterproof case." Norah sighed. "Let's go home."

CHAPTER TWENTY

Norah's phone woke her at eight-thirty in the morning. She was stretched across a giant tongue that was rough and seven feet long. Had she fallen into the clutches of some monster? She remembered that she'd fallen asleep in Stellan's workshop after disgorging every detail Ronni had given her about the haunted marionette eyes. Stellan was building an enormous dog's head for a children's television show, and the lolling pink tongue was as big as a twin bed.

Norah looked down now and saw that she'd made a Norah-shaped impression in the fleshy velvet. Apologizing to the dog, she punched the dent until it was approximately flat and looked at her phone.

Her mother had sent her a series of photos, which showed Petra, Jackie, and a relentlessly unsmiling light elf at Disneyland, on a beach in Malibu, at the Santa Monica Pier, and in the front row of *Hamilton*. Norah, hoping that her mother wasn't blowing through her life savings, sighed and headed back to her apartment.

Stan met her in the parking lot. "Do you know where Frondle spent the night?" he asked, snatching the sword out from under her arm. He unsheathed it, checked the blade, whispered something soft and comforting to it, and carefully slung it across his back with a look of disapproval on his face. "He showed up late last night, soaking wet and smelling like a day-old sushi buffet. Came in, banged on my door holding a lemon branch, and begged me to whip him with it. The thing still had full green lemons on it. It was disturbing."

"You didn't do it, did you?" Norah asked.

"I declined to participate in the zesty flagellation," Stan said, his dim expression now perilously lightless. "I thought he would go home and sleep off his indiscretions."

"We didn't… I mean, not really," Norah said, her face one or two shades brighter red than a beet.

Stan graciously ignored her protests. "Anyway, this morning, I woke up to discover that the sprinkler system had been turned on and Frondle had spent all night standing under the spray, reciting an elvish prayer for forgiveness. Billy saw him this morning and said that he looked like a blond wig fished out of a storm drain."

"Ew." Norah grimaced.

"The complex got a ticket for watering on an off day. I'd tell Frondle to pay me back, but it would send him into an even more pathetic tailspin, and California needs its water resources too badly for me to let that happen."

Norah, under attack, crossed her arms. "You're the one who loaned him your sword."

"Trust me, I regret it," Stan drawled. "I beg you to fulfill your oaths, Norah. When Frondle is happy, he's almost unbearably earnest. I don't think I can take him at his nadir."

A memory of Frondle's stricken salt-caked face floated through Norah's mind, and she nodded in agreement. "At least we made some progress. You don't have a lead on any pure souls, do you?"

"Normally, I would have pointed you at Frondle, but now I'm not sure," Stan said. Norah had a sudden urge to stand under a cold sprinkler herself.

Had she deprived the greater Los Angeles metropolitan area of its one pure soul among thirteen million? Damn.

"If you really need a pure soul, do what Hollywood does every time they need a new ingenue and import one from Kansas," Stan suggested.

"We might have to," Norah agreed. Maybe she could wipe her memories of everything she'd ever done and do it herself? If things got dire, she'd bring it up. "Is Frondle still here?"

Stan shook his head. "He ran off. Probably dunking himself in the LA River by now. I hope you like your men with skin infections."

"I'm an excellent healer," she replied.

Stan rolled his eyes. "In addition to the elf-pity, I had to cast a cone of silence over your apartment. 'Cone' is an understatement. 'Geodesic dome of silence' is more appropriate."

Castor and Sid.

Norah sighed. "I'm sorry, Stan. I'll fix it." Up she trudged to her apartment.

Pepe was curled on the tile by the door, having somehow weaseled his head into a pair of earmuffs. Norah understood why when she heard the volume of the argument in the next room.

"You said the script was done, then you went behind my back and changed the whole B-story!" Sid shouted. Norah tiptoed down the hall and peered into the apartment.

"I changed it because *you* refused to implement any changes that weren't *your* idea. You treated me like a dumb typist," Castor screamed back.

Their voices were ragged like they'd been at this for a while. When she strode in, they didn't bother with niceties.

"Sid drank all your wine," Castor tattled.

Sid's face twisted into a tight screw. "Castor opened a tin of smoked calamari at the back of your fridge, took one bite, and threw it away. I looked it up online. It was pretty expensive."

"Cheaper than all the wine you drank!" Castor screamed.

Norah thought for a beautiful moment about fusing their lips shut. Was this what being a parent was like?

"Hey!" she shouted at the thirty-something toddlers. Castor and Sid quieted, possibly to rest their raw vocal cords. "You two are worse than my seven-year-old nephew. May I remind you that this script, the one you wrote *together*, is your first big success?"

Castor snorted. "May I remind you that I was number *four* on Variety's *Ten Young Puppeteers to Watch* list?"

Sid made a strained noise. "How could we forget when you retweet the article twice a day?"

Maybe she *would* fuse their lips shut, or borrow a few Sleeping Beauty arrows from Frondle. She took a deep breath. "Whatever weird love-hate thing you've got going on, it produced some decent art. But instead of enjoying your moment on top of the mountain, you're spending all your time trying to push each other downhill."

Two snorts echoed in a porcine chorus. "Yeah, well, I wrote most of it," the men said in unison.

Pepe trotted into the room, raised his sharp hoof in the air, and quirked his head hopefully at Norah. She shook her head. "I'm sorry, Pepe, but I'm going to subject them to something much worse than your hooves. Which are admirably sharp," she reassured the goat.

She dug through her wallet for a dog-eared business card. After typing the number on the card into her phone, she hit call. Cyprine picked up in under two seconds, her greeting polite but brusque.

"Can you come to Los Feliz? My apartment." She gave the dark elf the address.

The subsequent pause was so long that Norah checked to see if she'd been disconnected. Finally, there was a curt yes, and Cyprine cut the call.

"Who was that?" Sid asked.

"You're not sending some bruiser with dwarven thumbscrews after us, are you?" Castor asked cautiously.

"You wish," Norah replied. "It's much worse than that."

"A Kilomea executioner?" Castor's voice sailed up into a nearly inaudible register.

"Worse. A lawyer," Norah told them.

"Not Cyprine," Sid whispered, turning the green of a fairy.

Norah smiled viciously. "If you leave without working out the intellectual property rights, I'll let her follow you home."

As she spun and went to stride back down the hallway, Sid weakly asked, "Do you want Frondle's message?"

"*What?*" Norah shouted.

"He came by early this morning and asked us to give you a message," Sid continued. "He was soaking wet. It was weird. Anyway, I guess Madge couldn't reach you, so she called him and told him the monster was seen at Universal Studios. It took a while for people to realize it wasn't a prop. Frondle said that despite his moment of weakness, he is going to redeem his oath. Those were his exact words."

"He went alone?" Norah asked, voice rising in panic. "Shit. I have to go."

Letting her first romantic prospect in years be sucked dry by a magic-hoovering monster was no way to start a new relationship.

CHAPTER TWENTY-ONE

Norah thought of two ways to sneak into Universal Studios. One involved borrowing some dwarven equipment from Stellan and tunneling in. The other involved Madge, a harness, and an antigrav spell. In the end, she decided it would be faster to buy a ticket.

A security wizard half-heartedly inspected her wand as she danced anxiously from foot to foot, and when he finally nodded, she pushed through overexcited children, put her thumb on the little electronic reader, and ran in. The crowds weren't bad on a Wednesday, but as she raced along Main Street, she realized she had no idea where to start looking for either Frondle or the monster.

The monster. She remembered her promise to Ronni. Did she really want to get the unhinged old witch involved? But a promise was a promise, and Norah reluctantly texted her.

Monster seen at Universal Studios. On the hunt.

A child screamed ahead of her. Norah stuck her phone in her pocket and ran toward the noise. A few seconds later, she pulled up in front of an actor dressed as Dracula making a hasty retreat from a crying five-year-old. The actor looked guilty under his white face paint.

Norah sighed. "If that was a real vampire, he'd have burst into flames by now," she told the boy, who wiped his eyes and looked at the actor with renewed skepticism. The boy's mother, burdened with an overstuffed fanny pack and several surly teens, shot Norah a thank-you look.

Norah tried to hide her disappointment. *If I were a magic-eating monster, where would I hang out?*

"I heard the WaterWorld show has real water elementals now," someone behind her said. The two surly teens were scowling at each other and talking in low voices.

"That sounds lame, but we could go check it out," the other teen replied.

Would the monster consider elemental magic a good snack? It was as good a place to start as any. According to a nearby electronic screen, the next WaterWorld show was at 11:00 a.m.

She joined a moderate crowd flowing toward the big WaterWorld show gates, passing under netting and rusty metallic fishing equipment into the elaborate show arena. It was like an outdoor theater, except instead of a stage, there was a large pool backed by fake cliffs, metallic scaffolding, and various zip lines and plunge pools. In front of the first row, well within the splash zone, two water elementals were making water sculptures like balloon animals, wet, twisted shapes that looked vaguely like cats or flowers. It was not the high-powered magic she thought the monster would be most interested in.

Norah searched the elaborate backdrop for matted black fur and oversized arachnid legs but saw only faint ripples on the calm surface of the pool. Still, she stayed alert as an usher pointed her toward the middle of a row of aluminum benches. As Norah plunked down, a boy somewhere near the water elementals shouted, "Do a goat!"

Norah knew that voice intimately. Standing up, she pushed through the incoming crowd, jostling through endless novelty t-shirts until she reached the front. One of the water elementals, a woman with brown skin, shiny hair, and dark eyebrows, had an annoyed expression on her face as she pulled a thin stream of water out of the pool behind her and formed it into a first draft of a goat, if Norah was generous.

"That's not what Pepe looks like," the annoyed boy said. Norah's heart sank. Facing down the water elemental was Leaf, wearing a fire-engine red tyrannosaurus rex t-shirt. As he watched the lame water sculpture form, he crossed his arms.

"Leaf!" Norah said. He looked up in confusion, then got excited.

"Auntie Norah! Mom and Grandma said you were too busy to come!"

"Where are they?" Norah asked. Leaf pointed into the stands. "Let's find them," she said.

As Leaf trotted away, he shouted, "Your goat sucks!" over his shoulder. The water elemental looked embarrassed, and Norah murmured in disapproval, "Leaf. Don't be mean about other people's magic."

"But her goat *was* bad," Leaf insisted. "If Pepe looked like that, we'd take him to the vet."

Norah couldn't imagine Pepe at the vet, at least not without bloodshed.

Petra and Jackie were sitting halfway up, well out of the splash zone. When they saw Norah, they looked even more confused than Leaf.

"What are you doing here?" Norah asked.

"What are *you* doing here?" Jackie retorted.

"I'm here with Frondle," Norah replied. "Or rather, I'm looking for him." In a low voice, she told the two women about the monster.

A tourist with a thick midwestern accent sitting just above them butted into their conversation. "Is there a new monster? Where? On the studio tour?" Norah ignored her.

"You have to get out of here," she whispered to her mother. "All of you."

"I'm not going anywhere," someone said imperiously. An ancient light elf sat board-straight on the aluminum bench beside Petra and Jackie. Norah recognized her from her mother's photos. The woman had an extra-large soda in one hand and a funnel cake in the other. Even weighed down with concessions, she looked elegant, like a well-made knife.

Petra introduced Glesselda. "We did the Santa Monica Pier last night, and now we're here." Her mother's voice was streaked with exhaustion. Norah hadn't seen that bloodless, drained expression since she and Quint and Andrew had been toddlers.

"I'm sorry, Glesselda, but you'll have to come back

another time. The monster eats magic. We'd all wind up sucked dry."

"Yet here you are, looking for trouble." Petra had a calculating look in her eyes.

"This is happening because of a script I chose. Look, someone has to take Leaf home."

"You want me to take my seven-year-old son home from an amusement park after *thirty* minutes? We were in the security line for longer than we've been here! They kept making Leaf go through the metal detector!" Jackie looked as if Norah had asked her to take a relaxing nap on some railroad tracks.

"I'm so sorry," Norah replied.

At the expression on her face, Jackie pulled herself together. "Leaf, I'm sorry, but we've gotta go." She dry-heaved. Apparently, funnel cakes had not alleviated her morning sickness.

There was no whine of protest. Amazing. Norah was about to compliment Leaf on his maturity, then realized he had vanished.

"Leaf?" she called, voice rising. "Shit. This is not the time for you to run off!"

"Leaf!" Jackie shouted with a *you're-in-trouble, mister* tone in her voice.

Norah ran back to the front to check the crowd of tourists around the water elementals, but her nephew was nowhere to be seen. A loudspeaker crackled, then announced that the show was about to start. Norah scanned the bleachers for an unruly boy.

Jackie, breathless, ran up behind her. "I think I know where he is." She pulled Norah toward the exit.

CHAPTER TWENTY-TWO

Jackie elbowed people to the side on the escalator while taking the steps two at a time as they were carried down the hill toward the lower half of Universal Studios. On the hilltop, a giant yellow Minion looked down on them mockingly.

"Where do you think he is?" Norah shouted after her sister-in-law.

"He wanted to go on the Jurassic Park ride when we came in," Jackie shouted over her shoulder. "He begged me. He said he was tall enough. I thought it was too scary and convinced him to do the WaterWorld show instead. Now I know why he's been obsessed with measuring himself. Ugh! Stupid growth spurt."

Leaf was wearing a red t-shirt with a cartoon T-Rex. Now he had gone to find the real thing or an animatronic approximation.

If I were a huge furry monster, where would I hide?

"With the other monsters," Norah whispered.

"What?" asked a dad. He had a Bart Simpson t-shirt

stretched over a huge potbelly. Norah pushed him aside and ran down the escalator after Jackie.

The atmosphere was less festive when they disembarked. An unpleasant murmur filtered through the crowd, and several people were griping about "technical difficulties." Nearby, a khaki-clad fake park ranger whispered something into the neck of a disturbingly realistic velociraptor puppet. Presumably, there was a human ear underneath. The velociraptor puppet trotted toward a screened gate, and the ranger made a beeline for the entrance to the Jurassic World ride. A chaotic, aggravated noise was rising from the crowd in that direction. As she and Jackie moved closer, people began to filter out.

"Due to technical difficulties, Jurassic World—The Ride is currently out of order. Please exit the line. We apologize for any inconvenience."

It was harder to make progress with the crowd pressing against them. Norah gave up on pushing through. She climbed onto an aluminum rail and quickly hopped from post to post. She and Jackie weren't the only ones moving toward the ride. Here and there, uniformed park employees and plainclothes security people talking into their earpieces approached. From her vantage point, Norah looked for her nephew, pausing as brown-haired kids who weren't Leaf complained to nervous parents.

Please tell me he didn't get on the ride.

"Leaf!" she shouted. Then, vowing to use every tool at her disposal, she reached inside herself and activated her radio magic.

Waves of emotions buffeted her from all sides. An upset crowd was the worst place for her to use empathic powers, and the currents threatened to drown her. Threads of emotion from individual people were nearly impossible to pick out, but she tuned in on a few themes. The visitors were mostly annoyed, with the ones who had been closest to the front the most aggravated.

Worse than that was the occasional flash of fear from the security guards and park employees, which confirmed Norah's suspicions. This wasn't an ordinary mechanical breakdown.

"I need all magical Security to Jurassic World," a plain-clothes guard with a buzz cut and a taupe polo shirt said. "We've got two witches up there, but they said their wands stopped working."

Norah jumped down and grabbed his collar.

"Are there people in there?" she asked.

"Ma'am, you need to clear out," the guard told her.

"My nephew's up there," Norah replied. The alarmed look on his face was underscored by a quick stab of pity. She pushed past him toward the line of empty boats waiting on their tracks in the dark water.

"Ma'am!" the guard shouted. Norah pulled out her wand.

"I'm going. If you try to stop me, I'll stun you." She leapt into the car at the front of the line.

"I'll stun your backup," Jackie called, then, following close on Norah's heels, leapt in beside her.

The seats were wet, and Norah shivered as a breeze blew across her skin. A mechanical dinosaur roared from the building above them, followed by muffled screams.

"You're not going anywhere without me!" Petra pushed through the crowd to join them.

"I've never seen a magic-eating monster," Glesselda added. Norah's mouth dropped open as the old elf floated over the crowd. She was riding a gleaming chaise lounge, a luxurious conveyance made of beams of light. Even more impressive, Glesselda was still holding her large soda, although the funnel cake had been replaced by a magnificent ice cream sundae, which she nibbled.

"You go along. I'll float behind," she called.

"You sure you don't want some popcorn first?" Norah shouted back with a brutal edge in her voice. If Leaf was in there, he would need more than an ice cream sundae.

Glesselda shrugged. "I'm all right for now. *Bon voyage*!"

Petra and Jackie took up positions at the side of the boat, guarding Norah against an influx of security personnel and park employees. Now free to work, Norah inspected the mechanical car with her magical senses. It was a complicated piece of equipment, and they were short on time.

There was another scream from above, and Norah made a split-second decision. Sending two bolts of magic into the raft, she severed it from the track, then drew a small pinwheel in the air with her wand. Blue magic crackled into the blades of a small propeller. She affixed this magical engine to the back edge of the boat just under the water.

"Wait!" a woman said. A shadow crossed the ride as Ronni descended from the sky on a jalopy of a broomstick. Norah wrinkled her nose at the formulaic construction of aged straw bundled around a dirty branch. At least she hadn't brought her cat.

The second Ronni thumped onto the plastic behind her.

Norah poured magic into the propellor, and it spun to life. As they escaped the people who'd tried to stop them, Petra joined her, pale green magic twining with Norah's blue. The propellor spun faster.

They were going much faster than the ride's design parameters, but their progress felt achingly slow. As they twisted through the lagoon, the loudspeakers shouted useless dinosaur facts at them, and animatronic parasaurolophus and compsognathus statues whirred back and forth. An announcement that their boat had been pulled off course, part of the ride, was cut off mid-sentence, and a nearby animatronic stegosaurus went still. Someone had shut off the electricity.

Soon, the ride's track rose out of the water and followed a long hill into the dark of a large building. Without the noise from the ride, she could hear alarmed voices above.

Norah reached out with her radio magic and *finally* felt a stream of emotion she was pretty sure was Leaf. He was determined but also very afraid.

"Leaf's alive!" Norah shouted. "I can feel him."

Jackie let out a huge sigh of relief, and they clambered out of the boat. There was a set of narrow stairs to the right of the track. They climbed up the steep slope into the building, which was lit by ugly fluorescent emergency lights. Under the yellow glow, the surroundings were eerie, but no animatronic velociraptors leapt out at them.

At the top of the stairs, they ducked under a lifeless statue of a velociraptor positioned near the ceiling, then climbed downhill as the river dropped a few feet.

"Stop it!" a small boy shouted.

"Leaf," Jackie cried, sounding half-relieved and half-terrified.

In the open space in front of them, next to a fake tree that looked even faker under the emergency lighting, was a yellow boat. It was empty.

"Are you here to save us?" A woman in a security uniform cowering behind a fake boulder pulled Norah in beside her. "It ate my wand!" she said, holding a dead piece of wood out in one shaking hand. Wand and woman had been drained of magic.

"Where's Leaf?" she asked, searching the cluster of twenty or so people cowering in the corner of the room. "The little boy. Where is he?"

The security witch pointed. As Norah looked, the monster screamed.

Whatever sound designer had created the ride's dinosaur screams could have learned a thing or two from Fuzzball. The monster straddled the boat with two legs on each bank and one in the water. Its furry articulated limbs were like compressed springs.

There on the bank was Leaf, wand out in front of him.

"No! Stop!" Norah cried, but it was too late. He shot a jet of green magic into the monster's many-toothed face.

Norah knew a few adult witches and wizards who could have learned a thing or two from Leaf's deft stunning spell, but no spell, no matter how skillful, would work against a monster that used magic as food.

Bright pleasure lit the monster's mossy small-pupiled eyes, and a mucous-coated tongue lapped at the spell. Instead of being stunned, the monster was delighted, like a dog drinking from a sprinkler. Leaf whimpered as the monster sucked up more of his green magic. Leaf backed away and started when he bumped into a dilophosaurus.

The monster took a step forward, the wet sucking noise from its lips pulling in a gust of air that rustled the leaves on the manmade trees. Pieces of green plastic flew off the resin branches into the tooth-lined maw. Leaf pulled on his wand, but it wouldn't budge. Magic was pouring out of it and out of Leaf and down the gaping throat. As the monster drank the magic, its rings of teeth pushed forward with a scrape of bone, and a row of incisors grew from the back of its jaw. The new white teeth gleamed against the slick loam-colored flesh.

Jackie raised her wand arm, and Norah hissed and smacked it down.

"It eats magic," she snapped. "Don't feed it."

Jackie dropped the wand and sprinted toward her son.

"What are you going to do?" Norah shouted after her.

"Punch it to death with my fucking fists!" Jackie shouted back.

Leaf's small, surprised intake of breath at hearing his mother drop the F-bomb spurred Norah into action. She had not planned her tactics carefully.

The monster eagerly took a step toward Leaf, front legs splashing in the water. Norah looked up at the corrugated aluminum.

The roof is never secure.

She raised her wand above the monster's head and coaxed out a thin, electric-blue jet of magic, thinning the stream to a hair's breadth. Working cautiously, she cut a ten-foot-by-ten-foot square out of the aluminum roof, then imagined it hurtling through the air and slicing the beast in half. The French hadn't been messing around when they'd invented the guillotine.

The monster sniffed, nostrils flaring as it sought the source of magic. After a second, it looked up, and Norah saw her electric-blue magic reflected in its greedy shining eyes.

The monster brought its legs together, crouched low, and leapt. It went thirty feet in the air, and Norah cursed the lightweight carbon steel frame Stellan had given it. It shouldn't be possible for something that big to jump that high, but there the monster was, catching her stream of blue magic between its moldy teeth.

The sensation was like having her intestines used in a game of tug-of-war. As the monster sucked the magic out of her wand and her, Norah screamed in pain. She pawed uselessly at the blue stream, trying to hang onto it. Drop by drop, the crackling blue magic that had been a part of her since she was a baby was yanked out of her. As the wrenching loss doubled her over, she waited for the monster to fall back to the ground. Maybe she would be able to salvage a few drops of power.

When the monster fell, it brought her magic down with it. The jaws had latched on and were consuming her from the inside out. It was like having her belly button vacuumed out or having her heart pulled from her chest, leaving behind an emptiness as cold as outer space.

As her magic ebbed, the monster's desires flowed into her. The monster had no goals or emotions, just a bottomless, aching hunger that the magic from a thousand witches could never fill. The magic that had been her joy, her life, vanished into that darkness. The monster didn't even feel it.

Norah stood, shattered. With a sinking heart, she realized that the monster had run out of magic to drink. She was a dry well, and it was still thirsty.

"Interesting," a woman said above her. Ronni, on her broomstick, was gazing at Norah like she was a zoological specimen. Norah's mouth dropped open as Ronni, balanced precariously on the broom's long handle, pulled her lab notebook out of a fold in her black robe and began to jot down notes. She only had a moment to gape before a monstrous howl diverted her attention.

The monster's long legs were clicking toward her, green eyes fixed on her neck. It ate magic, but did it *only* eat magic? A globule of saliva dropped into the water with a splash. As the ripples settled, the water reflected an onrush of movement.

At first, the scene confounded her. A resinous dinosaur was running toward the monster, dull claws raised.

"*You will not touch her!*" the dinosaur shouted and shook its shining blond hair.

It was Frondle. Apparently, he too had discovered the hard way that magic was useless against the monster, and, searching for a weapon, had retrieved the nearest mace-like object. Frondle swung the arm, and it connected with a wet crack. The monster screamed and turned.

"Norah! Catch!" Petra barked, her sharp tone meant to get her daughter's attention. Her mother pointed her wand at the fake tree above Norah's head and fired the faintest dab of magic at the place where the branch met the trunk as a yellow disk. It sliced through the resin and paint and the branch fell into Norah's hands, the severed end a vicious point.

The monster, smelling Petra's magic, had turned and jumped, but it missed. The nostril slits on the tooth-lined snout flared again, and it stalked toward Norah's magic-rich mother.

Petra was a very powerful witch, which meant she would be a lavish feast.

"Stay hungry, bastard." Norah ran toward the many-limbed monster, holding the severed branch in front of her like a spear. After getting a foothold on a fake boulder, she jumped, naked without the comforting crackle of magic coursing through her.

She was more than her wand.

As she accelerated toward the floor, she aimed the severed tree branch at the monster's spine, holding on tightly as it sank into the fur with a crunch. Norah let go and rolled out of its reach across the artificial forest floor.

The monster hissed and screamed. Black goop oozed around the branch like blackberry jam squeezed from a plastic bag, and it galloped away from the danger.

Frondle pulled Norah to her feet, dinosaur arm in his hand and a disbelieving look in his eyes.

"It sucked me dry like a vampire, Norah. Without my power, how will I fulfill my oath?"

"We're more than our magic," she assured him, squeezing his hand. A current passed between them that had nothing to do with magic.

A creak of movement stole Norah's attention back. The monster raised a long, furry limb and sank a talon into the fake branch, then pulled it down and out. There was a sucking slurp, and the branch fell to the floor, leaving a dark hole matted with wet fur. The black goop welled for another instant but then retreated, sucked back into the monster's body.

The wound was healing.

"Shit. It has to be a pure soul," Norah muttered.

Frondle raised an eyebrow, assessing her.

"I'm a human being!" Norah exclaimed defensively.

"And I am a dishonored elf." His voice was so strained that Norah would have been annoyed if there had been a whisper of reproach in it.

The monster raised each of its limbs in turn as if it were doing the Wave, talons clicking on the ground in rapid succession as it confirmed its bodily integrity. The nostrils flared again, cruel and black, then it turned toward the corner of the room where Petra and Jackie protected Leaf. The monster's movements were languid, like a cat with a cornered mouse.

Norah ran toward the severed blood-covered branch, Frondle at her heels. Then they rushed the monster like goons at hockey practice, swinging with desperate ferocity. The monster paid little attention as it batted them away like flies, focused on Jackie and Petra. Bone cracked and its jaws unhinged, then rows of new teeth glistened in their inexorable forward motion. Whatever magic was in Jackie's body, it was going to chew it out of her bones.

As Norah searched for an opening, metal flashed. A glowing blade emerged from a scabbard.

Leaf was holding his elven sword.

"Taste Steven, jerk-face!" Leaf screamed as he ducked

between his mother's legs. Norah cringed as the blade sliced through Jackie's jeans, missing her skin by a hair.

"Leaf! No!" Jackie shouted.

"Fly me, Grandma!" Leaf yelled.

Petra's eyes widened, then she tightened her grip on her wand and shot a burst of magic into Leaf's sneakers.

The spell flung him ten feet in the air. Norah's heart stopped as his small figure soared toward the monster's open tooth-lined jaws. At the last moment, the monster dove for Petra's stream of green magic. Leaf dropped onto its neck and brought the silvery blade down.

The elven metal flashed under the emergency lights, and the monster's jaws, forming that magic-vacuuming oval, went slack.

Everything went still. Then, with a wet noise like fish sliding over a cutting board, the monster's head parted from its body and tumbled to the ground.

Leaf was on the creature's back, hanging onto a clump of black fur with one hand like he was riding a bull. The decapitated body took one step, then two, and then exploded into a rainbow of loose magic, black fur, and coagulated guts that sprayed foully in a ten-foot radius.

Norah couldn't bring herself to be upset by the offal shower because as dark goo hit her face, she felt her blue magic pouring back into her body, as welcome and sorely needed as rain in the desert.

The knotted rainbow of power in the monster's stomach untangled into separate streams, returning to their original owners. Leaf's grassy green magic filled him like a teacup as he laughed in delight, and blazing light poured back into Frondle through his fingers and eyes.

They *hadn't* been too late.

The blue crackle of power was such a relief that Norah sobbed, her tears making tracks through the sheen of monster guts on her face.

With her magical sight, Norah noticed a smooth white stone glowing faintly on the ground. It crackled with magic the color of baked sand, shot through with a fetid brown.

Was that Duncan's magic?

"Do you have a handkerchief?" Norah asked her mother. Petra, looking lost, retrieved her quilted bag from the boat and handed a square of fabric to Norah, who carefully rolled up the magic-laden stone and tucked it into her pocket. Then, with a glance at Jackie and Leaf, Petra pulled an argyle blanket out of her bag and cautiously approached.

Jackie shot to her full height.

"How *dare* you send him hurtling toward a dangerous monster!" she screamed at Petra. "He could have been killed!"

"If there's one thing the Silver Griffins taught me, it's never to turn down an opportunity to survive," Petra replied. Her voice was steely, but there was a touch of sorrow in it.

"Grandma and I practiced flying," Leaf added, stepping protectively between his mother and his grandmother.

"And you!" Jackie turned on her son. "What were you doing with an *elven sword*? How did you get it through Security?"

Leaf looked at his feet.

"When the metal detector beeped, I glamoured Steven to look like a back brace."

"Is that why we had to go through *four times?*" Petra asked, exasperated and exhausted.

"Why are you mad at me?" Leaf protested. "The monster was going to eat you, and I held the blade just like Frondle showed me."

"A well-aimed stroke, young warrior," Frondle agreed, face serious.

Leaf puffed up with so much pride that Norah thought she might witness her second explosion of the morning.

Jackie's face was red with anger for another two seconds. Then, without warning, she burst into tears.

"Mama?" Leaf's voice quavered.

Jackie sank to her knees and wrapped her son in her arms. Norah gently took the unsheathed elven blade from him.

"You did a good job, sweetheart," Jackie assured him, wiping her face. "I was just scared."

Leaf suffered through the hug for a generous fifteen seconds, then squirmed away. Scrambling over the fake boulders and leaves, he picked up the monster's head. "Can I keep it?"

"The spoils of battle are the young warrior's right," Frondle intoned.

Jackie shot him a look that could have desiccated an acre of rainforest.

"We can take it home, and your father and I will discuss it tonight," Jackie told her son, nose wrinkling as the smell hit her.

"What an engaging show!" someone said from above

them. Glesselda floated in on her gleaming chaise lounge, taking a delicate bite of ice cream as the golden conveyance bobbed. "Not as good as *Hamilton*, mind you, but engaging."

"It's been a long few days," Petra muttered to Norah.

"You're Garton Saxon's mother," Norah stated.

"Yes, and I have decided to help you wake my son." Her voice held distaste, but her face was determined. "Now, if you'll excuse me, I want some of that popcorn you suggested earlier. I'll be in touch. Cheers."

The chaise lounge floated toward a glow of natural light, where the ride exited back into the open and shot down a waterfall. Glesselda disappeared around the corner.

Norah turned back to see Ronni trying to wrest the monster's head from Leaf's grip. She sighed and stomped over.

"If you stop that, I'll tell you what it felt like to have the monster suck out my magic."

Ronni paused, then quietly let go of the lump of fur. "I'd love to get those eyes back at some point."

A vein on Jackie's forehead looked like it was about to explode, and Norah shook her head. "I mean this sincerely, Ronni. Not a fucking chance."

CHAPTER TWENTY-THREE

Norah checked the black-hole onyx cuffs on Saxon's stiff wrists for the thirteenth time, then confirmed that none of the stones on the crystal coffin had disappeared in the past half-hour.

Petra and Jeronda sat on the sofa, drinking tea and quietly chatting.

"As soon as you check the wards again, we're ready to go," Norah stated.

Petra patted Norah's hand. "We've checked them three times already. Saxon's not going anywhere, especially not with his mother here."

In the corner, Glesselda was nibbling on a lemon tart and chatting with Quint. She laughed at something and placed a flirtatious hand on his chest. Norah's eyebrows almost crawled off her head.

"Please tell me Quint's not joining an omnipotently powerful light elf's boy-harem," she whispered.

"At least he's not whining face-down on the sofa!" Petra responded brightly.

Stan was glaring daggers at the pair in the corner, and Norah approached him cautiously. He still hadn't forgiven her for sending Frondle into a tailspin.

"Everything okay, Stan?" she asked.

"I'm fine," Stan growled. "I just haven't seen Glesselda in quite a few years. Since I was a young elf." This last statement was delivered as a barb at Quint. Norah's jaw dropped.

"Stan, is Glesselda your ex?" she asked incredulously.

"Our breakup was mutual." The old light elf sniffed.

Norah's eyes widened in a new appreciation of the woman who had flapped the unflappable Stan. Then she took a deep breath. "Places, everyone!" she shouted.

Glesselda knelt by the head of the coffin, and a large circle formed around her. Norah, Madge, Quint, Andrew, Lincoln, Petra, Jackie, and Jeronda raised their wands in a veritable wooden forest.

Despite his fervent protests that he was a ferocious, pure-of-heart monster slayer extraordinaire, Leaf had not been allowed to attend. Frondle nocked a Sleeping Beauty arrow, poised for action. Stan pointed his ancient elven sword at the coffin, and Pepe had positioned himself near Saxon's shins and raised his hoof in warning.

Stellan bore a large and heavy-looking hammer with cruel mechanical spikes that pistoned in and out on the flat end. "It's a meat tenderizer, but people seem to find it intimidating," he had explained earlier.

As Norah opened her mouth to call "Action," someone pounded on the door.

"Are we expecting anyone else?" Lincoln asked.

Norah shook her head. "Follow my lead," she whispered. Everyone but Glesselda crept after her in a v-formation. Norah readied her wand, touched the handle of her front door, and flung it open.

"Surprise!" a woman said, then shrieked in alarm at the bristle of ready wands and blades. Hovering just below eye level was a wooden cube held aloft by winged Hermes tennis shoes.

"Cleo!" Norah exclaimed and flung her arms around the box.

"Am I interrupting something?" Cleo asked hesitantly.

"Well, yes, but the more, the merrier. Can I explain later? We're ready to go."

"I can see that," Cleo replied as light reflecting off Stellan's hammer glinted across her flanks.

Norah locked the door, and they resumed their formation. Cleo, picking up on the plan, hovered near the ceiling over the coffin.

When everyone had settled back into their places, Norah raised her wand, looked at Glesselda, and said, "Smooch away, mama bird."

The ancient light elf bent over the coffin, puckered her glossy lips, and kissed Saxon's waxen forehead. Norah prayed that the well of motherly love had not dried up.

For a moment, the only sound in the room was the slow flap of Cleo's wings near the ceiling. Then there was the softest noise, a creak of bone and a whoosh of blood, and Garton Saxon sat up in his coffin.

"Hello, son." Glesselda's voice was carefully neutral.

Garton Saxon's jaw dropped when he saw his mother. He seemed less terrified by the smorgasbord ring of magical and non-magical weaponry, although he did draw back from Stellan's meat tenderizer.

"Mother?" he squeaked. His boyish chagrin rapidly transmogrified into outraged entitlement as he raised his hands before him and tried to summon a blade of light. Static crackled as the black-hole onyx stymied him.

"Take these off at once!" he ordered his mother.

"You've been a naughty little elf, and I will not remove your cuffs," Glesselda replied. Saxon pulled on the cuffs, but their dwarven construction was impeccable. The more he pulled, the more they constricted. He stood in the coffin, and the elven sword and dwarven meat tenderizer inched toward him.

Glesselda continued, "These people have helped me paint the town bright red, and I would like you to answer their questions."

"And if I do?" Saxon asked.

"I will consider letting you out of the box," Glesselda told him. Hands tensed around wands, and Stellan looked like he might turn his hammer on the old light elf. "In a hundred years or so," Glesselda amended. Norah relaxed. She didn't want to leave a mess for Leaf's grandkids to sweep up, but they could deal with that later.

"What do you know about Dark Hound?" Norah asked.

Saxon snarled, then glanced at the circle of faces. Zeroing in on Petra and Lincoln, his voice dropped. "I know it chased down and exterminated plenty of your little Griffin friends," he snapped in Petra's direction. A pea-sized globule of saliva landed on Petra's shoe, and Lincoln, looking offended, pulled a handkerchief out of his pocket, bent, wiped up the spit, and folded the handkerchief.

"Thank you, dear," Petra told him.

Pepe reared up and delivered a vicious kick to Saxon's tailbone. The producer's high-pitched squeal almost covered the sound of breaking bone.

"That's enough, Pepe," Norah said, wondering if the Geneva Convention had anything to say about goat-kicking. When Saxon spun and snarled, his eyes were watering.

"What's next? Thumbscrews?" he asked.

"No," Norah replied carefully.

"I did bring some!" Stellan piped up.

"It's not going to come to that." Norah hoped it was the truth.

Glesselda fixed Garton with a firm gaze. "If you ever want to get out of the box, son, it's time to start making amends. As Petra and Jackie have so graciously shown me, life is full of pleasures—have you ever had a funnel cake?—and if you want to have any hope of enjoying those pleasures again, you will answer their questions."

Try the carrot before the stick. What would an ancient, evil light elf consider to be a sufficient bribe? She could try to find out. Norah turned on her radio magic. Support and caring flowed toward her from the assembled crowd, and Norah was embarrassed when her eyes watered.

She focused on the black wave of emotions and impulses aggressively pouring out of Saxon. He wanted pain; that was one thread. Norah shuddered as the outlines of imaginative and terrifying scenarios reached her. Saxon also wanted freedom, but that desire was entwined with his craving for destruction. He wanted his hands free so he could bring an infinite amount of suffering down on their assembled heads.

Beneath the ferocious yearnings for pain and freedom lay a third impulse, smaller but no less insistent. The desire was hot and bitter, and when Norah realized what it was, she burst out laughing.

"Answer a few questions, and I'll bring you a cup of coffee," she offered. Saxon's eyes widened in surprise, but his face screwed up.

"I have no interest in your powdered slop," he spat.

Quint gasped at the accusation. "How *dare* you!"

Norah shook her head. "Nice try, Saxon, but there's a fresh pot brewed from Oriceran shade-grown arabica beans in the kitchen. You can smell it if you try."

Saxon, who had been asleep for months, followed the smell of the coffee with a yearning that was almost comical. He slumped into the coffin, crossing his arms.

"Do you take cream and sugar?" Petra asked.

"Cream," Saxon growled, and Petra padded into the kitchen.

"Now, tell us who is funding Dark Hound," Norah ordered.

Saxon stared at his feet, frowning. "Why am I covered in gold?"

"Long story." Madge zoomed in a wide circle around Cleo. "Answer the question."

Saxon picked a flake of gold paint off his trousers. "Domenico Consoli."

Norah sucked in her breath. "The caterer?"

"If Domenico Consoli is a caterer, Al Capone was a home-brewing enthusiast," Saxon shot back. "All that shipping in and out of Oriceran? It's not just sunfruit and drow chocolates."

"Why kill the Silver Griffins? They're disorganized and on the run," Petra blurted. Steam rose from an orange-and-white floral mug she held just out of Saxon's reach.

The light elf licked his lips, then sputtered at the taste of the gold spray paint. Norah, taking pity, shot a cleansing spell across his face. Saxon drew back at the crackle of blue magic, then grudgingly relaxed and accepted the coffee from Petra's hands. He sipped it like a drowning man surfacing in the water.

"This is good," he admitted.

"Of course it is," Quint replied sourly.

Glesselda touched Quint's arm. "Now, now. There's no need to meet rudeness with rudeness."

Quint quieted, and Jackie and Andrew exchanged horrified looks.

When Saxon had finished half the cup, he looked at Petra. "The Silver Griffins have the knowledge and experience to stop illegal importing. I suspect their cache of artifacts was not obliterated, as they like to pretend. Domenico wants anyone who needs Oriceran goods to go through him."

"So, he considers us a threat *and* competition? You'd think he would choose one or the other," Lincoln mused.

Saxon nodded. "Dark Hound was an easy way to keep the Griffins from re-forming. It's giving the old-timers something to fight that's not him."

"Old-timers?" It was Lincoln's turn to take offense.

Petra patted her husband's hand. "We're *seventy*, dear.

Many of our friends weren't lucky enough to become old-timers."

That mollified Lincoln.

Norah thought about Domenico's and Angelo's reach into Hollywood and shivered. It wasn't the first crime syndicate to be sucked in by the lights and money of Tinseltown, but she couldn't picture the elder Consoli typing on a computer.

"Domenico isn't the coding type," she stated.

Saxon pressed his lips shut and held out his empty cup. When Lincoln returned it to him full, he sipped it and nodded in approval. "Dom doesn't do the coding himself. He works with some hacker named UrbanWurm."

Had Norah seen the name on Dark Hound? Maybe in one of the forums.

"What's his real name?" she demanded.

"I don't know. He's a hacker folk hero. According to legend, he lives under Los Angeles, off the grid."

"Where?" Norah asked.

"I couldn't tell you. I've never met him."

Pepe raised his hoof and looked hopefully at Norah, but she shook her head. She focused on Saxon, trying to understand his wants and motivations. The coffee had diminished his craving for pain, which Norah could identify with, but he still meant them harm. She gave Frondle a quick nod, and he drew back the glowing string of his bow.

"Hey-" Saxon protested, but before he could say another word, a Sleeping Beauty arrow sank between his eyes. He collapsed and the mug in his hands shattered, splashing coffee across the interior of the crystal coffin.

"Sorry," Frondle muttered, but Petra waved it away.

"Nice shot, dear," she replied.

"You might be the first individual in history to make my son shut up," Glesselda told him approvingly. "What will you do with him?"

"He makes a perfectly good coffee table." Norah frowned. *As long as I can keep an oath-sworn elven bounty hunter off my tail.*

"Very good," Glesselda continued. "Now, let us celebrate. Quint, darling, pour me a glass of something extremely alcoholic."

To Norah's dismay, Quint leapt up. The faces around her were hopeful and determined, and she was bolstered. They didn't have to take down the crime syndicate in one night. Norah smiled and turned to Quint.

"Make that two."

CHAPTER TWENTY-FOUR

The six-legged, black-furred monster crashed through the chapel's floor-to-ceiling stained glass window. Shards of bright glass threw kaleidoscope patterns across the mossy stone as the monster stalked toward Duncan, opened its jaws, and swallowed the wizard whole.

Everyone on the set of *The Players* held their breath.

"Cut!" Bitta called and turned to Sinter. "Tell me we got it since we don't have time to rebuild that fucking window."

"We got it," Sinter replied with deep relief.

A cheer went up, and the crew extracted Duncan, who was shaking. Even after losing his magic, he'd wanted to push on, although Norah wasn't sure it was the right choice. She called to him, but he fled the scene.

Norah glanced at the now-limp monster. Its body had been rebuilt, but Stellan had kept the head, which he had obtained from Leaf through the simple expedient of bribery. Although the special-effects maestro had repeatedly assured Norah that the monster was inert, the sight of it trundling around the set had made her sick. Still, she was glad the production was back on track. She was about to track down Duncan when Stellan got her attention.

"Norah, wait!" the dwarf called urgently.

Norah's hand flew to her wand. "Is the monster alive again?"

"What? No. Besides, I have my meat tenderizer with me. I just wanted to give you this." He handed Norah a Cleo-sized wooden crate. Curious, she popped the lid open and almost dropped the box. Inside was a monster head, almost identical to the one Leaf had taken down but much smaller. Mossy green eyes with very small pupils stared up at her.

"Those aren't the cursed marionette eyes, are they?" she asked.

Stellan shook his head. "Your mum and dad have those. That weird, obsessed cryptozoologist witch has been following them around, begging to inspect them. She's persistent. I think she might wear them down. No, these are resin replicas," Stellan poked one to show her it was solid.

"It's very lifelike." Norah remembered the wrenching pain of magic being sucked out of her. "It's not, uh, for me, is it?"

Stellan frowned. "I didn't think you'd want one. No, it's for Leaf. He was so attached to the thing that I felt bad taking it from him, even at his extortionate rates. Still, the head smells like a dead sewer rat, so I think I did Jackie and Andrew a favor."

That was putting it mildly. "I believe Jackie is considering making you the godfather of her next child as a way of saying thank you."

Stellan beamed, and Norah glanced at the monster's head and then shut the lid. "It's horrifying," she announced. "I'm sure Leaf will love it."

"Have you figured out what to do with that weaselly puppeteer?" Stellan asked.

"I have," Norah replied. "But I have an errand first. Have you seen Duncan?"

"Maybe by Crafty? He's been putting down a lot of pastries since he lost his magic," Stellan said.

The quality of the craft services had gone down since Norah had unceremoniously booted Angelo off-set. He had sent her several apology gift baskets since then, which she'd subjected to rigorous magical and chemical testing before disposing of them.

Duncan stood by the folding table, eating a cheese Danish and staring at a plate of croissants.

"Hey, Dunker," Norah called. "You did great work back there. I'm sure it wasn't easy."

The wizard looked up and nodded grimly.

"I have something for you." Norah pulled a small object out of her pocket. Duncan frowned as she flicked open the embroidered handkerchief to reveal the stone she'd retrieved from the monster's exploded guts. It was crackling with sandy magic.

"The magic might be half-digested, but it's a start," she told him.

Duncan stared at the arcs of light-brown magic with longing and apprehension, then set aside his Danish. His hand shook as he took the stone. The sparking magic grew more agitated, and a tendril uncurled and buried itself in Duncan's skin. The wizard winced as the magic crawled up his muscular arms.

"It might be different than before," Norah continued. "My mom said you should sleep with the stone if it's not too painful. She said to call her in a week to talk about next steps."

Norah texted Petra's number to Duncan, and his hand tightened on the stone. The magic crackled with renewed vigor.

"Fuck," he whispered, teeth clenched. "You know how it feels when you move your arm after you fall asleep? It's like that, but for my whole body."

Norah nodded sympathetically. "You don't have to do it all at once."

The wizard shook his head. "I don't care if it hurts. I'm just glad to have some of my magic back. Thank you, Norah."

"You're welcome."

"Want a Danish?" Duncan asked. "They're okay."

She shook her head. "No thanks. I have to see a man about a puppet."

The door of the Bob Baker Theater was open when Norah arrived. The interior was dark except for the light spilling from a door in the back. Norah padded across the space, alert for wooden threats, but nothing rose to stop her. Peeking through the door, she found a small workshop. Inside, Castor was brushing a fresh coat of paint on a wooden clown's head. When he saw Norah, he scrambled to his feet, reaching for his wand.

"Please don't," Norah protested. "I'm very tired."

"What do you want?" Castor asked, hand hovering over the wand.

"You could start with an apology."

Castor grumbled, "You sent that lawyer to peel my skin off." Norah raised an eyebrow. "Metaphorically," he grudgingly added.

"*The Players* is a good script, and you should be happy it's getting made. *Both* of you should be happy."

Castor turned back to repair the damaged puppets from *Evening Wood*. Norah looked away from the disembodied anatomical correct carvings.

"You know, Duncan might not get all his magic back," she said quietly.

Castor turned back to her, remorseful. "I'm sorry. I didn't want it to go that far."

"I'm here to help you make amends," Norah replied.

Castor looked at his puppet. "I don't think I can help Duncan. I would if I could, but…"

"It's not that," Norah countered. "I have a project for you. It's better suited to your skills." She pulled some drawings out of her pocket and opened them. On the paper was a rough sketch of a crate with winged feet and two articulated hands.

"My cubic friend could use a few additional limbs," Norah explained. "I thought wooden hands might be well within your grasp and, hopefully, hers if you help."

"They need to be animated? What's your plan for that? And where did you get the flying shoes?"

Norah smiled as Castor's face took on the expression of an artisan with an exciting new project.

"I thought we could meet next week for some additional planning," she replied. "If you're willing."

Castor nodded, and he beamed. "This gives me some new ideas for my one-man show. The box isn't a performer, by any chance?"

"She's an old silent film star. She can tell you all about it next week."

Before Castor could babble anything else, she took her leave, dismayed at the prospect of a one-man, one-box show.

Would weaseling out of attending it be easier or harder than taking down the digital arm of a major crime syndicate? Only time would tell.

Get sneak peeks, exclusive giveaways, behind the scenes content, and more. PLUS you'll be notified of special **one day only fan pricing** on new releases.

Sign up today to get free stories.

Visit: https://marthacarr.com/read-free-stories/

THE STORY CONTINUES

The story continues in book three, *No Country for Old Agents*, available at Amazon.

Claim your copy today!

AUTHOR NOTES - MARTHA CARR
DECEMBER 12, 2022

I've started a project answering questions for my son about my life. I realized after last year's fifth round of cancer, and then chemo this time that he was expecting me to die sooner rather than later. It's been a lot for him to deal with and there isn't much I can do to make it better, except tell him stories that I can leave behind – eventually. Hopefully, a long time from now. I'm going to let you guys listen in as well.

My author notes for this year are going to be answers to questions and all of you can get to know me better, too. Maybe inspire, maybe give you a laugh along the way.

Today's question is: Who inspires you?

This may surprise you, but I'm inspired mostly by you. Sure, there are famous people that I've looked up to like Nelson Mandela. Who walks out of a prison after 27 years of hard labor - missing most of his working years - and figures out a way for everyone to be forgiven? And there are people I actually know who I admire, like our friend Jen who is always up to do anything, and is friendly and kind, inclusive. Like anyone, there are things about her life that are not easy and she's real about it but doesn't go on and on. She'd rather be out enjoying life, and she does. She sets, and inspires, a very good example.

But really, the person I marvel at the most, famous or not, is you, my son.

Life has handed you a few challenges and you haven't ignored them or denied them. Instead, you've worked with them and sometimes, even made hard decisions about leaving them in the past, forever.

However, more than that, it's the way you conduct yourself in the small moments that happen every day that has you at the top of my list to admire. You're a grown man now, creeping up on middle aged even, and I've gotten to see who you've become on a day to day basis.

When there's a problem, you work on the solution and without a lot of fanfare. At the beginning of quarantine when they cancelled SXSW weeks before the music festival was supposed to start, costing you and Jackie a lot financially, you were angry and worried for a day or two - and then you started looking for opportunities. First up was offering music videos of Jackie to closed clubs to keep their web sites fresh and active. That was some very clever thinking.

Being creative and proactive under stress was hard, especially when restrictions dragged from weeks to months to years, but you kept moving. And because of that, when the smoke finally cleared after two years, your position in the music world was actually stronger, sturdier than it was at the start of 2020. Just pursuing a career in any kind of art is tough. There's no building to go to for a job interview. No clear ladder to climb and a lot of it is very subjective. Often, it's about being ready when an opportunity strikes as much as it is about honing a craft.

I know that better than most, as you know. It was just you and me when you were growing up and you came along on some of my interviews or book signings as I slowly made it work. But when that's where your heart is, that's where you need to go. One day at a time, one step at a time, one deal at a time, you and Jackie are walking the music path and making it work. It inspires me, over here creating things. I know at some point the two of you are going to break big and the whole world will know who Jackie is and celebrate her music, in part because of your efforts. Your other clients will become household names, too.

Then there's the way you treat people. You're very loyal, always willing to show up, and very honest at the same time. There will be no half-truths told to 'spare someone's feelings'. I'm not a big fan of that behavior, either. It's a kind of disrespect to treat someone like they need to be taken care of all the time. And yet you do it without judgment.

Watching you around your grandmother in her last days when you sought her out just to hang with her was full of grace and love and respect. I'm glad I got to be there to witness it. You've always been like that around people that often others didn't want to be near. And you weren't doing it to be of service, you could see what others missed. What they had to offer if only someone would slow down enough, not make things about themselves, and pay attention. That's you - you pay attention with a kind heart. It makes space for others to be a better version of themselves.

That's probably enough for now. I look forward to seeing what comes next for you. It's always fun, exciting and interesting. I wouldn't have it any other way. Love, Mom. More adventures to follow.

AUTHOR NOTES - MICHAEL ANDERLE

DECEMBER 12, 2022

Thank you for not only reading this book but these author notes as well!

I HAVE A COKE® PROBLEM

The drink, not the white substance you snort from a tabletop and need a razor blade to cut.

So, I am an author, and I absolutely love Coca-Cola.

Recently (actually, yesterday), my wife and I went to the World of Coca-Cola in Atlanta, Georgia on a cold and wet day.

We were at a hotel two blocks from the place. We decided to walk. It was cold. It rained. Not a great choice.

I digress.

When we arrived at the museum, I was excited…to get out of the cold.

Judith and I browsed through the exhibits, learning about the history of Coca-Cola. It was invented in 1886 by a pharmacist named John Pemberton. I was surprised to learn that Coke was bought and sold as a company multiple times. I thought it was only sold once.

The "vaunted" secret recipe was taken to New York as collateral for the twenty-five-million-dollar loan when the company was sold the second time.

I wasn't surprised to learn that the recipe for the secret blend of flavors in Coca-Cola is known to only a handful of people and kept under tight security. If you have read my *Kurtherian Gambit* series, some of the characters steal the secret recipe before they leave Earth. Also, one of the couples grabs the Pepsi recipe. Fun was had by all ;-)

After exploring the museum, Judith I visited the gift shop. There, Judith pointed out a cozy Coca-Cola hoodie I just had to have.

Read, I was freezing my...*arms* off and didn't want to go back out into the weather without it.

I tried it on, and it fit nicely. That means that it was black and slimming ;-)

I made my purchase and wore the hoodie for the rest of my visit to the museum, feeling warm and comfortable. Since you MUST leave the building through the store, the rest of my visit was about ten feet before we stepped out. Hell, yeah! I was toasty.

Overall, my trip to the World of Coca-Cola was a memorable experience, and I left with a new hoodie to add to my collection, as well as some exciting knowledge about the history and production of Coca-Cola. As a devout Coke lover, I feel like I've made my required one-time trip to the hallowed halls and can feel ten percent more devout ;-)

Now, it's 7:45 in the morning and I'm going to go grab a Coke®.

Chat with you in the next book.

Ad Aeternitatem,

Michael Anderle

MORE STORIES with Michael newsletter HERE: https://michael.beehiiv.com/

OTHER SERIES IN THE ORICERAN
UNIVERSE:

THE LEIRA CHRONICLES
CASE FILES OF AN URBAN WITCH
THE EVERMORES CHRONICLES
SOUL STONE MAGE
THE KACY CHRONICLES
MIDWEST MAGIC CHRONICLES
THE FAIRHAVEN CHRONICLES
I FEAR NO EVIL
THE DANIEL CODEX SERIES
SCHOOL OF NECESSARY MAGIC
SCHOOL OF NECESSARY MAGIC: RAINE CAMPBELL
ALISON BROWNSTONE
FEDERAL AGENTS OF MAGIC
SCIONS OF MAGIC
THE UNBELIEVABLE MR. BROWNSTONE
DWARF BOUNTY HUNTER
ACADEMY OF NECESSARY MAGIC
MAGIC CITY CHRONICLES
ROGUE AGENTS OF MAGIC

OTHER SERIES IN THE ORICERAN UNIVERSE:

DIARY OF A DARK MONSTER
CHRONICLES OF WINLAND UNDERWOOD

OTHER BOOKS BY JUDITH BERENS

OTHER BOOKS BY MARTHA CARR

JOIN THE ORICERAN UNIVERSE FAN GROUP ON FACEBOOK!

CONNECT WITH THE AUTHORS

Martha Carr Social

Website: http://www.marthacarr.com

Facebook: https://www.facebook.com/groups/MarthaCarrFans/

Michael Anderle Social

Website: http://lmbpn.com

Email List: http://lmbpn.com/email/

https://www.facebook.com/LMBPNPublishing

https://twitter.com/MichaelAnderle

https://www.instagram.com/lmbpn_publishing/

https://www.bookbub.com/authors/michael-anderle

BOOKS BY MICHAEL ANDERLE

Sign up for the LMBPN email list to be notified of new releases and special deals!

https://lmbpn.com/email/

For a complete list of books by Michael Anderle, please visit:

www.lmbpn.com/ma-books/